The NEIGHBOR

GERRI HILL

BELLA
BOOKS
2018

Bella Books, Inc.
P.O. Box 10543
Tallahassee, FL 32302

Printed in the United States of America on acid-free paper.

First Bella Books Edition 2018

Editor: Medora MacDougall
Cover Designer: Judith Fellows

ISBN: 978-1-59493-600-5

Other Bella Books by Gerri Hill

Angel Fire
Artist's Dream
At Seventeen
Behind the Pine Curtain
Chasing a Brighter Blue
The Cottage
Coyote Sky
Dawn of Change
Devil's Rock
Gulf Breeze
Hell's Highway
Hunter's Way
In the Name of the Father
Keepers of the Cave
The Killing Room
The Locket
Love Waits
The Midnight Moon
No Strings
One Summer Night
Paradox Valley
Partners
Pelican's Landing
The Rainbow Cedar
The Roundabout
The Secret Pond
Sawmill Springs
The Scorpion
Sierra City
Snow Falls
Storms
The Target
Weeping Walls

About the Author

Gerri Hill has thirty-four published works, including the 2017 GCLS winner *Paradox Valley*, 2014 GCLS winner *The Midnight Moon*, 2011, 2012 and 2013 winners *Devil's Rock*, *Hell's Highway* and *Snow Falls*, and the 2009 GCLS winner *Partners*, the last book in the popular Hunter Series, as well as the 2013 Lambda finalist *At Seventeen*.

Gerri lives in south-central Texas, only a few hours from the Gulf Coast, a place that has inspired many of her books. With her partner, Diane, they share their life with two Australian shepherds—Casey and Cooper—and a couple of furry felines.

For more, visit her website at gerrihill.com.

CHAPTER ONE

Laura Fry stood at the edge of the driveway, looking at the two-story house she'd grown up in. Memories flashed through her mind quickly—like playing on the swing on the old oak tree in the back—bringing a smile to her face. Unfortunately, the swing was long gone. Then her eyes landed on the wheelchair ramp, and her smile vanished as quickly as it had come. With a sigh, she closed the door to her car, not even bothering to take anything with her. The car was packed to the gills with her stuff but…she could always change her mind. Couldn't she?

"No, you can't," she murmured. Her sister would kill her.

She still couldn't believe that Carla had talked her into this. Guilted her into it was more like it. Yeah, yeah…Carla was married. Carla had two kids. Carla had a *real* job. Laura? Not so much.

She took the steps to the front door instead of using the ramp. She noted the house was badly in need of a paint job. The flowerbeds were filled with weeds, not flowers. The yard needed to be mowed. She paused at the door, hand raised. Should she knock? Should she knock and wait or should she knock and go inside? Frankie wasn't here, she reminded herself. No need to be hesitant about going inside. She took a deep breath, then tapped her knuckles three or four times on the door.

"It's unlocked," a voice called from inside. Her mother's voice.

With another deep breath, she turned the doorknob and pushed the door open. Her mother was in the short entryway, waiting. Not using her walker, which Carla said she should be using. No, she was in the wheelchair. For effect. For sympathy. For guilt, maybe.

Well, this is getting off to a fine start.

"Hello, Mom," she said dryly.

Her mother pursed her lips together. "Laura. I hardly recognized you. Have you gained weight again?"

Again? *I'm going to kill Carla for making me do this!*

But she forced a smile to her face. As much of one as she could muster, that is. "No, I haven't. At least I don't think so. My clothes still fit."

"And what have you done to your hair? It's certainly not flattering on you."

Laura reached up, touching her now shorter locks. Dare she tell her she had a breakdown one day and cut it herself? No. As she'd told Thomas, she needed a change. It took him an hour to fix her mess. She liked it now. But she voiced none of that to her mother. Instead, she walked closer. "Are you having a bad day? Carla said you weren't supposed to use the wheelchair. She said you could get around with the walker."

"How would she know? She's come by only once since… since the funeral, as if I can manage on my own." Her eyes narrowed. "But at least she bothered to come by. You? How long has it been?"

Laura mentally threw up her hands. She wanted to scream. She wanted to run. But, no. She could do neither. Her mother was in a wheelchair, for God's sake. She couldn't just walk out on her. She wasn't however, going to play games.

"I don't know how long it's been, Mom. How long were you married to that jerk? Seven years?"

"Laura Sue Fry! The man has been buried less than a week. Have you no decency?"

Laura rolled her eyes. "I hated the man, Mom."

Her mother raised her chin. "He was my husband," she said, as if that mattered.

"He was an obnoxious jerk! Nobody liked him! Nobody could stand to be around him!"

"You never took the time to get to know him. He was a *good* man."

"No. Dad was a good man. Frankie didn't come close."

"Your father left me a widow at fifty-eight. What was I to do? Live the best years of my life alone?"

"No, Mom. But you didn't give it a chance. You grabbed the first jerk that came along. You let him move in with you!"

"I'll not have you talk about Frankie that way!"

She pointed at the wheelchair. "He's the reason you're in that chair! He's the reason you can't live alone at the young age of sixty-five!"

Her mother stared at her in disbelief. "How dare you?"

"I dare because it's the truth."

Her mother spun her chair around. "You are simply too hard to get along with. You always were. Your father spoiled you rotten! I told Carla this would never work."

"So did I! She made me come anyway," she yelled to her mother's retreating back. She grabbed the bridge of her nose and squeezed it.

Well, that actually went better than I expected.

CHAPTER TWO

"You knew that was going to happen. Mom knew you were going to talk trash about Frankie and you knew she was going to yell at you. It's over with. Now go unpack your car and move into your old room."

"You live forty-five minutes away," Laura complained. "Why the hell am I moving in with her? Ever since Dad died, we haven't gotten along."

"No. Ever since Frankie, you haven't gotten along," her sister clarified.

"Yeah, funny how that happened at exactly the same time!"

"We had six months with her. You two were as close as ever, if you recall. Frankie is gone now. Maybe it's time you grew up and gave her a second chance."

"Grow up? Says the woman who still sleeps in Mickey Mouse pajamas."

Carla laughed. "How do you even know that?"

Laura sighed. "You're probably right. I'll give it one month."

"And then what? We can't afford to have someone check in on her daily. She can't manage on her own. Since the accident—"

"Which he caused," she interjected.

"Frankie did everything. He cooked, he did laundry, he cleaned the house. He even—"

"Look, I didn't come here to be a damn maid."

"Laura…we talked about this. You're leaving an apartment you could no longer afford. This is a win for you. Mom pays the bills, Mom pays for groceries…you cook and do her laundry."

"Just because I've hit a rough spot doesn't mean I need to mooch off Mom. This is a temporary arrangement. As soon as I get another book deal, I'm out of here."

"Of course."

"You said that too quickly," she accused.

"I did not. This will give you more time to write."

Laura wrinkled up her nose. "More time? How do you figure? I'll be cooking—which I hate—and cleaning and doing the freakin' laundry!"

"Well…you're in a mood."

"That's because I'm stuck here against my will!"

"Can I help it if I have a family to take care of? A husband? Twins? A *job*?"

"You're patronizing me!"

Carla laughed. "Okay, yeah. I guess I am. But you're overreacting. You just need to give it a chance. It will do you good—both of you—to spend time together."

"I hate you."

"Now I know you don't mean that. You have a good week, a good weekend. I'll see you next Thursday. I'll bring pizza or something."

"I still hate you."

"I love you, sis."

"Love you too," she murmured as she tossed her phone onto the passenger's seat. She leaned back, staring at the house. She could do this. Carla was right. She and her mother used to be close. She and her mother used to talk. In fact, in those six months after her father had died, they'd talked almost daily.

Then Frankie came into the picture. She honestly didn't know if she hated him because he was an obnoxious jerk or if she hated him because he was living in her dad's house, sleeping in her dad's bed.

"Or both."

Well, she couldn't hide in her car forever. She got out, then grabbed a couple of clothes bags. She hadn't been here in seven years. Who knew what her old bedroom looked like? Frankie probably turned it into a game room or something.

But no. Her old room looked the same. Same bedspread, that's for sure. That would be the *first* thing to go. She tossed her bags on the bed, covering some of the hideous roses. She went back out into the hallway and peeked into her sister's old room. It, too, looked the same. The bathroom between the two rooms was different, though. New tile. New fixtures. She stood in the hallway and surveyed the upstairs. Yes, this might just work. She'd have the second floor to herself. Her parents' bedroom—now her mother's—had always been downstairs. Now that her mother could no longer manage the stairs, she'd at least have some privacy up here. Perhaps she could turn her sister's room into her writing room.

She went back into her own room, pulling open drawers. Everything was completely empty, including the closet. That seemed odd to her. Surely she hadn't taken *everything* when she'd left. She pushed apart the drapes that covered the large back window, hoping to get a view of the woods she'd loved as a kid. She frowned. The once familiar view of trees—woods— was gone. A house was there instead. A huge house. A house with a pool, which she could just see a corner of. A tall privacy fence separated her mother's property from next door. When had that gone up? She'd been so dreading her move here, she hadn't even noticed it earlier.

But who the hell had bought the woods? Who would tear down those beautiful trees and put in a house and pool?

She hurried back down the stairs, finding her mother in the kitchen, attempting to reach the microwave. A frozen Weight Watchers dinner was on the counter.

"What are you doing?"

"What does it look like?"

"Mom...I'm supposed to cook, remember?"

"Yes, well, Frankie's been gone six days. How do you think I've managed thus far?"

She took the dinner and tossed it back into the freezer but not before she spotted the six or eight additional dinners that were in there.

"You've been shopping?"

"I haven't left the house. Carla got those for me."

Laura put her hands on her hips. "I know you can get around with the walker, Mom. Why the chair? Or is it just for my benefit?"

"I don't know what you mean. The walker is difficult. Slow."

"At least you're on your feet." She bent down to eye level. "The doctor said the more you walk, the stronger you'll become."

"How would you know what the doctor said?"

"I *did* come to the hospital," she reminded her.

Her mother waved her hand in the air. "That was three years ago. That doctor didn't know what he was talking about. Why, if not for Frankie, I'd practically be an invalid."

Laura bit her tongue. If not for Frankie, she wouldn't be in the damn wheelchair to begin with. What was it? He blacked out? Or he swerved to miss a dog? She'd heard both stories. Somehow, she suspected neither was true. Regardless, he'd smashed the car into a tree. He walked away from the crash with nothing more than a few bruises. Her mother? Broken back. Broken pelvis. Broken legs. Broken body.

But...she wasn't going to go there. Not now. So she took a step away and held up her hands.

"Truce, please. Let me get a few things in from the car, then I'll see about dinner. Do you have anything here other than these frozen things?"

"There's a chest freezer out in the garage. I don't know what's all in there. Frankie did the cooking. And the shopping."

And the laundry and the cleaning, Laura added silently. Maybe she'd been too hard on old Frankie. He lived with her mother. He did everything around the house. The man was apparently a saint. Except he wasn't.

"Oh, who bought the lot next door?"

"Some woman from Dallas. Not friendly in the least. Frankie tried to make friends. Several times he went over there while they were building. She would hardly give him the time of day, he said. Next thing we knew, that huge fence was put up."

Again, she bit her tongue. Frankie was always rough around the edges. Obnoxious. One of those guys who had been there, done that—only much better. Loud. Laughed at his own stupid jokes. A jerk. Yeah, she'd have probably put up a fence too.

"So how long has she been there?"

"Sometime in December. I remember she had a Christmas party. That house was under construction for more than a year. Constant noise we had to deal with. But from what Frankie was able to get out of her, she won't live there. A weekend place, she said."

"I'm going to miss the woods."

"Why?"

"Why? I used to play in them when I was a kid. I loved to walk there. Dad always said he was going to buy it."

"Yes, well, your father was going to do a lot of things that he never got around to."

Laura shook her head. "You're still so bitter. He's the one who died, not you."

"And left me a widow."

"I'm sure if he had the choice, he'd have rather lived."

Her mother's expression softened. "I'm…I'm not over it yet. I miss him every day."

This time, Laura was unable to keep her thoughts to herself. "Yet a mere six months after he died, Frankie moved into your bedroom. And two months after that, you married the man!"

Her mother stared at her. "Six months is a long time to be alone. I had no one. All my friends had someone. I was always the odd man out. I stopped getting invited to places because… because it was couples and I was no longer a couple. I was lonely."

There were tears in her mother's eyes, and Laura cursed herself for being so blunt with her.

"We tried to be here for you, Mom."

"I know, but it wasn't the same as having a partner. Someone to do things with. Someone to talk to in the evenings. Someone to share meals with."

"I'm sorry. I can see your point." She held her hand up. "Truce, remember. Let me unpack."

CHAPTER THREE

After three days, Laura had settled into somewhat of a routine. That routine, unfortunately, did not involve writing. Writer's block was a terrible thing. A *horrible* thing. She must have started and stopped ten or twelve different outlines in the past month alone. Not a one of them had the makings of a novel.

"Breakfast on the patio again?" she called to her mother.

Her mother shuffled into the kitchen, using her walker. Since the first day, the wheelchair had come out only in the evenings, when her mother was tired.

"We should take advantage of the spring weather. It'll be too hot before long."

"I don't have anything fancy today. Oatmeal with fruit and toast," she said as she buttered a slice.

"I don't expect fancy, Laura Sue."

Laura had stopped complaining of her mother's use of her middle name. It had fallen on deaf ears. "Can you make it out or do you need help?"

"I can manage."

Laura resisted the urge to open the door for her. The more independence her mother had, the better it would be for the both of them. She loaded the serving tray with their bowls of oatmeal and toast and two glasses of orange juice. She had found that her mother, unlike her, was a one cup a day coffee drinker, which she usually had while she watching the morning news. Laura, on the other hand, took her first cup outside with her, usually before dawn or right at it. The empty bird feeders had been filled her first day here. The low branches of the oak tree by the fence—where three feeders were hung—were a flurry of activity and she enjoyed the sights and sounds as the new day began. That was her quiet time, before her mother got up. If it was a particularly pleasant morning, she'd have two cups outside before going back in to start breakfast.

"I hear music. Do you?"

Laura put the tray down, then tilted her head and listened. "Yes." She scowled. "The neighbor?"

"I imagine. At least it's not that godawful stuff those young people listen to."

"Young people? How old is she, anyway?"

"Oh, I have no idea. Frankie didn't say."

"Married? Kids?"

"I don't know. Frankie said there were some men over there sometimes. Maybe she has a husband. I never met her."

"So was Frankie spying on her or simply being a nosey neighbor?"

"He wasn't spying. No one has lived there—or even been out there—since we bought this house and you were three at the time. You're almost forty now."

Laura gasped. "I am *not* almost forty! I'm thirty-seven."

"Only for a few more weeks," her mother said with a smirk.

Laura narrowed her eyes and pointed a finger at her. "If you don't want me to start slipping nasty things into your food, you better be nice."

Her mother laughed and Laura thought it was the first time she'd heard her laugh since…well, since before her father had died. She couldn't imagine that she'd have anything to laugh about living with Frankie.

Laura smiled as she put their food out on the table. They had actually been getting along. Better than she would have imagined, really. After breakfast, her mother would retreat to the living room to watch TV and Laura—after cleaning up the kitchen—would go upstairs to her "writing room." She'd rearranged the furniture the first day and set up an office for her. So far, she'd done little more than sit and surf. Yesterday afternoon—after starting laundry—she'd gone to the grocery store. Frankie's freezer had been stocked as well as the pantry, but fresh food had been sorely lacking. There wasn't even an onion or potato to be found. She had immediately thrown out the box of instant mashed potatoes that she'd come across. Who ate that stuff? How hard was it to cook and mash *real* potatoes?

"I thought you didn't like to cook."

"I don't. What gave you the idea that I did?"

"The pork chops last night," her mother said. "Perfection. I hate to speak ill of the dead, but Frankie's were always dry, even when he baked them."

"He was cooking them on too high of a temp," Laura said as she scooped up a strawberry with her oatmeal.

"You never cooked at all when you lived at home. I tried to teach you."

"I wasn't interested. I'd rather have been outside playing."

"Or following your dad around. So how did you learn?"

Laura put her spoon down. "Remember Sandi?"

Her mother frowned and shook her head. "No, I don't recall her."

"Oh, yeah. That was after Dad died...and Frankie was here. Well, I was seeing this woman—Sandi—and she liked to cook. All the time. We never went out. I was forced to help...chop veggies and such. I may have picked up a few pointers. Not that I like to cook," she added quickly.

"Well, that's good. I take it she's not around any longer?"

"No." She held her hand up. "And before you ask, yes, I was the one who ended it, not her."

"I wasn't going to ask."

"You always blame me."

"Well, your track record is what it is."

"I just don't see the point in continuing to date someone when you already know that they're not 'the one,'" she said, making quotations in the air.

"I'm not sure you give them a chance," her mother said with a wave of her hand. "Of course, the only tidbits of your life I've had lately have been from Carla."

"It's not like I haven't *called* you in the last seven years."

"Phone calls that lasted perhaps five minutes."

She picked up her toast, which was now cold. "I'm sorry, Mom. I simply could not tolerate that man."

"You never gave him a chance either."

Laura held her hand up. "Please...let's don't go there again. We're getting along fine. Let's not bring Frankie into it, okay? Truce?"

Her mother took a sip of her orange juice, then seemed to study her. Laura sighed, then looked up, meeting her gaze.

"What?"

"I take it you're not seeing anyone now?"

"No. Not for a...a while," she said evasively. As her mother had said, her track record was what it was.

"Why?"

She blinked at her. "I've been focusing on my writing." *Yeah, right.*

"So you can't date?"

"Yes, I can date. It's just that the older I get, the choosier I get."

Her mother stared at her blankly. "I would think it would be the opposite."

Laura actually laughed. "It's too easy. My comeback...it's too easy. I won't even say it."

"I know you're referring to Frankie. I was fifty-eight, not thirty-eight."

"I'm thirty-seven!"

"Regardless, you'll wake up one day and you'll be fifty and alone. And your problem all along has been that you're *too* choosy. You were always that way, even in high school. You're looking for this perfect person. They don't exist, Laura Sue. You're going to have to lower your standards." Her mother's spoon clanked into her empty bowl. "Although I did like that cute fellow you dated in college."

"You only liked him because his parents were rich."

"Filthy rich," her mother corrected with a grin.

"He was kinda nice," she admitted. "He was my last attempt at being straight."

"Well, you are what you are."

Yes, that was one thing she always respected her mother for. When she came out to her, to her father, her mother hadn't blinked an eye. She'd said those very words to her. Even her father hadn't been thrown by the news. Perhaps it's true what they say; parents know long before you do.

They heard laughter coming from across the fence and she swore she heard a splash in the pool.

"It's still April," she said. "Even in Texas, who swims in April?"

"Well, the days have been warm, but I bet the pool is heated. It sounds like they're having a party."

"It's barely nine o'clock in the morning."

Her mother shrugged. "Sounds like fun. Maybe you should go meet her."

"I will not. I'm mad because the woods are gone. I might say something ugly to her."

"I think the reason her house is so close to us rather than in the middle of the property is that she left a lot of the woods on the other side. That's where most of the big trees were. It's one of the large lots, Laura Sue."

Yes, Laura had already seen that from her bedroom window. The lots here ranged in size from one and two acres up to ten. Her parents were on a two-acre lot. She guessed the neighbor's was the larger, at ten. At least from what she remembered when she was a kid, the woods had seemed to go on forever.

She leaned back, looking at the backyard. It had been neglected. Her mother's flowerbeds were crowded with grass and weeds. The neat cobblestone walkway had been encroached upon by the lawn. The lawn that needed cutting. Badly.

"You used to keep this so tidy, so colorful with all your flowers."

"For everything Frankie did for me after the accident, he was not into gardening. He kept the lawn mowed, that's about it."

"Is the riding mower still working?"

"Frankie bought a new one just last summer. That old one finally went to the junkyard."

"Well, I guess I'll tackle the yard this afternoon."

"It's Saturday. Our new neighbor is here. It would probably be polite to wait."

She nodded. "I'll wait until they go inside. How's that? I don't plan to schedule my chores so as not to disturb the neighbor."

CHAPTER FOUR

At the time, Cassidy had thought it extravagant to heat the pool. This was Texas and the few months of winter could be tolerated. However, after watching not two, but three ladies— all clad in bikinis—take the plunge on this April morning, she was glad she did. Well, Deb would be better served in a one-piece rather than a bikini, but who was she to complain.

"Come on in! It's fabulous!"

Yes. She already knew it was. She'd tried it last night after everyone had gone to bed. She turned her eyes to Claudia and smiled. After bed and after sex, she clarified. Claudia waved her in and she paused, pulling her T-shirt over her head and tossing it down before going to the board and diving in.

Oh, yeah, heating the pool had been a great idea.

"I can't believe we got to come early," Zoe exclaimed. "This is such a cool house, Cassidy."

"Thanks. It's my dream home, that's for sure." She swam over to where Claudia was holding on to the side of the pool. "Thirty guests might be pushing it, though."

"With more than an hour's drive back to Dallas, you might have every bedroom filled," Deb warned. "How are you going to feed everyone?"

"It's catered. There's a crew coming out about five to set up. We'll do it outside on the deck since the weather's good."

"Then we'll do it inside later," Claudia purred as her tongue snaked into her ear.

"Oh, yeah," Cassidy murmured. "Maybe even before that."

Claudia moved her mouth to Cassidy's. "Maybe right here. Right now."

* * *

Laura stared in disbelief as the anorexic blonde shoved her tongue into the dark-haired woman's mouth.

"Oh my God! They're *lesbians*! Are they going to have an orgy or something? There are four of them!"

God, I have got to buy some binoculars!

Staring, she couldn't pull her eyes away. But no orgy, no. They seemed to be coupled up and on opposite sides of the pool. But they were doing *much* more than swimming.

She finally turned away.

"That's disgusting," she murmured. It wasn't even noon yet! "Who does that?"

She slammed out of her room and went into Carla's...the writing room. However, Carla's room had a much better view of the pool than her own room. She was drawn to the window.

The large, rectangular pool was now empty.

Well, at least they took it inside, she thought as she let the drapes fall back into place. But who was that? Was there a nympho lesbian living next door? She groaned. How cruel would that be? She hadn't been on a date in eight months. She hadn't slept with anyone in...well, in a while.

"Of my choosing," she murmured as she opened up her laptop.

To say she was in a rut was an understatement. She was simply tired of the endless dates. Tired of meeting new people and none of them living up to her expectations. She was tired of pretending to be interested in someone when in reality, she was bored to tears. She'd told her friends to stop setting her up on blind dates. And they had. But like her mother, she often felt like the odd man out...and even some of her friends had stopping including her when they did group parties and such.

So yeah, she was in a rut. And living out here, more than an hour away from Dallas and her friends, she suspected that rut was going to get deeper. It wasn't like she knew anyone in the area any longer. She'd moved away when she was eighteen, losing touch with her old high school friends within months as she made new ones in college. She stared at the wall, trying to remember some of her friends from back then. While names popped into her head, the faces remained fuzzy. Oh, well. She turned her attention to her laptop and the blank page staring her in the face.

If only she could write.

Something.

Anything.

* * *

"Do you have binoculars?"

"Why on earth would I have binoculars?"

"You live out in the country. Everyone has binoculars."

Her mother motioned to the closet. "Look in there. Frankie may have had some. And why do you want them?"

"I want to spy on the neighbor," she said as she rummaged in a very cluttered closet. "What is all this stuff?"

"Frankie's stuff."

She found the binoculars and pulled them out from under a stack of fishing magazines. *Did he fish?*

"So we can throw all of this out now, right?"

"I spoke with his nephew at the funeral. I told him to come by if he wanted anything, but I haven't heard from him."

Laura closed the closet door. "Did he have much family?"

"None that live here, no. The nephew was the only one who bothered to come to the funeral. Terrible."

"Was there *anyone* at the funeral, Mom?"

Her mother sighed. "Not many, no. For some reason, my friends didn't warm up to Frankie."

Laura snorted. "Really? For some reason? Maybe it's the same reason your daughters didn't warm up to him." She held her hand up. "But we're not talking about this, remember? Truce."

"Truce. Now, why are you spying on the neighbor?"

"Because they're having a party."

"Oh? And?"

Laura grinned. "Women in bikinis."

Her mother laughed and waved her away. "Well, by all means, spy away."

She turned all the lights out upstairs, then pulled her chair closer to the window in her writing room. She hid behind the drapes, only opening them enough to stick the binoculars out.

"Oh my God," she murmured. Definitely lesbians. Hordes of them. Oh, okay. There were a few guys. Kissing. Great! Her neighbor was having a gay bash. Half of the people were in swimsuits. Some of them should *not* be in swimsuits.

Oh…there's that anorexic blonde again. God, she's pasty white.

"Who's she kissing now?"

I wonder who the owner is.

She scanned the crowd and the pool, trying to determine who their neighbor was. It had to have been one of the four women in the pool that morning. Surely to God not the anorexic blonde. No, not her. She spotted a woman—dark hair—making the rounds. She nodded. Yes, same woman from the pool, the one the blonde had been latched onto.

Tall, dark…handsome, almost. Certainly too handsome to be called pretty. Her dark hair was a little shorter than shoulder length, parted on the side. *Oh…she's got bangs. How cute.* Not young, though. In her early forties, she guessed. She rolled her eyes. Forty was sounding younger and younger, wasn't it? *Should you still have bangs when you're in your forties?* She had a nice body, though, regardless of her age. Skimpy bikini top, white shorts. Tan legs…firm. Really *nice* legs. A runner, maybe? Definitely athletic. She made the return trip up the woman's body, back up from her legs to her face, then gasped as the woman seemed to be looking right at her.

She froze in place, not even daring to breathe. Surely she couldn't see her. Surely to *God* she couldn't see her spying. Then the anorexic blonde approached, getting the attention of tall, dark and handsome. As soon as her head was turned, Laura literally dropped to the floor, below the windowsill.

"That was close," she murmured. Then she smiled. "But kinda fun."

CHAPTER FIVE

"So you survived the week?"

"That better be two loaded pizzas and I get to keep the leftovers."

Carla leaned forward and kissed her cheek. "Yes. As you requested." She pulled away. "So?"

"I survived. We've made a truce. We don't talk about Frankie. I pretend he never existed and she pretends I loved him."

"See? I knew you could do it." Carla paused to look around. "You mowed. It looks good."

Laura took the pizza boxes from her. "I'm a yard gal, yes. This week I have been cleaning out flowerbeds too."

"You got Mom's green thumb. I never was much into planting stuff." She bent closer. "Where is she?" she whispered.

"Living room. TV. Go say hello."

Laura went into the kitchen with the pizza. While the house had a separate dining room, they always used the small kitchen table for their meals. She put the pizza down, then pulled out three plates and put them on the table.

"What do you want to drink?" she called.

Carla came into the kitchen. "What have you done to our mother?"

"What are you talking about?"

"She's actually in a good mood. Have you been spiking her drinks?"

Laura laughed. "I told you she's been different." She opened the fridge. "I've got beer."

Carla shook her head. "No. Beer makes me sleepy. I'll just have a Coke or something."

Laura was about to go see if her mother needed help, but she came shuffling in with her walker. Laura hadn't wanted to say anything, but she could tell her mother was getting around better. Since the accident, Frankie had waited on her hand and foot—probably out of guilt. She used the wheelchair far more than the walker that first year. Now, she seemed to be getting some of her strength back, although she still had balance issues.

Carla noticed too. "That's as fast as I've seen you move in years. What gives?"

"Well, I've had to use this dang thing more. Laura Sue refuses to let me have my chair."

Carla turned to her. "Hiding the wheelchair, are you?"

"She's exaggerating. She uses it in the evenings to chase me around the house. My only escape is running up the stairs."

Laura noted the smile on her mother's face and she returned it. Yes, they had been getting along famously, which was scary. It was almost as if the last seven years hadn't happened. And really, she wished that could be so. That was seven years they would never get back. It was her fault, she knew. She was the one who stayed away. She was the one who wanted to strangle the very breath out of Frankie whenever she laid eyes on him. Maybe her mother was right. Maybe she never gave him a chance.

"Mom, I noticed that Laura has the yard looking nice," Carla said. "It'll be good to see flowers out once again."

"In the last seven years, you've been here three or four times. I'm fairly certain you don't remember what my flowerbeds looked like."

"Well, that's three or four times *more* than Laura was here. That should count for something."

"Hey, don't pull me into this." She opened up one of the boxes of pizza and offered it to them. "Mom, you want tea?"

"Yes, please." Her mother patted Carla's hand. "Laura Sue is such a good daughter."

Carla's eyes widened. "Oh my God! I knew it! You've been body snatched!"

Laura laughed. Oh, yeah. She and her mother were getting along great. They had always been close, but after Frankie...she was afraid they wouldn't be able to get it back.

"So did you know somebody moved in next door? Mom said December. Weekends only."

"I knew someone was building. Have you met them?"

"No." Then she smiled. "Not officially."

"What does that mean?"

"That means she spied on them last weekend. There was a party. Girls in bikinis," her mother explained.

"With binoculars," Laura added with a grin. "Frankie's. Found them in his junk closet. And I do mean junk."

Carla bit into her pizza, then talked with her mouth full. "What kind of spying?"

"From my writing room. Perfect view of the pool and outdoor kitchen from the window."

Carla frowned. "Writing room? You confiscated my old room, didn't you," she accused.

"I did. You'll never miss it."

An evil grin followed the frown. "So what have you written? Anything?"

"Nothing I'm ready to share yet. It's a slow, creative process. It doesn't just happen with a snap of the fingers, you know."

"So you haven't written anything, huh?"

"No," she groaned. She sat down at the table next to her mother. "I mean, I've written *words*. They just aren't going anywhere."

"So, sis, maybe this book writing gig isn't for you."

"How can you say that? I'm already published."

"That was seven years ago."

"Eight," she corrected with a sigh. Who knew writing a second novel would be so damn hard?

"I think you're afraid of success," her mother said. "You always hated calling attention to yourself. You hated speaking in public. You hated piano recitals."

"I hated *piano*, period."

"You were so good at it."

"That doesn't mean I liked it. And I'm not afraid of success." She bit into her own pizza slice. "It wasn't like it was a monster seller or anything."

"You made the Top Twenty," her mother reminded her.

"For all of one week. God, that seems like ages ago."

"It was," Carla said. "That's why I'm thinking, maybe, just maybe, you should have a fallback plan."

"Like get a job?"

"Yeah. Like normal people do."

"I had a job. I hated it."

"I could try to get you on at my place," she continued, as if Laura had not spoken.

"Really? So you'll quit your job then to stay here with Mom?"

Carla shoved pizza into her mouth.

"Thought so," Laura murmured.

CHAPTER SIX

Cassidy Anderson spun around in her chair when she heard her office door open. Tanya, her assistant and her friend, looked at her with raised eyebrows.

"It's nearly four. Are you not heading out to the country this weekend?"

"I am."

"Something got your attention?"

"No. Not really."

"What's wrong?"

Cassidy blew out her breath. She'd known Tanya nearly twenty years. Tanya could read her like a book. "It's Claudia."

"Claudia? Oh, yes. The flavor of the month. What about her?"

Cassidy shrugged. "I don't like her very much."

Tanya raised her eyebrows.

"Sex is great. It's just everything else."

"Another one bites the dust," she murmured. Tanya put her hands on her hips. "Do you know how many times we have this very same discussion?"

"We do not. The sex isn't always great."

"I have lost count of how many girlfriends you've had."

"Oh, please. Claudia is not my girlfriend. She's just…just someone I'm going out with."

"Let's see…this weekend makes what? Four weekends? Five? So yes, I suppose it's about time to move on to someone else."

Cassidy stood up. "It's hard dating. You have no idea."

"Spare me. You can have anyone you want. You *get* anyone you want. You're cute. You're successful. You have money. You now have a nice retreat out in the country—which I have yet to be invited to. How hard can it be?"

Cassidy crossed her arms. "We do have this discussion a lot, don't we?"

"Yes. At least once a month." She waved her hand in the air. "Move on from Claudia. It's time."

"She's friends with Erica and Amber. They like us together."

"So?"

"And I've already invited her out to the house. There's another couple coming, so that'll make it bearable."

"You never said how the party went last weekend."

"Oh, it was fun. Had a few people drink too much so I had them stay over. The pool was a big hit."

"I'm sure it was. Maybe one day I'll get to see it."

"Yeah. You and Derrick come out, bring the boys. They'd love it."

"Yes, they would. But teenagers…they'll think they're too grown up to go with Mom and Dad to a pool party."

Cassidy nodded. "I keep forgetting they're all grown up." She motioned to the door. "Why don't you head out early? I'll see you on Monday."

"You sure?"

"Yeah. Give Derrick a kiss for me, huh?"

"I will. See you Monday."

Cassidy sat down again and spun her chair around, gazing out of the high-rise window. Sometimes, it was still a shock to be sitting where she was. She worked hard for it, though.

Putting Anderson Heating and Air Conditioning at the top of everyone's list hadn't been easy. Her grandfather was probably rolling over in his grave at the idea that they even had corporate offices, much less that they took up the entire twentieth floor in a fancy office building.

Dispatch was done from here. Online scheduling was managed from here. Accounting. Payroll. Marketing. All here. And spread out over Dallas and Fort Worth were now ten hubs that they could dispatch from. They could be anywhere in the Metroplex within twenty minutes of getting a call. That kind of service couldn't be matched by anyone. No one could even come close to that.

That's not to say it hadn't taken years to get to ten hubs. No. When she'd come on board, they only had the one office, which her father ran. Her brother was out in the field. He had been the hardest one to convince to branch out. But now, fifteen years later, they'd more than quadrupled in size.

Their ads ran on TV and radio constantly. They had billboards all over the city. If anyone had an air conditioner go out, they called Anderson. Winter blues when the heater didn't work? They called Anderson. New home builders? They contracted with Anderson.

It was all working like the well-oiled machine it was intended to be. Yes…life was good, she mused as she spun back around to face her desk. Her professional life, that is. She'd spent so many years working to get the company to where it was, she'd sacrificed her personal life. Now, now that she had time—and money—she couldn't seem to enjoy her personal life. It wasn't fulfilling. Everything—everyone—seemed to be a stopgap to her goal: meeting the love of her life.

So far…she hadn't come close to meeting her. And now that she was approaching her mid-forties…she feared she would never find her. She feared she would have to settle. Settle for someone like Claudia.

"At least the sex is good," she murmured as she closed her laptop.

* * *

"Again with the anorexic blonde? She is so not right for you," Laura murmured as she stared through the binoculars. "Can't you see that?"

There was something different this time, though. Tall, dark, and handsome was being a little standoffish. She'd pulled away from the kiss.

"Oh...who's this?" She didn't recognize them from last weekend's party. Two women, both blond. They seemed young. They were giggling. Laura rolled her eyes. "Children," she muttered. Tall, dark, and handsome appeared to be fortyish, perhaps a little older. The anorexic one was in her thirties. These two looked to be early- to mid-twenties.

She lowered the binoculars and turned away from the window with a sigh. "I have *got* to get a life."

She firmly pulled the drapes together. She had no intention of spending this weekend like she'd done the last: spying on her neighbor. Sure, she was cute and a pleasure to look at, especially in a bikini. But her taste in women was sorely lacking.

She was fortyish and wore a bikini. Wore it nicely.

Laura shook her head. "I wouldn't be caught dead in a bikini," she murmured to herself. Then she smiled. "I think I'll mow today."

CHAPTER SEVEN

Cassidy floated idly in the pool, her mind closed to the laughing conversation coming from the float next to her. The neighbor was mowing. It was Saturday. Couldn't he mow during the week when she wasn't there? From what she remembered of him—what was his name? Frankie?—he wouldn't be considerate enough to mow on a weekday.

All she wanted was some peace and quiet. That's why she built out here. Peace and quiet. Not to hear some damn riding lawn mower buzzing by along the fence. She looked toward the noise, but the privacy fence was too high for her to see over. Yeah, she'd put the privacy fence up in the first place because of him. Six feet tall was the standard, but she'd wanted ten. Her builder talked her down to eight. Frankie popped over all the time, attempting to flirt with her. He annoyed the hell out of her. So...up went the fence, well before the house was even finished. He was probably still pissed about that.

She sighed. They had a couple of acres over there, mostly lawn. She imagined it would take an hour or so to mow it. She tipped off her float and swam into shallow water, then took the steps out.

"Be right back," she called to no one in particular.

Claudia was engrossed in a conversation with the two young women she'd invited. Claudia worked with Angie. The other—Yvonne—was Angie's girlfriend of two weeks. And Cassidy had absolutely nothing in common with either of them. Truth was, she had nothing in common with Claudia either. Of course, after this weekend, she wouldn't be seeing Claudia anymore. No, she was thinking of asking Larson out. She'd met her at a party a couple of weeks ago. A party Claudia had dragged her to.

She stopped to pull a T-shirt over her head, then slipped on her flip-flops. She contemplated going inside for shorts but didn't want to take the time. She walked down to the edge of her driveway, punched in the code for the gate, waited impatiently for it to open, then walked along the road to the Morrison place. She stopped. Flowers? She hadn't seen flowers here before. Seeing her obnoxious neighbor mowing in the back, she walked across the freshly mowed lawn, around the house, waving at him.

As he got closer to her, she realized the person under the ball cap wasn't Frankie after all. It was a woman. She scowled as the woman cut the blades off but kept the mower running.

"Do you mind?" she yelled, pointing at the machine.

With an exaggerated sigh, the woman turned the mower completely off.

"Yeah…thanks." She pointed across the fence. "I live next door."

The woman nodded. "I live here."

"Okay. Well, I was wondering if perhaps…you could stop mowing. It's Saturday. I have guests out by the pool. It's virtually impossible to have a conversation with this noise."

The woman stared blankly at her. "And this affects me how?"

Cassidy narrowed her eyes. *Really?* "Yeah…so where's Frankie?" she asked, thinking maybe she could negotiate with him instead of this woman.

"Frankie? He died."

"Died? When?"

"Several weeks ago. Why?"

Cassidy put her hands on her hips. "Who are you?"

"Laura Fry."

"So…you live here now? Frankie was your father?"

"Oh my God! No! He married my mother."

"Oh. Stepfather then."

Laura Fry actually clenched her teeth. "No, he was *not* my stepfather." She shook her head. "What is it you want?"

"I want you to stop mowing. Isn't this something you could do during the week when I'm not here?"

"So I should rearrange my schedule to suit you?" She gave a rather sweet smile. Condescending, but sweet. "I am *very* busy during the week. Very busy."

"So there's no compromise?"

"Compromise? Your yard people come very early on Fridays. *Very* early. Daybreak. It's impossible to sleep in."

Cassidy glanced at the house, guessing the bedrooms were upstairs. Their two houses weren't *that* close together. But…

"So you're suggesting I reschedule them?"

"After ten would be great."

"Ten? You sleep until ten?"

"Oh, no. I'm usually up by dawn."

"Then…?"

"Quiet time. Coffee on the porch. Birds. Quiet. No mowers."

"I see. Okay. So if I agree to that, you'll stop mowing on Saturdays so I can have *my* quiet time?"

Laura Fry nodded, smiling quickly in her victory. "Deal."

Cassidy stuck her hand out. "Deal." Their handshake was firm, but brief. "I'm Cassidy Anderson, by the way."

"Okay," Laura said as she started up the lawn mower again.

Cassidy stepped out of the way as the mower buzzed around her. At least the woman waited until she was past her before engaging the blades. So she was going to stop mowing, right? Their deal started today, not next Saturday. Right?

She blew out a frustrated breath, then turned and headed back to the road. The woman was wearing cutoff jeans. When's the last time she'd seen that? She chanced a glance at the house. It looked different than she remembered. Oh, the paint was still chipped and faded, but it looked inviting. All of the flowerbeds were stuffed with flowers. The grass was trimmed along the edges of the sidewalk and around the trees. If she hadn't seen this woman mowing she would assume they had a yard service too. Although her own yard service did not do flowers. Maybe she'd ask them to plant some for her. After she asked them to start coming at ten instead of seven.

She stopped at the road when she heard the mower shut down. The woman had pulled it into the shed at the back of their property. Cassidy stared at her as she walked back toward the house. The cutoff jeans were mid-thigh, leaving plenty of leg exposed. Long legs. The woman was nearly as tall as she was. The woman—Laura Fry—disappeared behind the house and Cassidy continued back toward her gate and driveway, conscious of the smile on her face. So her new neighbor was cute. That was a plus. And, if she had to guess, she would say Laura Fry was a lesbian. Although she wasn't particularly friendly. Maybe that was a good thing. Overly friendly, she couldn't handle. Weekends. Quiet time. No neighbors, even if they were cute lesbians. Quiet time.

However, loud laughter coming from the pool dispelled any notion she had of quiet time. Before going around the walkway to the back, she took the time to look at her yard. It was nice. Pristine, in fact. But sterile. No flowers. No colors. Not even any flowering shrubs, which she'd seen plenty of on her drive out. Her shrubs were all uniform and perfectly placed. She nodded. She needed some flowerbeds. She needed some color.

* * *

"I saw you talking to the neighbor. She looked younger than I imagined."

Laura lifted the lid on the slow cooker and tested the roast with a fork. Another two hours ought to do it.

"Fortyish," she replied.

"What did she want? That's the first time she's ever been over here."

"She asked me not to mow on Saturdays. Apparently it distracts from pool time." She smiled at her mother. "We struck a deal. She's going to get her yard crew to come at ten on Fridays and I'll stop mowing on Saturdays."

"Well, that's good. So who is she?"

"Cassidy Anderson." She held her hand up. "And before you ask, no, I did not find out anything about her." She was cuter up close than through binoculars, that's for sure, although she didn't share *that* with her mother. "I was a little rude to her."

"Why?"

"Because she came over with this attitude. Like everyone should work around her schedule so as not to disturb her on the weekends when she's got her groupies out by the pool."

"Groupies? What are you talking about?"

"The anorexic blonde, who is apparently her girlfriend, and two young, giggling blondes today."

"Laura Sue, have you been spying again with the binoculars?"

Laura took the potatoes and bowl of water over to the table where her mother sat. "Here, help me," she said as she handed her a vegetable peeler.

"For saying you didn't like to cook, that roast smells divine."

"Thank you. The Internet is a wonderful thing. Thousands of recipes."

"I could have given you mine. There's nothing to it. Although I never made mine in the slow cooker."

"It's a little different than yours, Mom. Chunked garlic, mushrooms, a sprig of rosemary, a dash of tamari."

"Onions? You have to have onions, Laura Sue."

"Of course there are onions. I was just giving you the highlights. I'll make gravy and we'll have that over mashed potatoes."

"Can you make gravy?"

"I watched a video. I think I can do it."

Her mother shook her head as she peeled the potato. "A video. A video on how to make gravy? Your grandmother would never believe it. She taught me to make gravy by the time I was ten."

"Good. Thank you for volunteering to make tonight's gravy," she said with a grin. Ah, it was too easy.

"You did that on purpose," her mother accused. "There was no video."

"Yes, there is a video. I just didn't watch it. Besides, you need to cook. You'll lose your skill."

"I haven't cooked since the accident," her mother said sadly. "I do miss it. I just can't—"

"Yes, you can. I'll stand beside you. You won't fall."

Her mother met her gaze and held it. "You trying to get me back on my feet? You tired of living here?"

"No, I'm not tired of being here," she said honestly. "And yes, I am trying to get you on your feet. But not because I'm tired of cooking—yet. It would be good for you. You must be sick of watching TV by now."

"I've gotten hooked on my daytime soaps, I know. But you're right. It would be good to be able to contribute some." Her mother looked out of the big kitchen bay window, her gaze settling on the flowers Laura had put out just yesterday. "I so miss being able to plant my flowers. I miss getting my hands dirty."

"Well, tomorrow after breakfast, you can get them dirty."

Laura had seen her mother watching her yesterday, had seen the wistful look on her face. And even though nearly every flowerbed was stuffed with flowers, the back patio, where they normally ate breakfast, was still bare. So yesterday, she'd gone out early—while the neighbor's yard crew was disturbing the silence—and bought some large planters, potting soil, and two big flats of impatiens. They had no impatiens anywhere else and the patio was shaded enough for them.

"What do you have planned?"

"You'll have to wait. I'll even let you use your chair."

Her eyes brightened. "I'm going to get to plant some flowers?"

"Yes. I've got some planters for the patio. There're still out in the truck." Frankie's old truck. It had come in handy, that's for sure.

"Thank you, Laura Sue. That was sweet of you."

"I try," she said with a smile.

Her mother smiled too. "I can't believe you were so mean to me when you first got here."

"Me? You called me fat!"

"You called my husband a jerk!"

"Was I lying?"

Her mother held her hand up, a half-peeled potato in it. "Truce, remember."

Laura laughed. "Yeah…you thought he was a jerk too!"

CHAPTER EIGHT

Cassidy had dinner with Larson on Thursday night. She'd been "delighted" that Cassidy had asked her out. So delighted, in fact, that she'd invited Cassidy in for a nightcap. A nightcap that lasted until morning. Cassidy—while still struggling to find her clothes—had invited her out to the country for the weekend. As expected, Larson readily agreed.

And now here she was, at midnight, swimming alone—naked—in her pool while Larson basked in the afterglow of sex and wine…passed out upstairs in Cassidy's bed. Cassidy moved into shallower water, slicking her hair back from her face, thinking about Claudia, not Larson.

Claudia had been hurt when Cassidy told her that they wouldn't be going out any longer. Claudia accused her of being a player…accused her of using her for sex and nothing more. Well…*using* was a strong word. But yeah, it wasn't like they were in a relationship or anything. They both benefitted. Claudia got wined and dined for a month. They both got sex. And now it was over with.

"On to another one," she murmured tiredly.

With a sigh, she ducked back beneath the surface of the water and swam across to the other end, resurfacing under the diving board. She held on to the side, enjoying the quiet of the late night, hearing the gentle lapping of the water as it rippled against the edge of the pool. The blue lights were still on, she having once again forgotten to change them at dark. Yellow, red...even green. She actually preferred the red lights. There was something sensuous about diving into a nighttime pool shaded in dark red.

She'd spent way more than she'd intended on the pool. Actually, she'd spent far too much on the house itself, but if this was going to be the one and only house she ever built, she wanted it to be her dream home. And it was. Not extravagant to the extreme. Her master suite—on the second floor—was huge, however. Six hundred square feet for the bedroom alone, big enough for a sitting area that overlooked the pool and opened to a small patio. A walk-in shower large enough for six. A floor-level Jacuzzi tub. An obscenely large, walk-around closet. Her office was nice and roomy and it looked out over the woods to the west. Four additional bedrooms—two of them upstairs—all with private baths. She had a workout room—her private gym with various machines and free weights—that she hadn't shown to anyone. That was *her* space. The entertainment room with theater seating had yet to be used. The formal dining room had yet to be used. The casual dining room had been used once. The breakfast nook in the kitchen got most of the eating action. And the kitchen itself was spacious and airy with a wall of windows looking out over the outdoor kitchen, the patio, and pool.

She looked at the outdoor kitchen now, envisioning steak dinners with friends, hamburger dinners with her brother and family. Tanya and Derrick coming out for ribs and chicken. So far, however, she had not gotten to use it. This weekend would be the exception. Larson said she loved a good steak.

Oh...Larson. Cassidy shook her head. Larson was nice. She was cute. She was closer to her own age for once—thirty-six. And the sex was...okay. Not mind-blowing, certainly, even though Larson made it out to be. And she had known within thirty minutes of their first date that Larson wasn't going to be around long. But still, she'd extended the weekend invitation. Selfish on her part, she knew. She simply had no one else to spend the weekend with and she couldn't remember the last time she'd spent an entire weekend alone. She liked being around people. She had a lot of friends. Truth was, she didn't really like being alone. Being alone gave her too much time to think. Like now.

She finally had her dream home, only she had no one to share it with. She looked up to her bedroom window, where Larson was sleeping. Was she using her? Was she using her as she'd done with Claudia? For company? For sex?

Yes.

Again she shook her head, then ducked down under the water as if that could hide her from the truth. She wasn't using them, she protested. She was dating—a lot. She was dating and hoping to find her soulmate. She was dating and hoping to find the woman of her dreams. That wasn't using them, she told herself.

She swam to the shallow end, walking slowly up the steps. The air was cool tonight, reminding her that it was still spring. She wrapped the towel around herself, pausing to look back at the pool.

It looked lonely. Much like she felt. Lonely, even though there was a naked woman lying in her bed.

Lonely.

CHAPTER NINE

Laura was tempted to start the mower at daybreak, hoping to wake the neighbor, but then that would mean cutting into *her* quiet time. No. She'd wait. She'd wait until she knew Cassidy Anderson was up. In fact, she might even wait until she was at the pool. It was a warm, sunny day. She had no doubt they'd use the pool.

She parted the blinds now, peeking out with the binoculars. The way the house was angled, she couldn't see inside it. From her writing room, the pool was in plain view, though, as well as the patio and enough of an outdoor kitchen to make her envious. It was after nine. Were they still in bed? Making love?

"Eww," she said. The anorexic blonde couldn't *possibly* be good in bed.

But no. She saw movement. Oh, there she was. Tall, dark, and handsome—Cassidy Anderson—was coming outside. A one-piece swimsuit? What's up with that? Her brows drew together as another woman came outside.

"That's not the anorexic blonde," she murmured. "Good. But who are you? God, I swear, Cassidy…your taste in women… it sucks."

She lowered the glasses. Oh, well. Not her concern. She needed to mow the lawn, she thought with an evil grin.

* * *

Cassidy nearly fell off her float when the lawn mower started up next door, right next to the fence. She closed her eyes and sighed. *Really?*

"We had a deal," she murmured.

"What?"

She looked at Larson and shook her head. "Nothing." She tipped off her float. "Be right back."

As she'd done last Saturday, she marched down her driveway to the gate, punched in the code, and waited for it to open, then she nearly stomped over to the neighbor's yard. The woman—Laura Fry—was down at the other end. Cassidy walked through the yard around the side, thinking that the grass didn't really even need to be mowed in the first place. The yard looked freshly manicured.

"Then what the hell?"

She waved at Laura, motioning her over. She narrowed her eyes, swearing she saw a smile on Laura's face. An evil smile. She put her hands on her hips as the mower approached. Laura was again wearing cutoff jeans—her mowing shorts?—and she gave Cassidy a flirty smile when she killed the engine.

"Good morning, Cassidy. What brings you around?"

Cassidy narrowed her eyes even further. "Really? I believe it's Saturday."

Again, a smile. "I believe you're right."

"Oh, come on. We had a deal. What gives? Your yard has obviously just been mowed. There's no need to mow it today."

"What gives is that yesterday morning, at exactly seven—while I was enjoying coffee on the patio—your guys showed up. My mother, who is an invalid and needs her rest, was roused from a sound sleep."

"Roused?" *Who says that?*

"Yes. Roused. She was grumpy all day."

Cassidy rubbed her temples with both hands. "So you're saying my yard crew didn't come at ten?"

"That's correct."

"So even though you don't really need to mow, you're doing it anyway, just to annoy me."

"We had a deal. I'm the only one who lived up to my part of it. So, yes, to annoy you."

Cassidy held her hand up. "Okay, look. I called them. I really did. They assured me they would come later. I don't live here, so I don't really have any control."

"Not my fault."

"Yeah…okay…so what? To just be a bitch, you're going to mow anyway?"

Laura Fry's eyes peered into hers, making Cassidy take an involuntary step away from her.

"Bitch? Did you just call me a…a *bitch*?"

"Oh…*Jesus*," she murmured. "I didn't…I didn't mean it like that."

"You didn't mean to call me a bitch? Or bitch means something else in your vocabulary?"

Cassidy threw her hands up. "Look, I'll give you a thousand dollars to stop mowing."

That statement was met with silence and a rather blank stare.

"Well?"

"I hate wealthy people who just throw their money around."

With that, Laura Fry started up the mower and engaged the blade, making Cassidy jump away as grass was shot in her direction.

She didn't know whether to be mad at Laura Fry or her yard guys. Should be the yard guys, she supposed…she'd called them and changed the time. But right now, it was her cute neighbor in cutoff jeans who her anger was directed at.

"You're unbelievable!" she yelled, even though she knew Laura couldn't hear her. Or could she? Was that a damn smile again? She spun on her heels and marched—stomped—back to the road.

* * *

"I don't find it that annoying," Larson said as she floated next to Cassidy. "I hear mowers all the time in my neighborhood."

"That's not the point. We had a deal."

"Oh, just enjoy the water and forget about her." Larson reached out and grabbed her hand as their floats bumped. "I've had a great time. Although I woke up and you weren't in bed last night."

"Couldn't sleep," she said. "The pool was calling."

"Oh? You got in the pool?" She tugged her closer. "Did you skinny-dip?"

Cassidy smiled. "I did."

"I meant to tell you, you have a fabulous body for your age."

Cassidy stared at her, trying hard not to frown. "'For my age'?"

"Well, after forty, I hear everything starts to sag." She smiled and winked. "You don't have that issue yet."

Cassidy gave a fake laugh. "Well…thanks. Maybe I've got a year or two left before I fall apart."

"I'm right behind you. I turn thirty-seven at the end of the year. And honestly, it's been so nice to spend time with someone older, like you. I mean, most of my dates lately have been much younger than me." Then she squeezed Cassidy's hand. "You've got *lots* more stamina than I expected."

"Gee…thanks."

Cassidy wondered how rude it would be to call a cab to haul Larson back to Dallas today. Probably very rude. She sighed. Was it too early to start drinking?

Probably. But…

She pulled her hand away from Larson's. "I'm going to get a beer. You want one?"

"I'm not much for beer. Besides, it's a bit early for me."

Cassidy flipped off her float and into the water, wishing she was alone. Maybe next weekend, she'd come out by herself. Take a break from dating. Take a break from…everything.

CHAPTER TEN

Laura pulled a small oscillating fan out onto the patio, then turned it on to high. It was a warm day, reminding her that April had flipped over to May a week ago. Soon they would no longer be able to enjoy breakfast out here, which she would miss. She sat back and twisted the cap off the bottle of beer she'd snagged from the fridge. Her mother was napping in her recliner—a daily occurrence. She took a swallow of the cold beer—one she'd stashed in the freezer for a few minutes—and gave an audible "ahhh" as she swallowed. The flowers were vibrant; hummingbirds buzzed around them and butterflies flitted about. The bird feeders seemed to have more customers every day and she enjoyed sitting and watching the activity. It cleared her mind. It was peaceful. She had hoped that all of that would carry over to her writing...but no, she *still* hadn't come up with anything worthy of being published.

She heard a splash in the pool next door and felt a stab of envy. Oh, how refreshing it would be to dive into a pool of cool water. Although, despite the afternoon heat, she imagined the water was still a little on the cold side. But they'd been using the pool for a while now. Maybe it was heated, like her mother suggested.

She took another swallow of her beer, listening. There were no voices, only the occasional splash of water. Laura had half a mind to run upstairs to see who was in the pool, but she'd told herself she needed to stop spying on the neighbor. For one thing, it was extremely rude and, well…a little creepy. Besides, she didn't really care what was going on next door. She was simply thankful the yard guys hadn't come at seven yesterday morning. She frowned. In fact, they hadn't come all week.

She looked across the expanse of their own yard…lush green and trimmed to perfection. Thursday was mowing day for her. Friday was when she used the weed trimmer around the trees and fence, the sidewalk, and flowerbeds. The yard looked nice. Very nice, in fact. Her mother was thrilled by the transformation she'd made already. Everything looked nice. Except the house. Next week's chore was to get quotes from painters. She'd already picked up paint samples and she and her mother had been arguing over colors ever since.

She smiled. Playfully arguing. She knew in the end, her mother would be the one to decide on the color. It was her house, after all. Laura was just…what? Maid? Cook? Caretaker?

Daughter.

She was content, though. Surprisingly so. She'd been keeping up with her friends sporadically through Facebook and the occasional phone call and text. Several had invited her to dinner, but so far she had no desire to head back to the Metroplex. She thought she'd miss the city more than she did. She only had two grocery stores to choose from here, but they were both as large and well-stocked as those in Dallas. Since she'd been cooking their meals, she hadn't really missed going out. And since she had her bedroom—and her writing room— set up the way she wanted it, she certainly didn't miss her overly expensive apartment.

All in all, this move had turned out so much better than she'd imagined. Now, that's not to say that in a few months, during the heat of summer, she wouldn't miss being in Dallas and at her fancy apartment that had not two, but three swimming pools.

She flicked her gaze to the fence. Shame she didn't get along better with Cassidy Anderson. If she did, she might be inclined to ask if she could use the pool during the week.

She heard a loud splash and wondered if someone had jumped off the diving board. That was nice. You didn't find many pools with diving boards anymore. Again, she felt a twinge of envy. Yes, it was a shame she and the new neighbor had gotten off to a rough start.

She called me a bitch, she reminded herself. Then she smiled. Well, she kinda was being one, wasn't she? But still…

"Hey…are you out there?"

She frowned, then looked at the fence. "Are you talking to me?"

A laugh. "Yeah."

Laura leaned forward in her chair. "What do you want?"

Another laugh. "Well, I've got a proposition."

Laura's eyebrows shot up. "Okay…no. Really not interested," she said to the fence.

"You don't even know what it is."

Laura stood up and walked over to the fence. "What do you want?" she asked again.

She heard Cassidy walk closer too. "My yard guys quit on me."

"They didn't like the change from seven to ten?"

"That…and I wanted flowers and stuff. We kinda had a mutual parting of the ways."

"And you want me to recommend someone?"

"I want you to do it."

"*Me?*"

"It pays well." Then she coughed. "Not that I'm trying to throw money around or anything."

Laura smiled, then wiped it from her face. "I don't know the first thing about being a yard girl."

"Not true. I've seen your yard. And flowers. I want mine to look like that."

Laura hesitated, then shook her head. "Look, you should probably hire professionals. You've got a lot of land. I'm not sure I could keep up with it and our yard too."

"It's less than you have. Most of it is wooded. It's only in the front and back here by the pool. The other side I left natural."

Laura hesitated again, wondering how much Cassidy would pay her. It would be nice to have some extra cash. Her savings was dwindling at a rapid pace and she had no intention of touching her investments. Even though she didn't have any living expenses here, she still needed *some* kind of income. Cassidy must have sensed her indecision.

"Listen, why don't you come over and take a look? Then you can decide."

Oh, hell...she was curious to see the house up close, after all. She'd only seen it through the fence in the front...and her binoculars, of course. "How did you know I was out here?"

"I saw you when I went off the board." A pause. "You coming over?"

"All right."

"The gate is locked. I'll meet you out there."

Laura stared at the fence for several seconds, aware that Cassidy had already left. *Why am I doing this?*

"Because your writing career is at a standstill," she reminded herself.

She walked through the grass, along the fence line. By the time she'd reached the front, she heard the gate opening next door. She went around the fence that separated the two properties and out onto the road. The gate wasn't in the center of Cassidy's property but much closer to the side by their house. Laura found her waiting under the oak tree, casually leaning against it. A T-shirt covered what appeared to be a one-piece swimsuit and, like her, Cassidy was wearing flip-flops. Her hair was damp from the pool, her skin tan. Laura had to admit—tall, dark, and handsome—she was even more attractive up close and personal.

"Ah, you like beer," Cassidy said with a smile. "Come on in. I was about to get one."

It was only then that Laura realized she was still holding the beer bottle. *Geez, she's going to think you're a lush.* She shrugged. Did she care what Cassidy Anderson thought?

As they walked up the driveway, Cassidy motioned to the yard. "See? Not a whole lot to mow. There's even less in the back."

Because of the woods, the yard was actually much smaller than their own. And of course, she knew what the backyard looked like. She had a perfect view of it from her writing room.

"I'm glad you left the woods." At Cassidy's raised eyebrows, she explained, "I used to play in them when I was a kid."

"Oh. So you grew up here."

"I was three when we moved here."

"I never had the opportunity to come out here. I wish I had."

Laura followed her around the house and to the back. "What do you mean?"

"The property here. My father bought it about thirty-five years ago. Thought when he retired that they would build out here." Cassidy smiled, showing off perfect white teeth. "My mother had a different idea, though."

"So you got it?"

"My brother had no interest in it. He's a city boy." She walked over to the outdoor kitchen area and opened up a full-sized, stainless steel fridge. "Another beer?"

"Sure. Thanks." She went to the sink and poured out what was left in her bottle and handed the empty to Cassidy. "This is pretty awesome," she said, pointing at the outdoor kitchen.

"Yeah...I haven't gotten to use it as much as I'd like to. I've got some friends coming later today, so I'm going to try my hand at some teriyaki beef kabobs."

Laura nodded, thinking that sounded good. Instead of commenting, she glanced out to the yard. "So...your yard guys left you, huh?"

"Well, like I said, it was mutual. They don't do flowers." She handed Laura a beer that she'd first slipped into a koozie. "I like what you've done over there." Cassidy walked toward the pool and sat down at one of the tables. "I was paying these guys four hundred dollars a month. They mowed the lawn, trimmed the grass, edged along the sidewalks…that sort of thing. If you'd do all that plus add some flowers—and take care of them—I'd pay you four-fifty. And of course, I'd pay for the flowers and whatnot." She raised her eyebrows. "Interested?"

Four-fifty? Laura tried to estimate how long it would take her. Using the riding mower, she figured she could have the lawn done in about an hour, front and back. The trees were mature, so trimming the grass around them wouldn't be much of a chore. Planting and tending to flowers would be more pleasure than work. Was she interested?

"Yes. I'll do it."

"Great! I only have one rule." Cassidy showed her smile off again. "Have it finished by noon on Fridays."

CHAPTER ELEVEN

Cassidy wasn't fond of blind dates. Never had been. But Erica promised her that she'd "love" Kathryn. Cassidy reminded herself that Erica had said the same thing about Claudia. However, Erica forgot to mention that Kathryn only ate chicken, never beef. So she'd had to scramble to adjust the teriyaki beef kabobs to include one with chicken breast. Sure, it wouldn't have the twenty-four-hour marinade on it—one hour, at the most—but it was the best she could do on short notice.

"So do you like her?"

"I've hardly talked to her. I've been busy thawing a chicken breast." She glanced over to the pool. "Besides, she and Amber seem like they have a lot to talk about."

"They haven't seen each other in months."

"I thought they worked together."

"Not anymore. Kathryn's in Irving now." Erica leaned closer. "How great would it be if you two started dating? We'd get to see you more often, that's for sure. I can't believe this is only the second time you've invited us out here."

"Is it?"

"I know you have a long list of friends, Cassidy. I'm glad we at least have warranted two visits now," she said with a laugh. "So what happened with Claudia? You were dating for over a month. That's a record for you, isn't it?"

Cassidy shrugged. "It was okay. I wasn't going to marry her or anything, so I didn't see the point in drawing it out."

"Still looking for that soulmate, huh?"

"Yep. I've never been one to settle. Not in business and not in my private life." She took the pitcher of margaritas from the fridge and topped off Erica's glass. "And…it's kinda fun to date."

"Well, you have variety, that's for sure," Erica teased. "Who was this last one?"

"Larson. On our first date, she invited me in for a nightcap and sex."

"Right up your alley," Erica smirked.

Cassidy stared out at the pool. Was that right up her alley? "I don't know. There's a huge difference between sleeping with someone—sex—and making love. And honestly, I can't remember the last time—if ever—that I've done the latter."

"I think you need to give them more than a month, Cassidy. It's hard to get to know someone in a few weeks."

"It only takes a few weeks to know if they're the one or not. Sex is just sex." She shrugged. "I don't know. Maybe it's my age."

"Your age? What? You don't like sex anymore?"

Cassidy laughed. "I like it as much as I always have. I would just like to get to know them a little first, I guess."

"How old are you again?"

"Forty-four. A few weeks ago."

"Did you have a party?"

"God, no. The last party I had was when I turned thirty. I may do one at fifty, though. Depends on my frame of mind at the time, I guess."

Erica touched her arm. "Well, you probably don't want to hear this, but Claudia was heartbroken."

"Come on. She knew the score. I never once said anything to make her think I was emotionally involved."

"That always seems to be your problem. You don't *let* yourself get emotionally involved."

"I know you're friends with Claudia. But she wasn't the one. I'm sorry if I hurt her."

"Oh, she'll get over you. They always do, don't they?"

Cassidy wasn't sure how to reply to that and she was thankful when she saw Amber hold up her empty glass. "Your wife wants a margarita refill. I guess we should join them."

"I'll take the pitcher. And I'd love to get in the pool if it's still heated."

"It is. But the weather is getting warmer. I'll probably turn it off after the weekend." She motioned with her head. "Go ahead. I'll grab some towels."

* * *

"Now who do you have over?" Laura murmured.

She'd resisted picking up the binoculars, telling herself once again that it was just wrong—*wrong!*—to spy. Especially now that Cassidy was going to pay her four hundred and fifty bucks a month to tend to her lawn. She didn't need binoculars to tell her that these other three women were new. Judging by the kiss she'd seen, two were obviously a couple. But…also judging by the way Cassidy treated the other woman, they weren't a couple. New date, perhaps? Blind date? Her friends trying to set her up?

This one wasn't for her either, Laura thought. *Who picks your dates?* Blond again. Thin, but not as bony as the anorexic one had been. Watching her throw her head back as she laughed… nauseating.

Oh? What was that? Margarita?

She couldn't stand it any longer. She snatched up the binoculars, focusing on the new blonde. Okay…pretty cute, although she'd bet a hundred dollars that blond wasn't her natural color. Early thirties, maybe. She looked at the other two. They appeared to be a little older. Then she found Cassidy. She was smiling. She was chatting. It looked forced. Then Cassidy stood and pulled her T-shirt off. Not a bikini, but a black one-piece again. Oddly disappointed that it wasn't a bikini, Laura lowered the glasses, just in time to see Cassidy look her way.

She ducked down below the windowsill. God, did the woman have a sixth sense or what? That's the second time she'd almost gotten caught.

"You have *got* to stop with the damn binoculars."

A margarita sounded good, though. Pity she had no tequila. She leaned against the wall with a sigh. How sad was it that her sole entertainment was spying on her neighbor? Maybe next weekend, she'd plan a trip to the city. Surely she could find someone to have dinner with. Or she could pop over to Carla's house, see the kids, talk Carla into springing for dinner. She thought her mother might actually like to have the house to herself for a night. Yeah…maybe that's what she'd do. Of course, that meant she'd have to tolerate the twins. Was it worth it?

She sat there for a while longer, twirling her hair in her fingers. She had thick, unruly hair, not thin and silky like the women at the pool. Maybe she should go blond. They seemed to be having much more fun than she was. Then she remembered when she was in her twenties and the hair color episode from hell. He assured her it would be a beautiful, light blond. It would look great on her, he'd said. Nope. Ronald McDonald red on the first try. Orange when he tried a second time. And then a shocking off-white was the last result as he attempted to "tame" the color. Her hair was so frazzled, she was afraid to touch it for fear it would break off.

She sighed. Maybe she'd stick with her natural color. Nothing exciting about light brown, but it wasn't all that bad. She ran a hand through it. She could stand to have a trim, though. Maybe she'd do that on Monday.

* * *

Despite Kathryn's obvious willingness, Cassidy had no desire to have her share her bed. Perhaps it was true what she'd told Erica. What was wrong with getting to know someone before jumping into bed? Did everything have to end in sex? Couldn't they at least wait until a second date? Claudia had been a sex machine and even she hadn't suggested bed on their first date.

But Larson? Yeah. Cassidy didn't even remember their dinner, what they'd talked about. All she remembered was being pulled into an apartment and not leaving until the next morning. The weekend here? Much of the same.

And now Kathryn? Hell, they hadn't said more than a handful of words. Apparently margaritas, and then wine, had made Kathryn lose any inhibitions she may have had. She'd run her fingers up Cassidy's arm teasingly after dinner. She'd flirted. She'd touched. And no doubt, after being initially disappointed to be going to bed alone, she'd crashed into a deep, alcohol-induced sleep.

And now here she was, sitting alone on the patio, the water of the pool rippling in the light wind. Erica and Amber were in bed. Kathryn was in bed. And she, after attempting to sleep, was sitting here listening to the night sounds—frogs in the trees mostly—and feeling a heavy sense of loneliness settle over her.

Was it her age that was making her feel this way? She'd never given her age much attention before, but turning forty-four had been more traumatic than she'd let on. Because forty-four was one very short year from forty-five. And forty-five was too damn close to fifty.

And she *still* hadn't met the love of her life.

She stretched her legs out, staring into the darkness. Maybe she was trying too hard. Or maybe she wasn't trying at all. Flitting from date to date, bed to bed, never settling long enough to really get to know any them.

Oh, she knew them, all right. Take Kathryn, for instance. They had zero in common. From what she'd learned, Kathryn was a movie buff. Rarely missed a new release. Her? She could think of twenty things she'd rather do to kill a couple of hours than sitting in a movie theater with a hundred other people. Kathryn also liked shopping and malls. "I could spend hours just browsing." Cassidy would slit her wrists. And, of course, there was the whole "I don't eat beef" thing. Who didn't like a tender, juicy steak, medium rare? And the teriyaki beef kabobs? They were sinfully delicious. Add to all that, she simply wasn't attracted to her in the least.

So, yeah, she already knew that there would be no second date with Kathryn, if you could even call this a first. But Cassidy would be a good hostess. She'd already planned brunch for tomorrow. And if the forecasted rain showers held off, they could enjoy the pool a little before heading back to Dallas. She would then tell Kathryn she'd enjoyed meeting her and leave it at that.

And the next time Erica—or any other friend—tried to set her up, "No thanks" would be her answer. She could find her own dates. That had never been a problem.

Or maybe that *was* the problem. There was always—always—a date.

CHAPTER TWELVE

Laura had made quick work of Cassidy's lawn. As expected, she had it mowed in less than an hour. She turned the mower off and sat there, mentally estimating how long it would take to complete the tedious trimming and edging. Another hour? At least. Then she turned and glanced at the pool.

Inviting, to say the least. It was nearly noon. The sky was clear. The temp was over eighty. Sweat clung to her skin. How wonderful would it be to strip off her clothes and…

"Don't even think about it," she murmured. With her luck, Cassidy would come home unexpectedly and catch her. But it was Thursday. Surely Cassidy wouldn't pop over on a Thursday.

She would finish trimming and edging. She would map out where she would put flowerbeds…and *then*, she would get in the pool.

Laura found herself humming as she walked around a particularly large oak, buzzing off the grass along its base with the weed trimmer. At the edge of the lawn, where the woods grew, she paused, wondering if any of her old trails were still there. Probably not. How many years had it been since she'd played there? Twenty or more? Of the ten-acre lot, she guessed the house, pool, and lawn took up only two. As Cassidy had said, she'd left most of the woods intact. When she was a kid, Laura had thought the woods went on forever. She never seemed to run out of places to explore. She smiled as she remembered the leaning tree. It was at the edge of a clearing and—after climbing the tree—there was a perfect view of the summer sunset. The land wasn't hilly by any means...just gently rolling hills here and there. But from that tree, she'd felt like she was on the top of a mountain, looking down as the sun disappeared below the horizon. She made a mental note to sneak over one afternoon and see if she could find the leaning tree again.

But not today. No, today—after the yard was done—she was going to sneak into the pool.

And pray that Cassidy didn't come home early.

* * *

Maybe stripping off her clothes wasn't the brightest idea, but she was hot and sweaty and going home to change into one of her two swimsuits did not sound appealing. Besides, in the backyard and pool area, no one could see her. No one. Unless, of course, they were upstairs in her writing room, using binoculars!

So, without delaying any longer, she tossed her clothes into a pile at the edge of the pool, went over to the outdoor shower to rinse off the grass that still clung to her legs, then jumped feet first into the water. She was smiling as she swam across to the other side. It was refreshingly cool and felt like silk against her skin. Oh, yeah. This could become a habit.

She spent a good half-hour splashing around, cooling off. If this was to become a habit, she would need to get a float of some kind. She knew Cassidy had some but, looking around, she couldn't tell where they were kept. There appeared to be a closet of some sort at the edge of the outdoor kitchen. Maybe they were in there. Of course, "borrowing" her pool was one thing. Rummaging through her closet looking for pool toys was quite another.

She finally made herself get out, and she stood in the sun, letting the breeze dry her off. She wished she had thought to bring a towel and clean clothes. Putting on her filthy mowing clothes seemed quite uncivilized after her swim in the pristine pool. But she shrugged and put them on anyway.

She went back to the front where she'd left her weed trimmer. She took a look around the yard and nodded. It looked good. Tomorrow morning she'd get out Frankie's old tiller and work up a flowerbed for Cassidy. She would at least get a few flowers in before she came for the weekend.

CHAPTER THIRTEEN

"Nice kitchen. I love it," Becki cooed. "Do you cook?"

Cassidy nodded. "I do."

Becki smiled seductively. "With all of this…*and* you love to cook, how is it that you're still single?"

Cassidy laughed appropriately but didn't bother with an answer. She walked through the double doors that opened up onto the patio. "Do you feel like a swim before dinner?"

"Oh, I'd love one." Another seductive smile, then red-tipped fingers glided up her arm. "Clothing optional?"

Cassidy glanced over to the two-story house next door, wondering what their vantage point was. Could Laura Fry see into her yard? She smiled then—a true smile.

"Yeah…clothing optional."

* * *

"Oh my freakin' *God*," Laura murmured, her eyes glued to the pool. Did the blonde really just drop her clothes? "And where are you…tall, dark, and handsome?"

Laura felt her pulse increase when she saw Cassidy walk up with towels and a float. Was she going to strip too? Cassidy tossed the towels onto a chaise lounge and flipped the float into the pool where the blonde was waiting.

"What do you *see* in these women?" she whispered. "They're so...*ugh*. You have such bad taste in women."

Then her eyes widened. *Oh. My. God.* Cassidy unbuttoned her shirt slowly, the blonde's eyes fixed on her. She was wearing a black bra and Laura had to remind herself to breathe. She knew the binoculars were within arm's reach, but she adamantly refused to grab them. Not out of a higher moral code or anything. No, she was afraid she'd faint.

Before Cassidy removed her bra, she slipped her shorts off, revealing matching black panties.

"Jesus..." Laura hissed. *She's a goddess.* She frowned. *Did I just think that?*

She held on tightly to the windowsill, resisting the urge to fling the curtains open so she'd have a better view. The bra came off first and Laura felt the blood rush to her face. Her mouth was dry and she had difficulty swallowing. Then Cassidy paused, her head tilting slightly. Laura ducked down to the floor a nanosecond before Cassidy looked her way.

She leaned her head against the wall, her eyes closed. "God, she's gorgeous." Then her eyes opened. This was at least the fourth different woman she'd seen her with. What was she? Some female Casanova?

"That figures," she muttered, shaking her head.

* * *

Cassidy wasn't at all self-conscious about swimming naked. She took care of her body. She exercised. She ate reasonably well. She was quite comfortable in her nakedness. But if one more person told her she had a nice body "for her age," she was going to scream. Especially a woman ten years younger than herself.

"I went out with a woman who was forty-eight," Becki continued. "She looked *nothing* like you." She made a face. "Things were starting to sag, if you know what I mean. Of course, she had huge breasts. You won't have that problem."

Cassidy silently groaned. So she had a nice body for being an old woman, but she had tiny boobs. Why did she invite Becki out for the weekend? Oh, yeah. Wednesday night's dinner date hadn't ended in sex, despite the passionate kiss Becki had drawn her into.

She ducked under the water and swam to the other side, holding on to the edge as she slicked her hair back. Whatever happened to her vow to spend the weekend alone for once?

"I love a woman who cooks, by the way. So what delectable meal are you planning for me?"

"I'm going to grill steaks for tonight. The delectable dinner will be tomorrow night. Chicken scaloppini. I've got a nice Riesling to go with it." She raised her eyebrows. "Unless steak is not to your liking. I can grill you something else."

Becki nodded. "I'm not really crazy about steak, but I suppose I could eat a little."

Great. Another one who doesn't like beef. "I've got extra chicken breasts. I'll be happy to grill one for you."

Becki swam over to her. "That would be super. I much prefer chicken." She brushed her naked body against Cassidy. "But I'm not in any hurry for dinner."

Cassidy looked past her, noting that dusk was approaching. She'd also skipped lunch. Her gaze drifted up to the neighbor's house. There was a light on upstairs. She sighed, wondering why she wasn't more attracted to Becki—a very attractive woman of thirty-four. Oh, well. She supposed she could fake it. It wouldn't be the first time.

"Let's go inside."

CHAPTER FOURTEEN

Laura sipped her coffee, absently listening to the rapid hammering of a woodpecker over in one of Cassidy Anderson's trees. It was barely daylight, but cardinals were already at the feeders, their sharp, metallic calls piercing the air. Thick clouds drifted over, and she wondered if they might get rain this morning. The lawn could use it, that was for sure.

She stretched her legs out, mentally planning her day. She would take a few hours to write. *Yeah, right.* Then, her mother had wanted to get out of the house so they were going to meet Carla for lunch. Laura was having Mexican food withdrawals, and Carla was happy to recommend a place. On the way home, they would make a quick trip to the grocery store—her mother had requested an old-fashioned roast with potatoes and carrots for their Sunday dinner.

She had to admit, it had been fun cooking. When she lived alone, it wasn't something she did often. Even though she complained to her mother that she didn't like to cook, she had been enjoying it. And occasionally her mother would venture into the kitchen to help, if only to peel potatoes or chop veggies.

"Hey…you out there?"

Laura's head popped up and she stared at the fence. "It's not even seven. What are you doing up?"

"What? Do you know my sleep schedule?"

"Just assumed…since you have company and all."

"Oh? How do you know I have company?"

Damn! "I heard voices."

"Oh? Now you're hearing voices? Have you seen a doctor for that?"

Laura rolled her eyes. "What do you want?"

"The yard looks nice. And the flowers."

"Yeah…I'm just getting started with the flowers."

"Did you keep the receipts?"

"I did."

"Okay." A pause. "So I'm having coffee."

Laura raised her eyebrows. "Is that…not a good thing?"

Cassidy laughed. "I mean, I'm standing here with a cup of coffee. I'm assuming you have coffee too. I thought I'd pop over and pay you for the flowers and…and maybe discuss what else you're going to do."

"It's…it's seven."

"And? You're up. I'm up."

"I have bedhead," she said as she quickly ran a hand over her hair, trying to tame it.

Cassidy laughed. "So do I. I'll be over in a second."

Oh, crap. She was still in her sleep shirt. She was barefoot. Did she have time to run upstairs and put on a bra? No. But she shouldn't care. This was *her* time. Her quiet time. She shouldn't have to be concerned with neighbors popping over at daybreak!

She narrowed her eyes as Cassidy walked through the dew-dampened grass in flip-flops. She was dressed similarly in a T-shirt and loose-fitting cotton shorts. However, that's where the similarities ended.

"You so do *not* have bedhead," she accused.

"No? I just assumed. I haven't looked in a mirror yet." She smiled. "Or brushed my teeth."

God...so this is how she looks when she gets out of bed? That is so not fair, she thought as she again ran a hand over her unruly hair.

Cassidy pointed at one of the patio chairs. "May I?"

Not only did she probably look a hot mess with her bedhead, but she'd apparently forgotten all her manners. She nodded. "Of course."

"This patio is great. Inviting," Cassidy said as she looked around. "Love all the flowers. Have you always had a green thumb?"

Laura shrugged. "I'm not sure. This is my first attempt at it."

"Really?"

"My mother...well, flowers—plants—that was always her thing. She can't do it anymore, so when I moved here..."

Cassidy nodded. "Oh, that's right. You said your mother was an invalid."

Laura felt herself blush. "Well, I may have exaggerated a bit. She uses a walker to get around, mostly. Wheelchair too." At Cassidy's raised eyebrows, she explained. "She was in a car accident three years ago. Frankie was driving."

"Ah. Your stepfather."

"Again...*not* my stepfather. I couldn't stand the man."

"Yeah, he was a bit on the obnoxious side. To be honest, I couldn't get that privacy fence up fast enough."

"I guessed he was the cause of it. But with the pool and all...I suppose you need one."

Cassidy met her gaze and smiled. "Yes. Especially since I enjoy skinny-dipping."

Laura tried. She really, really tried. But the blush started at her toes and crept up to her face anyway. She wanted to look away, mainly because she was embarrassed. Cassidy's expression told her she knew Laura had seen the activity at the pool. Well, there was no sense in trying to deny it.

"You have the worst taste in women," she blurted out.

Cassidy raised her eyebrows. "You think so?"

"So what happened to the anorexic blonde?"

Cassidy laughed. "You must mean Claudia. She…well, she wasn't really my type. I ended that."

"And the tall brunette?"

Cassidy frowned, then nodded. "Oh…Larson."

"Interesting name. What happened with her?"

"Yeah. She was a little…well, she called me old…in so many words. But she was very complimentary about it."

"She called you old, but it was a compliment?"

"She said I had a nice body for my age and that nothing was sagging yet."

"Oh my God."

Cassidy wiggled her eyebrows. "Well, I don't really have enough to sag," she said, pointing at her chest. "I was told that yesterday."

Laura refused to stare at her breasts. And why should she? She'd seen her at the pool, naked. She had nice breasts. Small, but nice. At least from a distance. It wasn't like she'd had her binoculars trained on her. *And that was a damn shame*. She leaned forward, resting her elbows on her thighs. "So really…where do you find all these women? The only time I go out is when friends set me up on blind dates."

Cassidy gave her a flirty smile. "What? Do you want to share?"

"God, no. Like I said, you have bad taste. I'm just wondering where you find them. They're all thin, pretty…girlie. If you like that sort of thing. I don't," she added quickly.

"I meet them through mutual friends, at parties. Some blind dates too, which I hate."

"Me too. They're the worst."

"Some are straight."

"That's creepy."

Cassidy smiled. "They're being adventurous."

"They're being stupid."

"Okay, yeah, they are. But at least we got that out of the way. You know…I'm gay, you're gay."

"And you have horrible taste in women."

Cassidy laughed again. "If you say so." Laura watched her watch a male cardinal at the feeder. "The flowers you did for me look good." Cassidy turned back to her. "What else do you have planned?"

"That small flowerbed was something I put in so you'd have some color when you came this weekend. Begonias. Nothing fancy. I think you need at least two more—larger ones— in the front."

"Okay. What else?"

"I was thinking some sort of planters out by the pool would be nice, but I didn't know how much you wanted to spend. Those large pots are quite expensive. I was thinking I could fill them with something that would flow over the sides, like portulacas—moss rose—or purslane or something like that. Those flowers will last all summer long."

Cassidy waved her hand in the air. "Whatever you think. Flowers out by the pool would look good. How much do I owe you so far?"

"That little flowerbed, including the compost and mulch, was only about thirty bucks. I thought, though, since you've got stone on your house, you might want me to get some stone to line the bed with."

Cassidy nodded. "Sure. Can you do that?"

"Hauling stone is a little more labor intensive than just mowing," she said.

"So you want more money?"

Laura smiled. "I was thinking we could trade."

Cassidy raised her eyebrows. "Trade?"

"Yes. I'll do labor intensive—for the original agreed-upon price—if I can use your pool afterward."

Cassidy met her gaze and grinned. "I think that's a fair trade. You're not going to drown, are you? Or slip and fall and sue me?"

Laura stood up. "I won't drown. I won't sue you. Can't guarantee I won't slip and fall." She motioned to the house. "You want another cup of coffee?"

Cassidy hesitated. "I should probably get back. My company might be looking for me."

"Oh, that's right. The young blonde."

Cassidy stood up too. "Yes. Becki. And unless you need the thirty bucks now, I'll add it to whatever you do next week."

"Sounds good."

Cassidy nodded. "Well...then I guess I'll see you later."

"Enjoy the rest of your weekend."

Cassidy sighed. "Yeah. You too."

Laura watched her walk away, wondering at the heavy sigh. Well, not really wondering. The blonde she'd seen her with at the pool would make Laura sigh heavily too.

She went back in the house and poured another cup of coffee. Cassidy was nice, she decided. For that reason alone, she should ditch Frankie's binoculars. And she should also stop spying on her when she knew Cassidy had company out at the pool. That would be the proper thing to do. In fact, she vowed right then and there that she would not peek out of her window later today when they were at the pool.

That is, of course, providing they weren't naked. If they were, then all bets were off.

She rolled her eyes. She *really* needed to get out of the house.

CHAPTER FIFTEEN

Cassidy closed her eyes, relaxing as the sun's rays peeked through the clouds. It was a little cooler today, especially after the brief rain shower they'd had, but it wasn't enough to keep her out of the pool. Becki, on the other hand, had opted to stay inside. She was in the entertainment room, watching a movie on the giant TV in there. Theater seating, surround sound, a bag of popcorn, and a bottle of water—Cassidy had left her on her own. Becki hadn't seemed to mind as she'd settled down onto the comfortable seat, waving Cassidy away.

When she'd left Laura and gotten back inside her house, Becki had been pouring a cup of coffee. She'd told Cassidy that she looked adorable. She'd tugged Cassidy back up the stairs and into bed. Cassidy had pretended to enjoy the sex, much like she'd done last night.

She was beginning to wonder if something was wrong with her. She had *lots* of practice making love with women she wasn't in love with. Why, suddenly, had it become such an issue with her? Had turning forty-four really been that traumatic? Or was she simply tired of it? Tired of playing the game. Tired of feeling lonely—alone—even with a woman in her bed.

She heard a car start up next door. Their garage was at the back of the house with their driveway on the other side. She looked up at the house, wondering where Laura's bedroom was. The first set of windows was closer to the street with the maple tree blocking most of the view. The second set, though, would have a clear view of the pool. Judging by Laura's blush earlier, she guessed her bedroom was the second one.

She smiled as she remembered Laura's expression when Cassidy had mentioned skinny-dipping. It wasn't the first time she'd sensed someone watching her. Laura had obviously been embarrassed but not so embarrassed that she hadn't voiced her opinion on Cassidy's dates.

"You have the worst taste in women."

Was that true? Did she? Granted, she tended to ignore personality in favor of looks. That was a habit that had started in college. She wasn't blind to her own looks. She had known she could go out with anyone she wanted to. She took that for granted. Now that she was older, she realized how conceited she must have been back then.

But had anything changed? Sure, she was forty-four, but she took care of herself...and her body. She had financial security, she had a successful business. She never lacked for female company—gay or straight. Had anything changed?

She moved her hands lazily in the water, putting the float in motion. No, the only change was that she had gotten older. She was still alone...still searching for that one special person. That person who could steal her breath with just a look. That person who could make her smile, make her laugh. That person who could read her, who knew what she was thinking, feeling, without the need for words between them. That person who she couldn't wait to see, to be with—every day. That person who could be both best friend and lover. That person. She feared, however, that that person didn't exist. At least not for her.

"*You have the worst taste in women.*"

Yeah…apparently it was true. But how was it that Laura Fry could see that—from a distance—and Cassidy—up close and personal with them—could not?

CHAPTER SIXTEEN

"So you haven't written *anything*?"

Laura grabbed a chip and dunked it in the bowl of salsa that had been placed in front of her. She paused before eating it, meeting her sister's eyes.

"I have written *something*, yes. Just not...you know, the makings of a book."

"No offense, but have you considered the possibility that you were only a one-hit wonder?"

Laura stared at her. "It's been eight years. What do you think?"

"Maybe this isn't your calling." Laura looked at her mother, who simply shrugged. "If you're meant to write another book, you will. I think you're pressing too hard. Maybe you should take a break from it."

"I've been breaking for eight years."

"No, from what you've told me, you've been trying to write another book."

That was true, of course. She had not really ever taken a break from trying. She couldn't even begin to guess how many she'd started, then discarded. Fifty? Some she'd toss after only a few pages. Others, months' worth of words—going nowhere—would be shelved, hoping she could someday salvage them. She never could.

"I guess maybe I could give it a rest, but that just seems wrong."

"I think Mom is right. You're trying too hard. Focus on something else."

Laura snatched up another chip. "Well, I do have a part-time job."

"Really? What?"

"She's mowing the neighbor's yard," her mother supplied.

"What? Why?"

"Because she asked me. And she wants flowers."

"What does she pay?"

"Four-fifty a month."

"Four-fifty? That's it?"

Laura smiled. "Four-fifty for a couple of hours of work a week...plus use of her pool. I think I got a great deal."

"So you like this yard stuff, huh? Maybe you should start a business."

She knew Carla was teasing, but honestly, it had crossed her mind. There were several retired and elderly couples in the area, and she'd seen them struggling to maintain their lawns. She just didn't know if that was something she wanted to commit to. Taking care of her mother's place and now Cassidy's...that was enough—for now—to occupy her, given that much of the rest of her time was spent staring at her laptop, hoping words—a novel—would come to her. If she took a break, as they'd suggested, might she find that she had too much time on her hands? She smiled to herself. Of course not! She now had access to a pool. She was fairly certain she could kill multiple hours per day lounging in Cassidy's pool.

With that decided, she found it safer to change the subject. "So what is Stephen doing today that you were allowed to escape without the twins. Not that I wouldn't mind seeing them," she added quickly.

"I know you think they're brats. Quit lying."

"They're just at that age," she said evasively.

"You've been saying that since they were two."

Laura smiled and shoved a chip into her mouth. "Okay... brats."

"Stephen took them to a movie," Carla continued.

"Pity the poor souls who sit by them," she said without thinking.

"Bryson was looking forward to the movie. I'm sure he'll behave. Brooke, however, didn't really want to go. She'll be the problem one."

"How could you let them get to be eight years old and still be little terrors?"

"Holy terrors," her mother chimed in, causing Carla to stare at her with an open mouth. "As if you don't know," her mother added with a wave of her hand.

Carla sighed. "I blame Stephen. We tried for so long to have kids that when it finally happened, he spoiled them rotten." She pointed a finger at Laura. "And you didn't help things, Aunt Laura. Always bringing them presents and toys."

"I at least try to discipline them when I'm around. They don't even like me anymore."

"They don't like anyone right now." She stared past them. "Lunch is served. Don't forget, I get one of your enchiladas in trade for a taco."

"Not so fast, sis. I said I would see how the taco looked first," she reminded her. The plate placed in front of Carla contained three large, stuffed-to-the-gills, crispy tacos. Laura smiled. "And I approve. Gimme one."

CHAPTER SEVENTEEN

Laura felt a twinge of guilt—albeit a very tiny twinge—for playing in Cassidy's pool before she'd even done one single thing that constituted yardwork. She was mentally planning flowerbeds, she'd told herself as way of an excuse. But she really didn't need an excuse, did she? No. Cassidy had given her permission to use the pool. She never once put qualifiers on it.

And it was simply glorious. The water looked crisp and blue. Refreshing. And oh, it was. And she'd had two beers. And she was relaxed. No, there would be no yardwork this afternoon. She'd make up for it tomorrow. She'd head into town—in Frankie's old truck—and buy the materials she'd need for the flowerbed. She'd also buy two large planters for out here at the pool. She'd definitely get those done before Cassidy came on Friday.

She sighed as she looked up into the sky. *Wonder who she'll bring this weekend?* She shook her head as the float bumped an edge and she shoved off with her foot, pushing her back into the middle. She didn't profess to know Cassidy in the least. They'd only had a handful of conversations, after all. But still, she seemed nice. Normal. Attractive. *Really* attractive. Obviously wealthy enough to afford this huge ass house. She'd seen her car—a Mercedes. So yeah, she probably could get any date she wanted. Why then would she settle for these bimbos that she'd had over?

Oh, in all fairness, bimbo might be too strong a word. She'd not actually spoken to any of them. No, but she'd seen them through binoculars, seen enough to know that not a single one of them was a keeper. But even though those women weren't *her* type, that didn't mean they weren't Cassidy's type.

"The worst taste," she murmured.

The ringing of her phone brought her around and she paddled as fast as she could to the side, sliding the towel toward her, the towel that her phone rested on. Her eyes widened when she saw who it was. *Crap!*

She cleared her throat before answering. "Hello."

"Hey…it's me. Cassidy."

"Hi." She looked around her guiltily, hoping Cassidy couldn't hear the sound of the pool water lapping at her float.

"Am I calling at a bad time?"

"No, no. I'm just…just…actually, I'm over at your place. Scoping out possible flowerbeds," she lied.

"Oh, that's great. I was just thinking, it was presumptuous of me to expect you to pay for everything and get reimbursed later. I mean—"

"A couple of hundred bucks won't break me," she said.

"Well, I didn't know. I assumed you didn't have a job."

"Actually, I don't."

"Independently wealthy?"

Laura snorted. "In my dreams. I'm…" What? A writer? "I'm taking a break from…from my job. My mother needed someone to stay with her after Frankie died. I got the short straw."

"Oh, I see. Well, this weekend, if you could give me an idea of what you're spending, then I'll leave some cash for you to use. In fact, I should have done that anyway."

"Cassidy, you don't—"

"I'll leave it in the pool closet," she said, ignoring Laura's protest. "Whatever you take out, put a receipt in. That's fair, right?"

It would help, she acknowledged. Lately, if she kept more than five hundred dollars in her checking account, it was an anomaly. She had been milking her savings account for the last year, touching it as little as possible. Still, to be thirty-seven years old—thirty-eight in two days—and barely have ten thousand dollars in savings was a little scary.

"Okay. Deal."

"Great." A pause. "So...how's the pool?"

Laura rolled her eyes. "I swear, do you have a sixth sense or what?"

Cassidy laughed. "Don't drown. It's so hard to find good yard help these days." Another light laugh. "I'll see you over the weekend."

Laura was smiling as she placed her phone back on the towel. So much for feeling guilty. There was no need to now. Cassidy knew she was in the pool. She flipped off the float, dipping under the water to cool off.

Yep, she had a pretty sweet deal going on here.

* * *

Cassidy twirled around in her chair, a smile still playing on her face. So Laura Fry was in her pool. She wondered what she was wearing. She didn't picture her as the bikini type. She was a little too tomboyish for that. Of course, she'd been called a tomboy more times than she could count and she still wore a bikini on occasion. But hell, at what age do you give up the bikini and go to a one-piece?

"When your body tells you to," she murmured. "Or your friends tell you to."

She tapped her thigh absently with her fingers, her mind still on Laura. She was...nice? Would she call her nice? Their first couple of conversations weren't exactly pleasant. She grinned quickly. She'd called Laura a bitch. Oh, that was so bad, she thought, still smiling. But yeah, she would call her nice. And honest. She could have very well denied being in the pool, even though Cassidy had heard the subtle sound of water. And she could have denied watching the pool from her upstairs window, but she hadn't. All she'd accused Cassidy of having was a sixth sense, thus admitting that it was true.

She turned back around to face her desk, wondering how she was going to kill the last few hours of the afternoon. The company was running like a well-oiled machine. Her brother had a handle on the crews. Tanya managed the office staff without much help from her. She'd already gone over the new marketing plan and had approved it. There was no crisis for her to handle since the glitch with the online appointments had been fixed. There was actually *nothing* for her to do. Maybe she should take a page out of her father's book. He was out at the lake, on his boat.

But she needed something to do. Something to organize, to plan. She smiled slightly. A party. A pool party. A real pool party. The one she'd thrown earlier had been more party and less pool, even though some had taken advantage of the heated water. But a daytime party sounded like more fun. A casual party with burgers or hot dogs on the grill. Or catered again. She mentally went over her list of friends, trying to come up with twenty or twenty-five who would mesh in that casual setting. Memorial Day Weekend was coming up. Could she plan a party in less than two weeks?

She decided she could.

CHAPTER EIGHTEEN

Laura wiped the sweat from her forehead, wishing she'd started on the flowerbed earlier. She should have started yesterday after she'd finished mowing, but the pool had beckoned—again. In fact, she'd been in the pool every day this week except Tuesday. That's the day Cassidy's pool guys came to clean. The only day she hadn't done any yardwork—either at her mother's or here—was on Wednesday. She didn't want to do anything to celebrate her birthday and she'd already told her mother not to make a big deal out of it. Another year older... what was there to celebrate? But she did take the day off from "work." She had packed herself a picnic lunch and a small cooler for refreshments. She had beer. She had a sandwich. She had wine and cheese. She blasted music from Cassidy's outdoor stereo. And she had the pool to herself on a blissfully cloudless, windless day. She sang, she floated, she napped. By the time she dragged herself out of the water, she was as limp as overcooked spaghetti. Still in a waterlogged state, she slept as soundly as she had in years. All in all, it was a good birthday.

But her day of play had set her back. Two large planters out by the pool were stuffed with colorful flowers. They looked so nice, she thought she'd get two more, if Cassidy approved. But designing and digging the flowerbeds out front proved to be harder than she'd thought. Actually, she'd been a bit exuberant in her plans, and she was nowhere near finished with either one. Her hands were dirty so she wiped them on her shorts before pulling her phone out to check the time. Just after three. Cassidy usually didn't arrive until after five, although last weekend it was four thirty. She wondered where she worked that she was able to sneak off early on Fridays. If she lived in the city—with Friday afternoon traffic—she'd be lucky to get here by seven if she worked until five.

She leaned on the hoe for a minute to rest, then went back to work, chopping at the grass that the old tiller hadn't pulled up. The back of Frankie's truck was loaded with mulch and compost and a pallet of stone. She'd hoped to get all that put out today, then pick up flowers on Monday. By the looks of it, she'd be finishing up the flowerbed on Monday and flowers on Tuesday. That is, if she could stay out of the pool.

The sound of Cassidy's gate opening made her jerk her head up. The familiar black Mercedes drove slowly up the driveway, managing to squeeze by Frankie's old truck by inches. Cassidy smiled at her as she drove up to the house and parked.

"Great," she murmured as a rather thin, rather young, rather bleached-blond beauty got out of the passenger's side. "I look like Farmer Brown and she's got a model with her."

Cassidy headed her way, still smiling, followed closely by the model. Laura leaned on the hoe again, barely resisting the urge to yank her ball cap off and tidy her hair.

"Hey," Cassidy said in way of greeting. "This is Ashly," she said, pointing at the model. "Ashly…meet Laura, my neighbor."

Laura nodded at her with a brief smile, then turned accusing eyes at Cassidy. "You're early."

Cassidy nodded. "Yeah. A little."

"You must have a cushy job."

Cassidy laughed. "Well, I'm the boss."

"Of course you are," she said dryly. "In the future, if you could let me know you're going to be early, I'll be sure to get out of here before you come home."

"It's no problem that you're here." Cassidy stepped closer. "You've got some…some dirt here," she said, rubbing Laura's cheek with her thumb. Laura's breath held as their eyes met. "And some here," Cassidy continued, brushing across her eyebrow.

Laura swallowed with difficulty. "Thank you." She finally took her cap off and ran a hand through her hair, conscious of the model staring at her.

Cassidy took a step away, still smiling. "So…this is how you build a flowerbed, huh?"

"Yes, well, it's a little more elaborate than I'd planned." She put the cap back on, hiding her sweaty, dirty hair. "I'm sorry I won't finish it today."

"No hurry. Although if you could have it finished by next weekend, that would be great. Memorial Day Weekend. Party."

"Oh. Goody. Can't wait."

Cassidy laughed. "We'll try not to be too boisterous."

The model cleared her throat and Cassidy glanced at her apologetically. Laura wondered if Cassidy had forgotten she was there.

"Well, I guess we should leave you to it," Cassidy said, motioning to the mound of dirt. "I promised Ashly an afternoon swim."

Laura forced a smile. "You two have fun. I'll clean up out here before I leave."

Cassidy turned back around as if to say something, then—after a quick smile—left her in peace. Laura tried not to be nosy, but she was. The garage door opened and Cassidy drove inside. The trunk popped open and two large bags were retrieved. Was the bleached-blond model planning to stay for a week or what? Then the garage door closed, slowly enough for her to see the blonde laugh flirtingly, then lean closer to Cassidy, presumably to kiss her. Thankfully, the door closed before she had to witness *that*.

"God, where does she find these women?" She shook her head. She'd bet a hundred bucks this one was as straight as an arrow. *Disgusting.*

* * *

Cassidy sat at the edge of the pool, dangling her feet in. Ashly was on a float. Ashly was young and strikingly gorgeous. Ashly was naked. Ashly bored her to tears.

She lifted her head, flicking her gaze to the house next door. She'd heard Laura start the truck up not more than twenty minutes after they'd gotten there. She'd given Ashley a tour of the house, listening to her "oohs and ahhs" indifferently. She absolutely "loved" Cassidy's bedroom. The disappointment was evident on her face when Cassidy took her two bags and deposited them in one of the downstairs guestrooms instead.

Ashly was a friend of a friend. She'd gone out with her once, a couple of months ago. Then this week, Macie had invited Cassidy to dinner at their house and Ashly was there. As was her habit, Cassidy invited all three of them to stay the weekend with her. Macie and Karon couldn't come up until Saturday. Ashly, on the other hand, said she was free all day Friday and would love to ride up with her.

And here she was, entertaining a woman who apparently had preconceived notions of how the weekend would unfold. Granted, their first date had ended with a rather heated kiss, one that Ashly had initiated and one that Cassidy hadn't pulled away from. However, there was nothing about Ashly—other than her looks—that attracted Cassidy so there had been no second date. Dinner the other night had been fun, but Cassidy had given no indication to Ashly that she thought of her as anything other than a friend.

"So what was your neighbor doing over here?"

Cassidy looked over at her, for the first time noting her all-over tan, the result of too much time spent in a tanning bed. "She's putting in some flowerbeds for me. Takes care of the yard."

"Why?"

"I asked her to."

"Do you pay her?"

"Of course."

"She must be hard up for money. That looked like a filthy job."

Cassidy felt the need to defend Laura, then realized she didn't know enough about her to contradict Ashly. Was Laura hard up for money? She didn't come across that way at all, but you never know. She looked over at the two new planters, smiling as the different colors burst from the top.

"I think she enjoys it," Cassidy said. "The yard crew I had wasn't working out so...I asked her."

"She seemed kinda old to be doing stuff like that."

"Old?"

"She's probably close to forty. Of course, the way she was dressed..." she said, her voice trailing off as if it was a bad thing.

What was wrong with the way she was dressed? Laura had had on her usual cutoff jeans and baseball cap. Today she'd been in sports sandals instead of the grass-stained sneakers she'd had on the other times. She frowned. And old?

"How old do you think I am?" she asked Ashly.

Ashly smiled at her seductively. "I'm going to guess thirty-five or six," she said. "But that's no problem. I like older women."

Cassidy sighed wearily. "And how old are you again?"

"Twenty-nine." She laughed. "I'm dreading turning thirty."

Cassidy fell into the pool, fighting the urge to swim over to Ashly and tip her off her float. But that would be childish. She was too old to be childish, so she played along.

"Thirty was tough. I recommend a big party with lots of alcohol."

"You're the second person to tell me that." She rolled her head in Cassidy's direction. "Why am I the only one naked?"

"I actually need to go inside. I'm grilling chicken tonight—green jerk. I need to get it in the sauce. It has to marinate for a few hours."

"What's green jerk?"

"It's Jamaican. It's a spicy, sweet green sauce that goes over drumsticks. I made the sauce last night."

"I'm not much for real spicy."

Cassidy bit her lip. "It's not all that spicy. It's just got a unique hot and sweet mix."

"I suppose it'll be okay."

Cassidy put her hands on the side of the pool and lifted herself out. "Great. Be right back." She paused, remembering her manners. "You want another wine cooler? Or perhaps a margarita? I could mix up a batch."

Ashly's eyes lit up. "I love margaritas."

"Okay. I'll bring one right out."

She gave a relieved sigh as she headed back inside. The outdoor kitchen had all the makings for margaritas, but she escaped into the coolness—and quiet—of the house to make them instead.

* * *

Laura refused—*refused!*—to look through the windows of her bedroom. Not only because these windows didn't offer much of a view of the pool, but because she didn't want to be that nosy, creepy neighbor who spied. Instead, she gathered clean clothes and went across the hall to the bathroom. She would take a long, leisurely shower. She wouldn't give another thought to Cassidy Anderson and the super-thin, super-blond model who was lounging naked in her pool.

"So I peeked," she murmured as she closed the bathroom door.

Just a little. Just enough to make her roll her eyes and turn away. Seriously, what's with women stripping naked in Cassidy's pool? She, herself, was guilty of that too.

But at least I was alone.

Her leisurely shower took twenty minutes, which was quite lengthy for her. After dressing and donning flip-flops, she found her mother in her usual spot—the recliner.

"Don't you get tired of watching TV?"

"What else should I do, Laura Sue? You barely let me in the kitchen anymore."

"It's going to be a nice evening. How about we eat out on the patio?"

"What do you have planned?"

"Steaks—ribeye. Baked potato. A salad."

"Sounds wonderful. Frankie used to make us a steak once a week."

"You should have told me. I just yesterday found the stash of steaks in the freezer."

Her mother struggled to her feet and Laura went over to help her. "Thank you. I get stiff when I sit for too long."

"We need to start walking in the mornings before it gets too hot." Her mother was about to protest and Laura held up a hand. "Just around the block. You can take your cane and hold on to me with your other hand."

"Oh, Laura, I don't know. Planting flowers with you the other week about did me in."

"But it was fun to get out and do something, wasn't it?"

"Yes, it was. But you shouldn't worry about me. I enjoy my TV." She gripped her walker with both hands and took a couple of shuffling steps. "I noticed that you haven't been holed up in your writing room this week."

"I'm taking your advice," she said. "No writing. Taking a break."

"Having access to a pool must have helped spur you," her mother said with a smile.

"Yes. And speaking of that, I thought maybe you might want to give it a try."

"The pool? You know I can't swim, Laura Sue."

"Just get in the shallow end, float around, move your legs. I've been doing some research. Water exercises are the best thing for you. I'm sure Cassidy wouldn't mind."

"Oh…I don't know. I've never been very comfortable around water."

"Let's try it next week," Laura pushed. "I'll hold on to you the whole time. What do you say?"

"What would I wear?"

"I have a swimsuit you can use. You can put shorts on over it if that would make you feel more comfortable."

"I don't know, Laura Sue. We'll see. Help me to my room. I'll get cleaned up before dinner."

CHAPTER NINETEEN

"I hear voices," her mother whispered.

"Yes. Cassidy has company," she said as she settled back in her patio chair. "And there's no need to whisper. They're not."

"I like this cocktail. Frankie was partial to beer." Her mother took a sip. "A little strong for me, though."

"I barely put a splash of bourbon in it."

Her mother took another sip. "It is a nice evening, isn't it? I hear frogs calling, but there was no mention of rain."

"I think they're in the woods behind Cassidy's house."

She had yet to put the steaks on—the potatoes weren't quite ready. But there was a delicious, enticing smell coming from Cassidy's outdoor kitchen. She was grilling out too, it seemed.

And playing in the pool, she added. She'd heard splashing... and laughing. Most of the laughter appeared to be coming from the model. She wondered what Cassidy was doing that was so amusing. She also wondered what it was that she was grilling. It made her mouth water.

"Time for the steaks," she announced. She put her drink on the small table between their two chairs and turned the grill up a bit, wanting to sear the steaks before turning the temp a little lower.

"Do you still sit out here before you go up to bed?"

"Some nights," she said. Actually, most nights. Especially this week since she'd been avoiding her laptop. A splash in the pool made her lift her head up.

"Oh, they're swimming," her mother whispered.

"Probably naked," she murmured.

"Are you still spying over there, Laura Sue?"

"Of course not. I told you, I gave that up." She turned the temp down on the grill and closed the lid. "How do you like your steak?"

"Just a little pink, nothing more. In fact, no pink would be better."

Laura wrinkled up her nose. "That's overdone."

"I don't care. I refuse to have red juice on my plate." She smiled smugly. "Frankie made them perfectly."

"Wait until you taste my seasoning. You'll forget all about Frankie's steaks then."

"I will admit, he was mainly just salt and pepper. What did you use?"

"It's a Tuscan blend for the seasonings. I mix a dash of balsamic vinegar with olive oil to moisten the steak, then season it. And if we had a rosemary bush, I'd put a couple of sprigs of that on it." She pointed to the corner of the flowerbed. "In fact, I think I could squeeze a bush in here. What do you think?"

"Whatever you want," she said with a wave of her hand. "I doubt I'll ever be well enough to take my yard back."

"Next week…walking and swimming. You've just got to get your strength back. And your balance."

"The doctor said if I fell again and injured my back, it could paralyze me."

"Mom, I think he meant that only at first, when you left the hospital. Your injuries are long healed."

"They don't feel like they're healed."

"Look, not to blame Frankie, but he waited on you hand and foot, Mom. He never gave you a chance to get back to normal."

"The doctor said I'd never walk without a limp."

"Yeah...a limp. Not a walker or a wheelchair."

"I went to physical therapy. It didn't help."

Laura held up her hand. "Let's don't argue. I can imagine you at physical therapy."

"Are you saying I didn't try?"

"I'm saying, you got back home from physical therapy and Frankie treated you like an invalid...thus you stayed one." She held her hand up again. "Truce. It's too nice an evening to argue."

Her mother nodded. "The patio table looks nice."

Laura followed her gaze. The little round table with the red cloth was already set for dinner. A square candle sat in the middle, the light bouncing around as the gentle breeze moved the wick back and forth. Yes...nice. Romantic, almost.

She blew out her breath before taking a sip of her drink. Not romantic, no. Romantic was probably next door...with the outdoor kitchen, the pool...Cassidy...and the naked model.

She let out her breath again with an audible sigh, suddenly feeling a twinge of loneliness.

Where did that come from?

* * *

Cassidy moved the chicken to a cooler side of the grill and closed the lid. There was a divine aroma of steak coming from next door and she was quite jealous. It didn't surprise her, however, that Laura would like steak.

"Come on back in," Ashly beckoned from the pool. "The water is simply wonderful."

Ashly was in a bikini now, but it barely covered more than when she was naked. Cassidy was in her most conservative one-piece, ignoring Ashley's attempts at getting her to toss the suit. Actually, she was ready to toss the suit—for clothes. The air was a little cooler this evening and now that she was out of the water, she felt the chill.

"I need to get the chicken off pretty soon. I think I'll head in for a change. Will you be okay out here alone?"

"Oh, sure. I wouldn't mind another margarita though."

"Of course. There's still some left in the pitcher." The pitcher that Ashly had been drinking from since the afternoon. She was going to have a wallop of a headache in the morning, no doubt.

Before going inside, she turned the grill down to its lowest setting. She didn't want to overcook the chicken. The rice was already done—spicy rice with peas—and a couple ears of corn on the cob were grilling next to the chicken.

She took a quick shower before slipping into dry clothes and choosing sandals instead of flip-flops. The table at the edge of the outdoor kitchen was already set for dinner. Instead of lighting the candle, she moved it back into the cabinet. No sense in having Ashly think she was trying to seduce her. Quite the opposite.

The wine she'd chosen for their meal was a sweeter zinfandel to offset the spiciness of the jerk sauce. The smell permeating from the grill told her that Ashly was not going to enjoy the chicken unless she scraped off all of the sauce...which was blasphemy, of course. The jerk sauce was what it was—green and spicy. And delicious.

"Everything is just about ready. Do you want to change before eating?"

Ashly walked up the steps of the pool and grabbed one of the large towels to wrap around herself. She stumbled slightly and Cassidy rushed over to help.

"That margarita just hit me, I think," Ashly said with a laugh.

"Yeah, a pitcher will do that," she murmured. "So? Change first or eat?"

"I'm starving. If you don't mind me being in a bikini, we can eat first." She spotted the wine on the table. "I think I better go with water, though."

"Have a seat," she said as she guided Ashly into a chair. "I'll serve you."

As expected, Ashly took one bite of the chicken—"Oh my God...my mouth's on fire!"—and gulped down most of her water. She then removed as much sauce as she could before taking a second bite.

Cassidy sipped from her wine before sampling the corn. Grilled to perfection, it exploded in her mouth with juicy flavor. The chicken was moist and tender—and spicy. The corn was perfect. The rice fluffy. The wine sweet. She picked up her glass again, watching as Ashly daintily held the corn with her thumb and index fingers, all the others were pointed appropriately skyward.

She sighed. How could she possibly be sitting here, out by the pool, having dinner with a beautiful young woman—in a bikini, no less—and feel as lonely as she was? She suspected, had she been alone, she would feel less so.

She heard quiet laughter come from across the fence and she smiled, recognizing Laura's voice. So they cooked steaks and ate outside too. She looked at Ashly, who—instead of picking up the drumstick—was trying to cut the meat from the bone. Ashly looked up and smiled.

"It's very good."

"Thanks." She picked up her own chicken with her hands. "Much easier to eat this way."

"Oh, I always use a knife. I can still hear my mother. 'It's not ladylike to use your hands.'"

Cassidy sighed yet once again and reached for her wine. By the looks of it, she would have lots of leftovers. Dinner for next week, she reasoned.

CHAPTER TWENTY

Laura sat down with a contented sigh and took a small sip of her hot coffee. A male cardinal was singing from the tree branch above the feeders. Soon, a female joined him and she watched as they flitted between the branches. Their patio faced west so there was never a view of the sunrise. Of course, there was never a view of a true sunset either. There were too many trees for that. Which reminded her that she still hadn't explored Cassidy's woods. She would make it a point to go out there one day next week and see if she could find the leaning tree. She wouldn't mind taking in a sunset from there. If she could still climb the tree. She wasn't a teenager anymore, she reminded herself.

"Hey…you out there?"

Laura smiled at the sound of Cassidy's voice. "Yes."

"Can I come over?"

"Sure."

She automatically ran a hand over her hair, wondering how bad it looked this morning. Again, she shouldn't care. Bedhead or not, this was *her* time. If Cassidy chose to come over, she would have to take her as she was.

Cassidy came walking through the grass in flip-flops and even from here, she could see the steam coming from her coffee cup. She matched Cassidy's smile and remembered her manners this time, motioning to the chair beside her.

"Thanks. Beautiful morning, isn't it?"

"It is. You're up early."

"So are you."

"I'm always up early."

"So am I."

"Yeah…but *you* have company and I don't. And where did you find the model?"

"The model? Ashly?" Cassidy nodded. "Yeah, she does kinda look like a model, doesn't she?" Cassidy took a sip of her coffee. "She's a friend of a friend."

"Blind date?"

"No, no. Not really a date. Well, I did go out with her a few months ago, but there was nothing there. No, I had dinner with friends this week—Macie and Karon—and Ashly was there. They're coming out this afternoon to spend the night, but Ashly was free on Friday so she came out early with me."

"So you just have what? An unlimited list of women to choose from?"

"She's young. And she's going to have a hell of a hangover this morning. She drank an entire pitcher of margaritas by herself."

Laura made a face. "I like margaritas, but two is my limit. I'd rather have a cocktail with bourbon."

"Yeah, me too. So how was the steak?"

Laura stared at her. "How did you know I had a steak?"

"It smelled divine."

Laura nodded. "It was. Medium rare. My mother likes hers like shoe leather, but I refused to ruin the steak. She complained the entire time she ate it, although not one bite remained."

"I love a good steak."

"How was your chicken?"

Cassidy laughed. "So we smelled each other's dinner, huh?"

"It had an unusual aroma, though."

"Green jerk chicken."

"Ah. An old girlfriend made that for me once. I've never tried it myself. You'll have to share your recipe."

"Gladly. Ashly wasn't too impressed. A little too spicy for her."

"Is there such a thing?"

"I know, right?" Cassidy's gaze was drawn to the bird feeders. "The flowers out by the pool look great, by the way."

"Good. I think there's room for two more, if you're game."

"Sure. Would you have time this week?"

"Maybe. It depends how long the front beds take. I still have to go get flowers for those too."

"Oh, which reminds me. I put an envelope with money in the closet out back."

"Where you keep your pool stuff?" she asked without thinking.

Cassidy laughed. "I see you found the floats, huh?"

Laura did have the good grace to blush. "Sorry. I hope you don't mind."

"Of course not. Make yourself at home. But yeah, I put it on the top shelf. I put a thousand dollars in there. Is that enough?"

"Good God! You have no idea how much flowers cost, do you?"

"Not a clue."

"I told you last week that little flowerbed only cost thirty bucks."

"Yeah, but I want to pay you for your time and labor."

"You already are."

"That's just for mowing. That didn't include hauling stone and bags of dirt and stuff."

"You don't have to pay me extra, Cassidy. We had a deal, remember? I get to use your pool in exchange for manual labor."

"No. I feel like I'm taking advantage of you. Let me pay you something. Just a one-time thing for the flowerbeds."

Laura tilted her head, studying her. "What is it that you do for a living, anyway? You said you were the boss."

"Anderson Heating and Air Conditioning...at your service," she said with a smile.

"Oh, God. That's you?"

"What?"

"All those obnoxious ads and billboards?"

Cassidy laughed. "Obnoxious? But hey, if your AC goes out and it's a hundred and one, who are you going to call?"

"I'm going to call Anderson and if your butt's not there in twenty minutes, my service call is free."

Cassidy smiled. "See?"

"I never imagined a woman owned that company." Laura stood up. "You want another cup of coffee?"

"Please. Black with just a pinch of sugar."

Laura went into the kitchen. What was a pinch of sugar? She poured coffee into the two cups and added a full teaspoon to hers and about a half of one to Cassidy's. She didn't see the point, but whatever.

Cassidy sipped it immediately and nodded. "Perfect."

"So? The company?"

"Oh. Family-owned. My grandfather started it. My father and brother followed. I went to college—business and marketing—and made a few changes."

"Like?"

"Well, expanded it quite a bit, for one. We've now got ten hubs around the Metroplex. My brother manages the crews, hires and fires. I manage the corporate office downtown. That's where everything is coordinated. We keep the servers there still. I haven't outsourced that yet." At Laura's blank stare, she continued. "We've got a pretty extensive online system for making appointments."

"Are there that many people who have AC problems?"

"Not just that, but yearly maintenance scheduling. And new homes. We have contracts with several of the major builders in the city to install new units." Cassidy held her hand up. "Boring stuff, really. What about you? You said you were taking a break."

"Yeah," she said slowly. "I...well, I quit my real job a few years ago. I hated the whole office atmosphere, dressing up, all that crap," she said, remembering the suits she used to have to wear. "Investment firm," she said by way of explanation. "But really, I'm a writer."

"A writer?"

"Yes. And I'm taking a break."

"What does that mean? You're in between books?"

"Yes. I'm in between my first one and my second one."

"I see. So you're published."

"Yes." Laura shifted uneasily in her chair, debating whether to tell Cassidy the whole truth. She decided there was no need to confess her eight-year drought. "It's been a few years, but I'm taking my time with the second one."

"I've never met an author before. I don't actually read much, though. Would I have heard of your book?"

"It was a murder mystery type thing. My heroine was a medical examiner. The intent was to have a series, like Patricia Cornwell." It was Cassidy's turn for a blank stare. "You know... Kay Scarpetta."

Cassidy shook her head.

"Well, anyway, my heroine didn't quite have the personality to compete with those kinds of books. I haven't been able to come up with a second book for her."

"What's the name of the book?"

"*Murder by Day*. Day was the man's last name. The murderer," she explained.

"Hmm. Don't think I've heard of it. Was it successful?"

"Mildly. I cracked the Top Twenty for one week."

"So you've got like...writer's block then?"

"I guess you could say that." Laura sighed. "Okay. So it's been eight years."

"Eight years? Good Lord! Eight years of writer's block?"

"Yes."

"What is that, anyway? Is that like something that writers made up? Like, you know, as an excuse for not writing?"

"What are you talking about?"

Cassidy shrugged and Laura wondered at the smile playing on her lips. "Writer's block. If you're a writer, you write. If you're a painter, you paint. Do they have painter's block?"

Laura narrowed her eyes at her. "Really?"

"If you're a car mechanic, you fix cars. Do you think they come into work one day and say, you know what, I just can't fix this car today. I'm totally blocked."

"Are you *serious*? Really?"

Cassidy laughed. "No. Teasing, of course. I can't imagine writing a book. Good for you."

"A car mechanic," she muttered disgustedly, causing Cassidy to laugh again.

"Well, I guess I've taken up enough of your time this morning. I need to go see if Ashly made it through the night."

"You don't know?"

"No. I didn't look in on her this morning."

"Oh. She wasn't—"

"In my bed? No." Cassidy smiled. "She *wanted* to be."

"Well, who could blame her?" Their eyes met and Laura felt a blush from head to toe. "I didn't mean that like it sounded," she said quickly with a shake of her head.

Cassidy laughed. "You're blushing."

"I know I am," she snapped.

"Don't forget to pay yourself," Cassidy called as she walked off. "Don't worry about receipts. I trust you."

Laura watched her until she rounded the corner of the fence, then sunk down in her chair with a groan. "I'm such an idiot."

CHAPTER TWENTY-ONE

"I love your house, Cassidy," Karon said as she linked arms with her. "How can you stand your apartment in the city after this?"

"I will admit, it's getting harder and harder to leave here," she said, surprising herself with the answer. She'd grown up in Dallas. Had gone to college in Dallas. Her family was in Dallas. Their business was in Dallas.

But that business was now practically running itself. If she wanted to, she could spend more time out here. Her upstairs office had everything she needed if she wanted to work from home a day or two a week. The problem was…she didn't think of this as "home" yet. This was still a weekend place she invited friends to and held parties at. Her apartment—where she'd lived for the last six years—still felt like home. When she'd decorated the house, everything was new. She hadn't taken anything from her apartment. There was nothing personal here. Maybe that's why it didn't feel like home to her.

Macie and Ashly were in the pool, standing in waist-deep water, leaning against the side. Karon joined them, walking gracefully in, using the steps. Cassidy opted for the diving board. As she sprang high in the air, she peeked over the fence, but Laura was not on her patio. She splashed into the water headfirst, surfacing near the others. It was a warm afternoon, bordering on hot. No wonder Laura wasn't outside. Then she smiled. Maybe she was upstairs in her room. Maybe she was watching. She gave an impish grin as she stared at the windows, but she saw no movement and the blinds were closed. She was oddly disappointed.

"I was just commenting on your flowers," Macie said. "Ashly tells me your neighbor does your yard for you."

"She does. She's great with flowers. You should see her patio and flowerbeds."

"Why on earth would your neighbor do your yardwork?"

Cassidy shrugged. "I asked, she agreed. I do pay her, you know."

"She's kinda…different," Ashly interjected.

Cassidy frowned. "Different?"

"I mean, I only saw her the one time, but…" She looked at Macie and Karon. "Baseball cap, dirty shorts. She was filthy!"

"She was working," Cassidy said, feeling the need to defend Laura. "In the dirt." And Cassidy happened to think that Laura looked really cute in her baseball cap.

"Is she gay?" Macie asked.

"I assumed…the way she was dressed," Ashly said.

They both looked at her and Cassidy nodded. "Yes, she is."

"Well, that's a plus for a neighbor," Karon said with a grin. "A dyke who does yards."

Cassidy cringed. Laura? A dyke? They were so off base. Sure, she was a little on the tomboy side. She certainly wasn't like these women. She'd never seen Laura with makeup on. In fact, she'd seen her only in her cutoff jeans while working and her gray, cotton shorts while having coffee on her patio—with a T-shirt and no bra. And yes, she wore a baseball cap while working and she had bedhead in the morning. She smiled at that thought, then noticed that the others were looking at her. Her smile faded.

"Not a dyke. Tomboy."

"Well, I guess we don't have to worry about her stealing you away. A tomboy is so not for you."

"She was kinda cute, though," Ashly conceded.

Cassidy smiled again. Yeah, Laura was kinda cute, especially with that streak of mud she'd had across her cheek.

CHAPTER TWENTY-TWO

Laura pushed the tree limb aside and went deeper into the woods. They were thick and green...and heavy, much like the air around her. It was a hot and humid day and her tank top clung to her skin. Back here in the woods, there was no breeze to stir the air.

Nothing looked familiar to her, though, and she knew the only way she'd find the leaning tree was if she blindly stumbled upon it. She had to remind herself that she'd been seventeen the last time she'd walked out here. It was kinda strange knowing that Cassidy's father had owned the woods all that time. She didn't remember ever seeing anyone out here, but surely, over all those years, Cassidy and her family had come out, if only to check on it. Although she did remember Cassidy saying she'd never had the opportunity to come out, so maybe she hadn't. She made a mental note to ask Cassidy the next time she saw her.

Sunday morning, Cassidy had popped over as usual, but they hadn't even finished their first cup of coffee when her company had come outside. She'd gone back over—albeit reluctantly, Laura had noticed—and entertained them. They were out at the pool until nearly one and by three, all was quiet after they'd headed back to the city…Cassidy included.

Laura didn't quite know what to make of their friendship. Was it even a friendship? Did a few minutes sharing coffee time count? Still, she liked her. Their time chatting was always entertaining. She wondered, though, why Cassidy felt the need to always have someone with her over the weekends. Whether it was only one—whoever she happened to be dating that week—or another couple…or a party, as she'd warned Laura there'd be one over the upcoming long weekend. Laura hadn't given the holiday much thought. When she lived in Dallas, there was always a cookout at someone's house. She supposed she could do burgers for her and her mother. Or…she could invite Carla over. But that would mean dealing with the twins.

"No," she murmured. Why ruin the holiday?

She kept walking, shocked to come upon a barbed wire fence. Had she made it all the way across Cassidy's property already? She looked around, trying to get her bearings. She had a moment of panic, fearing she was lost, then reminded herself it was only ten acres. Surely she could find her way out again.

She looked overhead, finding the sun. It had been one o'clock when she'd left. She figured Cassidy's pool boys would be finished by the time she returned. Not that she was anxious to get in the pool or anything.

"Yeah, right," she said with a smile.

But she did have flowers to plant. She'd gone into town yesterday and picked up two new planters and several flats of flowers, along with the potting soil mix that she used. She would get that finished today, then cool off in the pool. Tomorrow, she would tackle the front flowerbed. She'd already unloaded some of the stones and bags of compost and mulch for the larger bed. She figured she could get that one done in a couple of hours. Thursday would be mow day. Friday morning she'd try to finish up the smaller bed nearer the driveway. Everything should be ready to go for Cassidy's weekend party. However, trying to cram all of that into a few days meant there'd be no time to have her mother over to the pool. She'd shoot for next week on that.

She heard the tap, tap, tap of a woodpecker on a tree and looked around, trying to find him. He was hammering on a small, dead oak, and the ringing of her phone startled both him and her. She found herself smiling, though, as Cassidy's name appeared.

"Hey," she answered.

"Hey, yourself. What are you doing?"

"Trespassing," she said with a grin.

Cassidy laughed. "Figured you weren't in the pool. My guys should be there by now." She paused. "Trespassing where?"

"I'm out in your woods. I'm trying to find the leaning tree."

"And the leaning tree is what?"

"Something from my childhood. I used to climb it. Great sunset view."

"That's right. You said you used to play out there when you were a kid."

"I did. Almost every day. Did you really never come out here?"

"Not that I remember. Certainly not when I got older. I think my father almost forgot he had the place."

"We never knew who owned it. When I was a kid, I mean. To me, it was like this giant park that I had all to myself."

"I can hear the smile in your voice," Cassidy said, causing Laura to smile broader.

"Good memories." She leaned against a tree. "Why are you calling, anyway?"

"Oh. Just…you know, checking in."

"If you're worried I won't have your yard looking presentable for your party, don't be. I've got a handle on it."

"Not worried. Have you spent all my money yet?"

Laura laughed. "Hardly. I got two more planters to match the other two by the pool. I plan to get those planted this afternoon, after your pool guys leave."

"Okay." A pause. "So…listen. Why don't you plan on coming to the party on Saturday?"

Laura's eyes widened. "*Your* party?"

"Yes, my party. You might, you know, meet someone."

"Oh, I don't think so. I've seen the women you've had over."

"That's right. Bad taste," Cassidy said with a laugh. "You can still come over," she offered.

"Okay, again, I've seen your women in their bikinis. No way I'm going to be seen in a swimsuit next to them. That would just be wrong."

"I can't picture you in a bikini."

Laura grinned. "Why are you picturing me in a swimsuit?"

"I mean...I just meant...you know...I'd bet you were a one-piece kind of gal."

"When I wear a swimsuit, yes." That statement was met with silence and she smiled. "What? Skinny-dipping is not allowed in your pool?"

Cassidy cleared her throat. "Yes, it is certainly allowed. I enjoy it myself."

"I know. So did the model," she said without thinking. *Damn!*

But Cassidy laughed. "So which windows can you see the pool out of?"

Damn, damn, damn! "Mostly my writing room," she confessed. "Not that I spy on you or anything."

"So the room by the maple tree...that's your bedroom?"

"Yes. My mother's rooms are downstairs."

"Good to know."

Laura frowned. "Why good to know?"

"Just...good to know." Laura heard voices and the sound of a door opening. "Listen, I need to go," Cassidy said. "But think about the party."

"No."

Cassidy sighed. "Okay. Talk to you later."

"Bye."

She continued to lean against the tree. Should she reconsider the party? She shook her head. No. As she'd said, she'd seen the women who Cassidy had over. She couldn't imagine having anything in common with *any* of them.

* * *

Cassidy opened the blinds to the sliding glass door, then opened the door as well. It was a warm, humid evening, but she wanted to be outside. For some reason, her apartment was stifling her, the walls seeming to close in around her. So she took her drink out to the balcony and sat down in one of the two chairs, trying to relax. Her view was not great—more apartments across from her—but at least there were large trees to make it seem as if she had some privacy.

She could imagine being at her house, sitting out by the pool. It would be cooler there, for sure. Maybe she'd go up Thursday instead of Friday. Even though she was having the party catered—fajitas—she still had some things to get. Namely, beer and the makings for margaritas.

Of course, if she went up Thursday, she might spoil Laura's work plans. She smiled, thinking of the other woman. So she'd trespassed today, huh? Looking for a leaning tree, something from her childhood? She did regret that she'd never had the opportunity to explore out there like Laura apparently had. Even through the whole process of building the house—and saving most of the woods—she hadn't taken the time to actually go out *into* the woods, to explore, to hike around. She'd been too busy.

Or maybe it simply hadn't occurred to her to take a hike in the woods. Maybe this friendship she'd started with Laura would be good for her. Laura was different.

She had a lot of friends, she noted, but none were quite like Laura. They were more...what? Refined? Professional? Most, yes. Some younger, some close to her age. None older, none that she could think of. That was a little strange in itself.

She had a lot of friends. She just couldn't think of a single one that she would call her best friend. She couldn't think of a single one who she could bare her soul to, if she needed. Was there anyone in her group that she ever confided in? Erica would probably be the closest. She'd known her ten years or more. But if she truly needed to take someone in her confidence, would it be Erica? No. They had a lot of mutual friends and Erica was a bit of a gossip. So no, not Erica. Of course, there was Tanya. She'd known her forever. She'd played matchmaker with her and Derrick. But Tanya was more sounding board than anything. Tanya was straight. Tanya couldn't really relate.

Again, a sense of loneliness settled over her. She had a lot of friends…yet sometimes, she didn't have any friends at all.

CHAPTER TWENTY-THREE

"Are you kidding me?" Laura murmured as the black Mercedes came through the gate—a day early. She stood up and put her hands on her hips, eyebrows raised as Cassidy lowered her window.

"Hey."

"Hey? *Really?*"

Cassidy laughed. "I knew you'd be mad if I came early. I promise I'll stay out of your way."

"Oh, no. You're here now. Go change into work clothes. You can help." Cassidy stared at her blankly for a moment, and Laura smiled at her. "You don't have any work clothes, do you?"

"I can find some old shorts, yes. And I know for a fact that I have a T-shirt with paint stains on it."

"Perfect. My back's killing me. I don't think I can lift another stone." She wiggled her eyebrows. "I'll put you to good use."

"Okay. I'm game. I've got a few things to unpack first, then I'll be right out." She started to drive on, then stopped again. "You want a beer?"

"God, yes. Thanks."

Laura was smiling as she went back to her flowers. Her back wasn't hurting her *that* much, but she thought Cassidy might enjoy helping with the flowerbeds. And she was actually alone today. That had to be a first. But it was Thursday. Probably whoever she had lined up for her date this weekend wouldn't come until tomorrow.

Where does she find all of these women?

Was she envious? No. It had to be exhausting to date like that. But she wouldn't mind going out on a date occasionally. This dry spell that she was in had lingered and lingered until it had become the norm. And her chances of meeting someone out here were slim to none. Of course, Cassidy had invited her to the party, had suggested that she might meet someone there.

"I've seen her party friends," she murmured. "Way too girlie for me."

"Who are you talking to?"

Startled, she jerked her head around, finding Cassidy standing beside her, holding two beers shoved into koozies. The shorts she wore did not seem old in the least, but the T-shirt was splattered with not one, but two different colors of paint. She reached for one of the beers.

"I'm alone too much," she said as way of explanation.

"Ah. Talk to yourself, do you?"

Laura smiled. "Yes, but I rarely argue."

Cassidy laughed. "I would hope not."

Laura took a big swallow of the beer. "Thank you. I was parched."

"I'm sure you've seen the fridge out back by the outdoor kitchen. Help yourself."

"How do you know I haven't already?"

"Because even though you sneak over to use the pool and go trespassing in the woods, I don't think you're the type to swipe beer."

"You'd be right. I bring my own."

Cassidy took a swallow too, nodding. "I checked out the new planters by the pool. They look really nice. You've done a great job."

"Thank you. This is the last one. I finished the other one this morning before I mowed. I was going to finish this one up tomorrow, but since you're here…"

"Free labor, huh?"

"Yes. I've got one more flat of flowers, then we pile on the mulch. Then the stone goes around the sides. Then we water."

"All of that today? How about we finish the flowers, then get in the pool? I'll help with the mulch and stone in the morning."

Laura shook her finger at her. "You haven't even started yet and you're already trying to get out of working."

Cassidy laughed. "Actually, I think it'll be fun to play in the dirt with you. But you've been working all day out here. I thought you might be ready to call it a day."

"Well, if you hadn't shown up early, then yes, I was going to spend an hour or so in your pool," she admitted.

"So? What do you say?"

Well, it was awfully hot, she reasoned. No need to finish this up today when—with Cassidy's help—she could have the project completed in an hour or so in the morning. She nodded at Cassidy.

"Okay. We'll finish it all tomorrow, flowers included. Let me go get cleaned up and changed. I'll meet you there."

"Great. I'll supply the beer."

CHAPTER TWENTY-FOUR

Cassidy hadn't planned on interrupting Laura's day. In fact, she was sincere when she said she was looking forward to helping with the flowers. But Laura looked hot and tired. She had dirt stains on her knees and elbows, a streak of mud on her cheek again—which Cassidy barely resisted cleaning off—and her tank top was soaked in sweat. Laura accepting as readily as she did confirmed Cassidy's assumption that she was indeed hot and tired.

And they could take their time with the flowerbed. They'd have all day. For once, Cassidy hadn't invited anyone over early. The pool party started at noon on Saturday with fajitas ready by six. She did extend an overnight invitation to a few friends, though. Erica and Amber were staying, this time without their friend Kathryn. And Macie and Karon, even though they'd stayed last weekend, had opted for another weekend in the country...without Ashly.

It occurred to her then that she didn't actually have a date for the weekend—a first. There was always Claudia, who she'd run into at lunch one day. She had blurted out about the party without thinking and Claudia had accepted with a wink and a light touch on her arm. Yes, Claudia would be willing. But Cassidy shook her head. Claudia might be willing, but she was not. She smiled, remembering Laura's name for Claudia—the anorexic blonde. And Ashly—the model. Didn't she refer to Larson with some name too?

"No laughing at my farmer's tan," Laura warned as she walked around the pool.

There was no farmer's tan to see as Laura had on shorts and a T-shirt. She raised her eyebrows. "If that's what you swim in, no wonder you have a farmer's tan."

Laura held a foot up and wiggled the flip-flop. Her feet were definitely whiter than her legs and there was a sock line at her ankles. Then Laura pulled her T-shirt off, revealing a rather conservative Speedo, the color pattern a splatter of multiple shades of purple mixed with black and white. She appeared to have tan lines from both a T-shirt and a tank top, as well as the straps of the suit. Cassidy wasn't shy as she watched Laura remove her shorts. And yes, there was a tan line from the cutoff jeans that she normally wore.

She was smiling as she met Laura's eyes. "Nice variation of tan lines."

"Thank you. I *do* work outside for a living," she said with a grin. "And this is why I won't come to your party. I'll be the only one with tan lines."

"You'd probably be the only one with a natural tan and not the result of a tanning bed. I like yours much better," she said, surprising herself by the comment. At Laura's raised eyebrows, she said, "Real. Not fake. Much better than the perfection you get from a bed." Then she smiled. "Of course, swimming without clothes would get you that same perfection."

"Maybe I'll work on that during the week when you're not here," Laura said with an exaggerated wink, then dove into the water.

Cassidy was still smiling as she tossed in two floats, then pulled her T-shirt over her head. She, too, was wearing a one-piece—black. As was her custom, she walked around to the diving board. She glanced over at Laura, who had already scrambled onto one of the floats.

"Hey, wait a minute," Laura called. "Where's that beer you promised?"

"Under that towel." She pointed. "There's a bucket, with ice."

She waited while Laura paddled over and lifted up the towel, revealing the small bucket, big enough to hold four beers with heaps of ice. Laura pulled two from it and shoved the bottles into the koozies Cassidy had placed beside it. With a quick nod, she went to the edge of the board and jumped, diving into the cool water with barely a splash.

"You have great form. You took lessons as a kid, right?"

Cassidy shook her head. "Believe it or not, I hated the water when I was young. I was forced to take swimming lessons, but I hated it. It wasn't until college that I really got into swimming."

"Let me guess…girls in bikinis."

Cassidy laughed. "Guilty." She got on her float first, then took the beer from Laura. "I liked to fish, though. My dad has a boat. Fishing is his passion."

"Do you go with him?"

"Not much anymore. He's kinda semi-retired from the business so he does most of his fishing during the week."

"Semi-retired? Meaning retired, just not officially?"

"Exactly. The last couple of years, he's let me totally run the show."

"So really, you're responsible for those ads?"

"I am. And they're not that obnoxious. We change them up every year."

Laura splashed water at her. "I especially loved the one with the cranky wife complaining to the husband about the AC not working. I mean, she went after him until he snapped!"

"And we were there at his door in a flash," she said with a laugh. "Record time."

"Saved a marriage, I'm sure." Laura spun her float around to face her. "Why Cassidy?"

"Huh?"

"Your name."

"Oh. My mother had a huge crush on David Cassidy. Huge."
She grinned. "Guess what my brother's name is?"

"Oh, no…she didn't."

"She did. Although everyone calls him Dave, except her.
He's three years old than I am," she offered.

"I have an older sister. Carla. She has twins. They were cute
when they were babies, until they turned into holy terrors. She's
just a year older than me."

Since they were sharing personal things, Cassidy didn't think
it was out of line to ask why she was living here. She wondered
if this eight-year writer's block—and no job—had turned her
destitute. It wasn't really any of her business, but… "So what's
the story with you living with your mother? I know you said she
was an invalid. I don't think I've ever seen her."

Laura met her gaze for a moment, and Cassidy wondered if
maybe she should have kept the question to herself.

"My mother and I used to be very close. Always were, really.
But I was the tomboy tagging along with my father, following
him everywhere. After he died—my mother was only fifty-
eight—we got even closer. Then she met Frankie. Six months
after my dad died, Frankie moved in with her. They got married."
She shrugged. "I couldn't stand the man. My relationship with
my mother deteriorated."

"Your sister?"

"Yeah, she stopped coming around too. Then the car
accident three years ago. He was driving and wasn't injured.
She was in the hospital for weeks. Came out in a wheelchair.
I blame Frankie not only for the accident, but for not pushing
her to walk." Laura waved her hand. "Doesn't matter. Frankie
died. Heart attack, out by the shed. My mother can't get around
enough to be on her own…so here I am."

"Gave up your own life? That's admirable."

Laura once again splashed water at her. "I'm no saint. I came
kicking and screaming. But we couldn't afford to hire someone
to stay with her so…I had no job, no family."

"Sister guilted you into it, huh?"

Laura laughed. "Pretty much. But it's worked out. My mother and I have gotten close again. We called a truce regarding Frankie. And I'm making her use the walker instead of the chair. She's gotten stronger. I don't know if she'll ever feel confident enough to live on her own, but I hope she can at least gain some independence."

"You ought to get her in the pool," Cassidy suggested. "Water therapy is supposed to be great."

Laura smiled at her. "That's so sweet of you. I was going to sneak her in next week."

Cassidy shook her head. "You don't have to sneak. I'm not paying you nearly enough for all the work you've done."

Laura stretched her arms out. "Reminds me that I'm not as young as I used to be. Hauling that stone about killed me."

"How old are you, anyway?"

"Just turned thirty-eight. Last Wednesday."

"Really? You had a birthday. You should have told me."

"I spent the day here in your pool. I had a picnic. I blasted music. It was a good day."

"You were alone?"

"Yes."

Cassidy thought that sounded like a depressing way to spend her birthday but not everyone needed to have people around all the time. Laura, obviously, was comfortable being alone.

"What?"

Cassidy brought her attention back to Laura. She sighed. "I envy you."

"Why on earth?"

"I'm not very good at being alone."

"I've gathered that. You almost always have company with you when you come here."

"I don't really know what the reason is. I always feel compelled to invite someone or a couple…or have a party."

"So you don't like being alone?"

"Apparently not."

"Do you not like yourself?"

Cassidy frowned. "Meaning?"

"Meaning…do you not like your own company? I like you. You obviously have a lot of friends, so you must be nice. But is there something that *you* don't like?"

Cassidy moved her foot, using Laura's float to push off, setting her in motion. What didn't she like? How honest was she willing to be here?

"I sometimes feel like I'm…entitled."

Laura raised her eyebrows questioningly.

"This is going to sound so conceited."

"Oh, I get it. You're attractive. You have money. You have a nice house. You own a successful business. You can have any woman you want. Conceited like that?"

Cassidy smiled. "Yes. Except I have horrible taste, according to you."

"God, yes. What do you see in those women?"

"I'm not sure. They're just…who I've always dated."

"Yet you're still looking. You know what they say about insanity, right?"

Cassidy nodded. "Doing the same thing over and over but expecting different results."

"Exactly. But at least you have options. The last real date I went on was six or eight months ago. And it wasn't even a blind date. I went willingly." Laura shook her head. "I knew she wasn't the one, but you have to give it at least two dates before you give up on them." Then she smiled. "Now I'm sounding conceited. She probably didn't like me either."

"I told you to come to the party. There will be single women here, you know."

"And I told you, those skinny, girlie types are not for me."

"Claudia will be here," Cassidy said with a wiggle of her eyebrows.

"The anorexic blonde?" Laura rolled her eyes. "God, are you dating *her* again?"

"No. I saw her out at lunch one day and felt obligated to invite her."

"Why?"

"Well, she was into me a whole lot more than I was into her. She was hurt when I called things off." Cassidy bit her lip, wondering if she should tell Laura the real reason Claudia was hurt. "She insinuated that I was only using her. For sex."

Laura met her gaze. "And were you?"

"I tell myself no. And really, most of them—like Larson—initiate the sex, not me. I…I find myself just going through the motions and I don't like myself very much for that."

"Every date doesn't have to end in sex, Cassidy."

"I know. Now that I'm older, I actually hate first-date sex. What about you? This last one?"

Laura shook her head. "No. I have this rule. Well, since I turned thirty, I have this rule. If I'm not emotionally invested, I don't sleep with them. Sex, to me, is too personal."

"If I had that rule, I'd never have sex."

"You've never been in love?"

Cassidy shook her head. "You?"

"Yes. A couple of times."

"So what happened?"

"The first time, I was apparently in a little deeper than she was. And the second, Sandi—she's the one who taught me to cook—just fizzled out. For both of us. We ended things in a friendly, very civilized manner."

"You lived together?"

"Yes. And I introduced her to her current girlfriend and they are head over heels in love. I see her now and I realize how different it was with us." Laura shrugged. "So maybe we weren't really in love after all."

"I'm not sure I'd recognize it if it happened to me. I'm forty-four and still looking. I have this fear it's never going to happen."

"It'll happen when you least expect it. That's what my mother always tells me." Laura's foot bumped hers and she pushed off. "With all the dating you're doing, you're bound to find someone. Me? Living out here? My chances have dropped significantly."

"Yeah. Well…maybe being in love is overrated."

Laura laughed. "Yeah…let's go with that."

* * *

"Just because I spent a lazy afternoon in the pool—"

"Drinking beer," her mother added.

"—doesn't mean that you have to eat leftovers." She smiled. "Besides, I'm starving. I could eat a whole pizza by myself."

Actually, the pizza was Cassidy's idea. She'd invited Laura—and her mother—to have dinner with her. Laura had protested, of course. She'd just spent the better part of three hours with her. But Cassidy had persisted and Laura had been too relaxed to offer much resistance after that, other than to insist they eat at her mother's house.

She enjoyed Cassidy's company. A lot. Cassidy was cute and charismatic, pleasant to be around and just witty enough to be charming. Add to that, she looked fabulous in a swimsuit. No wonder she could date anyone she wanted.

"So you've made a new friend? You were worried about that when you moved here, I know."

"Yes, we've become friends. She's nice." And they had, even though Laura didn't recall ever having a friend she enjoyed looking at—especially in a swimsuit—as much.

"Have you told her about the binoculars yet?"

Laura pointed a finger at her mother in a mock threat. "Not a word," she warned. "She knows I can see the pool from the windows upstairs, that's all." God, she would be so embarrassed if Cassidy knew she'd spied on her with binoculars. But not lately, she reminded herself. She'd refrained. Even that one time when Cassidy had stripped and gone skinny-dipping with that blonde. She frowned. That particular blonde had only lasted the one weekend. She didn't remember Cassidy even mentioning her name. Or had she? Then she frowned even more. What if Cassidy wanted to go upstairs? Then she'd see exactly the view that Laura had from the writing room.

She had a moment of panic. Were the binoculars still there? Out in plain sight?

A knock on the back door—the patio—signaled Cassidy's arrival.

Damn! She turned to her mother. "If you mention the binoculars, I'm putting you in a nursing home!" she threatened teasingly.

Her mother smirked at her. "I think you have a crush on her."

"Don't be ridiculous!" She hurried over to the door and jerked it open, finding a smiling—and dressed—Cassidy Anderson. "Pizza's not here yet."

"That's okay. I brought wine," she said, holding up a bottle. Then she produced another smaller bottle. "And bourbon."

Laura grinned. "My kinda gal. Come on in." She motioned to the table where her mother sat. "This is my mother, Maggie Fry."

"It's Maggie *Morrison*," she corrected as she shook Cassidy's hand.

"Whatever," Laura murmured. "This is Cassidy Anderson."

"Nice to meet you, Mrs. Morrison. Thanks for allowing me to join you for dinner."

"Please…call me Maggie. Welcome to our home."

Cassidy eyed the walker next to the table. "Laura tells me you're getting around a little better."

Her mother nodded. "I have no choice. She hides my wheelchair from me."

At Cassidy's shocked expression, Laura laughed. "She's kidding, of course."

Her mother laughed too. "Yes, I'm kidding. Laura's been a godsend."

Cassidy nodded. "She certainly has. My yard has never looked better." Cassidy pulled out a chair and sat down. "You should see the flowers she's put in. They look great."

"Don't forget you promised to help me in the morning," Laura reminded her.

"Looking forward to it."

Laura pointed to the two bottles that Cassidy had set on the counter. "Bourbon or wine?"

"What will you have?"

"I'm going to have bourbon with Coke." Cassidy made a face and Laura laughed. "What? Ruining the bourbon?"

Cassidy smiled. "You know what? I'll try that too. Easy on the Coke."

"I'll have the same," her mother said. "Easy on the bourbon."

Laura was smiling as she took three cocktail glasses out of the cabinet. She'd only had two beers—well, three, if you counted that first one Cassidy had brought her out by the flowerbed—but she was still feeling a little mellow. Maybe she should go easy on the bourbon too. But why? It was a pleasant night. She was already at home and there was a very attractive woman having dinner with them.

She paused in mid-pour. Did she have a crush on Cassidy Anderson? She shook her head. No. Of course not. She wouldn't blame herself if she did...but no. She'd made a new friend, that was all. A cute, fun, charming friend. Yes, a new friend. Not a crush.

She was still smiling, however, as she brought their drink glasses to the table. Cassidy reached for hers and—as their fingers brushed—their eyes met. Laura felt a rather odd sensation flow through her as she watched Cassidy take a sip.

"It's perfect, Laura...thank you."

Laura swallowed and turned away.

Oh, God...I do have a crush. She closed her eyes for a second. Friend. She's a new friend. That's all. A friend.

For God's sake...a crush?

CHAPTER TWENTY-FIVE

Cassidy plopped down onto the grass and leaned back, staring up into the blue sky. She felt Laura nudge her leg with her foot.

"Get up. We're not through."

"You're being a slave driver," she complained.

Laura laughed. "We haven't even started on the stone yet."

Cassidy groaned. "Is it too early for a beer?"

"Yes. No beer until you're finished."

Cassidy lifted her head. "We could take a break. Hop in the pool," she suggested hopefully.

"No, no, no. If we get in the pool, we'll never get out."

"And what's wrong with that?"

"You have a party tomorrow," Laura reminded her.

Cassidy leaned back down. "Why am I having a party again?"

"Because you don't like to be alone. Now get up."

Cassidy sighed. That's right. She didn't like to be alone. Although she had to admit, she slept like a baby last night. She pushed herself up into a sitting position, smiling as she remembered Laura nearly devouring her pizza, then them playfully fighting over the last piece. Laura won, then she proceeded to cut it in half and share it anyway.

After pizza, they had swapped their drinks for water and gone to sit on the patio, both complaining of full stomachs. They'd chatted for a bit, then Cassidy had made her way home with Laura calling after her, reminding her of their flowerbed project.

And this morning, after coffee, they'd tackled it. It had proven to be more work than she'd imagined and she knew she'd not paid Laura nearly enough for all the labor she'd already done.

"Why are you smiling?"

Cassidy arched an eyebrow. "Can't I smile?"

"You just accused me of being a slave driver."

"And you are." Cassidy finally got to her feet, standing in front of Laura. "I'm smiling because I was picturing you having pizza last night—inhaling it—with tomato sauce on both cheeks."

Laura playfully punched her arm. "You could have told me! When I went up to brush my teeth, I nearly screamed when I saw it."

Cassidy laughed. "Yeah, I probably should have told you." She stared at her now, seeing a streak of dirt on her face. "How is it that you get so dirty?" She reached out a hand and gently wiped it away.

"Because I'm not a dainty girl, apparently," Laura said.

"No, you're not." And Cassidy found she liked that about Laura. She tried to imagine any of her other friends out here, playing in the dirt like Laura was and she couldn't even envision it.

Laura had dirt stains on both knees and sweat clung to her skin. A baseball cap covered up her bedhead—which she'd spied that morning when they'd had coffee—and her ever-present cutoff jeans were soiled as well. She wondered how many pairs of them she had.

"How about I finish spreading the mulch and you start bringing the stone over?" Laura suggested.

"Seems like I'll be doing more work than you. Is that fair?"

Laura gave her a rather flirty smile. "And whose idea was the flowerbed again?"

"It was mine. But—" Cassidy pointed her finger at Laura. "Whose idea was it to put stone around it?"

"Hey, I simply offered that as a suggestion. You were the one who agreed to it." Laura pushed her toward the truck. "Off you go. The more you complain, the longer it'll take."

"And the longer it takes, the less pool time we'll have."

"Exactly."

Cassidy found herself smiling as she slipped on her gloves. In her life, professionally and personally, she was used to being in charge. Certainly at work, she was the boss. And in her personal relationships—both with friends and lovers—she found most, if not all, deferred to her. Not Laura. She wasn't afraid to take charge. It was refreshing, really.

She picked up the first stone and lugged it over to the flowerbed where Laura was once again on her knees, spreading mulch carefully around the colorful flowers. Laura had told her the varieties, but Cassidy had already forgotten. The names didn't matter to her. They were beautiful and colorful and a feast to the eyes. As she went back for a second stone, she paused, watching as Laura lifted the petals of a flower before placing mulch around it.

"Hey…you want to come over for a steak tonight?" she asked, the question out before she could fully comprehend it.

Laura turned to look at her, her brow furrowed as if contemplating an answer. She finally nodded.

"I'll need to see about my mother's dinner first, but sure."

"She can join us too."

"No. Fridays are one of her favorite TV nights. She'd probably be happy to have me out of the house."

"Okay. Good."

She went back to her stone hauling, wondering if she wanted Laura's company simply because she didn't want to be alone… or if she simply wanted Laura's company.

* * *

Laura was full—stuffed, in fact—but she managed the last bite of steak anyway. It had been cooked to perfection and she refused to waste it. Instead of using the table by the outdoor kitchen, they'd brought their plates over to the pool, using one of the round patio tables instead. Cassidy had tilted the umbrella slightly to block the breeze and lit a candle. It was a very intimate dinner with only the lights from the pool and the candle flickering back and forth.

Intimate and romantic. And Laura wasn't quite sure what to make of it. She admitted that she had a tiny—teeny-weeny, itty-bitty—crush on Cassidy. But how embarrassing would it be if Cassidy suspected as much? Well, about as embarrassing as it was when Cassidy guessed she'd been spying on her pool from the upstairs windows. She'd blushed head to toe.

"Don't take this the wrong way, but I've cooked steaks for quite a few people over the years, and I do think that you are the very first woman to have finished one."

Laura smiled. "Yes, the polite thing to do would have been to leave some, as well as some of the potato," she said as she picked up her wineglass. "It was simply too good and it would have been sinful to leave it." She made a show of looking across the table at Cassidy's plate. "I see the only thing that survived you was an asparagus spear."

Cassidy stabbed it with her fork and shoved it in her mouth with a grin.

"Next to my own, of course, this was a pretty darn good steak," Laura said. "I'm impressed."

"What? That I can cook?"

"Cook to perfection," Laura corrected. She leaned her elbows on the table. "The next time—if there's a next time— I'd like you to make your green jerk chicken. That smelled wonderful."

"I like that about you."

"What?"

"That you like to eat."

"Oh. You mean compared to the overly thin blondes that you bring around?"

"Yeah, them."

"Yes, well, I do like to eat. I fear when I'm older, I'm going to plump out."

Cassidy laughed. "But your mother is thin."

"My mother claims she's gained six pounds since I've been living here. How do you stay in shape? Run? Gym? Both?"

"I hate to run. But gym, yes. I've got one in the house. Lots of fancy workout systems. Got an elliptical that I like and a rowing machine. Weights. Things like that."

Laura nodded. "That's one thing I miss about my apartment—the gym. Well, that and the three pools." She smiled and motioned to the pool beside them. "Thank you for allowing me to use yours."

"You know, if you want to use my gym, I wouldn't mind," Cassidy offered.

"Thank you, but I couldn't possibly intrude into your home. It's bad enough that I'm taking advantage of your pool."

"Well, when I give you a tour of the house and you see the gym, you might change your mind."

Later, when Laura stood inside that very same gym—seven weight systems, a fancy elliptical that she probably wouldn't know how to use, free weights, stationary bike, rowing machine—she nearly started salivating.

"Are you kidding me? This is bigger than the one at my apartment." She turned to Cassidy. "Your house is huge. Your bedroom is obscenely large. This gym is ridiculous."

Cassidy laughed. "Yes to all. The guy who drew up my plans added the sitting room in the bedroom. The entertainment room, with theater seating, that's over the top. I don't even like to watch movies. My master bath, my office, my kitchen…and my gym; all my designs. The rest, even the outdoor kitchen, the guy drew up."

"And all the extra bedrooms?"

Cassidy shrugged. "Weekend company."

"Family?"

"No. Not yet, anyway. I keep thinking I need to have my brother out here."

"Kids?"

"He's got three."

"I'm sure they'd love the pool."

Cassidy shrugged again. "They've got their own."

"Of course they do," she murmured, getting a smile from Cassidy.

"He built his new house about three years ago. Took me a bit longer."

"But yours is bigger?" she guessed.

"Yes."

"Sibling competition?"

"Not really, no. We get along fine. Separation of duties and all that."

"But you're the boss?"

"If we have a disagreement about something, we usually defer to our father."

She said that so easily, Laura knew that meant that her father then deferred to her. After all, Cassidy apparently was the brains behind the operation. She studied her for a moment, trying to decide if Cassidy truly liked being the boss or not. It must come with pressure—stress—to keep things running smoothly. Obviously the company was a huge success, judging by this monstrosity she'd built.

"You hate my house, don't you?"

Laura shook her head quickly. "Not at all." Then… "Well, it is a little sterile. There's nothing here that's *you*."

"I know. I was thinking that same thing. Personal things… they're all still at my apartment."

"So this is just a weekend place? That's still your home?"

"Exactly."

"Damn huge, expensive weekend place."

Cassidy laughed loudly but said nothing.

CHAPTER TWENTY-SIX

Cassidy stood back, looking at the activity around the pool. Judging by the laughter and splashing, she'd say the party was a success. She lost count of how many pitchers of margaritas she'd made and several empty wine bottles lined the bar. The table with appetizers and dips had been mostly ravished and it was still another hour before the caterers would come with the fajitas. Everyone seemed to be having a good time. Everyone but her.

Her gaze was drawn to the upstairs windows of Laura's house. Was she up there? Or was it too noisy? Was the music too loud? She'd hoped that Laura would make an appearance, even though last night she'd politely declined the invitation once again.

"There you are! Thought you'd disappeared."

Cassidy turned, automatically smiling at the woman who stood before her. What was her name again? Patty? Patsy? Pam?

"No, just checking on things. Are you having a good time?"

"Wonderful party. Randi was looking for you. I told her I'd help in the search."

Ah…Randi's girlfriend. Paula?

"They're trying to get a volleyball game going in the pool. She thought you had a net."

"I do." Cassidy watched as a beach ball was being bounced around by laughing women. "And a ball."

She forced a smile to her face as she attached the net, much to the delight of the splashing crowd.

"Come join us," someone beckoned.

"Maybe later. I've got to get set up for the caterers," she lied.

She walked back to the outdoor kitchen, then turned again, watching the party from afar.

* * *

"What's wrong?" Laura murmured as she watched Cassidy.

She had told herself she wasn't going to spy on the party. For one thing, she wasn't really interested in it and she didn't care how many skinny, blond women were in the pool. But the incessant laughter could be heard up in her bedroom even with the oscillating fan going for extra noise. Curiosity got the best of her and she went to the window and parted the blinds. Unfortunately, she could only catch a glimpse of the pool so— without too much thought—she went into her writing room and peeked out of the window there.

And sure enough, the pool was full of bikini-clad, skinny blondes. The party was mostly women, maybe six men out of the twenty-five or thirty that she counted. She couldn't find Cassidy so she picked up the binoculars, scanning the crowd, looking for her. She finally spotted her back by the outdoor kitchen. She had a rather indifferent look on her face…distant, as if she wasn't really there.

Laura frowned. "What's wrong with you?" she murmured again as she saw Cassidy sigh and head into the house.

Without thinking, Laura dropped the binoculars on her desk and headed out the door. She wasn't dressed for a party and she had no intention of staying, but the look on Cassidy's face tugged at her heart. It was more than simply being distant— aloof. It was something else, something Laura couldn't see from way up in her bedroom.

The gate was opened and she hurried through it. Instead of going around the back like she usually did, she went to the front door. Should she ring the bell? Knock?

She turned the knob, finding it unlocked. She went inside and headed for the kitchen. Cassidy was leaning against the island, her gaze drawn to the window and the activity outside at her pool, yet she remained detached from it.

"Are you hiding?"

Cassidy jerked her head around, obviously startled.

"Sorry. Didn't mean to scare you."

Cassidy's face broke out into a smile. "You came."

Laura shook her head. "No, no. Not to the party."

Cassidy frowned. "Then…"

"What's wrong?"

Cassidy sighed and pushed off from the island. "Not up for a party, I guess. I thought I was faking it pretty good."

"No one seems to have noticed."

"Yet you did." Cassidy raised her eyebrows questioningly.

"I may have peeked out of the window," Laura admitted. She would never, ever admit to the binoculars, though. She walked around the island to face Cassidy, unconsciously reaching out a hand to touch her arm. "Can I do anything?"

"Stay?"

Laura smiled. "Not my kind of party." She dropped her hand. "I just wanted to check on you. You looked kinda…I don't know…sad."

Cassidy took a deep breath, her shoulders slumping as she let it out. "Sad, huh? Maybe."

Laura tilted her head. "These are your friends, right?"

Cassidy nodded. "People I know. The normal party crowd."

Cassidy seemed so withdrawn, Laura was concerned. She took a step closer. "Are you okay?"

"Yes. Ready for it to be over with, that's all."

Cassidy's eyes were shadowed, not the sharp, clear brown that she was used to. Laura thought she was maybe overstepping her bounds, but she moved closer, pulling Cassidy into a hug. She had no right to be this familiar with her, did she? She was surprised when she felt Cassidy's arms circle her waist and pull her even closer. So close, in fact, that they were touching in all sorts of places that had no business touching.

Laura gently pulled away from the embrace, almost embarrassed to meet Cassidy's eyes. She took a step back, separating completely. She was about to apologize, then a rather sweet smile appeared on Cassidy's lips.

"Thank you. It's been a very long time since I've had a hug."

Laura smiled too. "Well, glad I could help."

"Sure you don't want to stay?"

"Positive." Then she wiggled her eyebrows teasingly. "Save me a couple of fajitas."

Cassidy laughed. "Okay. I'll save some back for you."

Laura pushed her toward the door. "Go out to your party before you're missed."

Cassidy nodded. "I know." Then she paused. "See you tomorrow?"

"Yeah." Laura met her gaze and smiled. "See you tomorrow."

CHAPTER TWENTY-SEVEN

Cassidy paced in her office, wondering at her restlessness. The day after a holiday was usually busy but she could find nothing to hold her attention this morning. Well, there was something, but she'd analyzed that to death already.

Laura.

Laura was unlike any of her friends. She was so different, really, she doubted that any of her friends would even like Laura…and vice versa.

But *she* liked Laura. She had quickly become a friend. In fact, Cassidy thought that if they nurtured this friendship, it could end up being a very good one. They obviously enjoyed each other's company.

She stopped pacing and stared out the window, a slow smile forming as she remembered their conversation over coffee Sunday morning—after Cassidy had delivered the promised fajitas to her.

"So, if you don't have a hot date next weekend or anything, I thought I'd make that green jerk chicken that you want to try."

Laura's eyebrows had shot up. "You mean there's no skinny blonde coming with you? Or is it a threesome?"

Cassidy had laughed. "No skinny blonde, no. Just us. If you want."

Laura had smiled sweetly at her. "Then I'll look forward to it."

Yes, Cassidy was looking forward to it too. And she was looking forward to having the weekend to herself. No company. No date. No skinny blonde to share her bed.

So what in the world was wrong with her? She hated being alone, she reminded herself for at least the fourth time that morning. She was used to having romantic company, whether she wanted it or not. She was used to people being around... used to parties.

But she'd hated the party, hadn't she? Laura had somehow known, even seeing her from a distance through an upstairs window. She'd looked sad, Laura had said. And Laura had come over, just to check on her.

Laura had hugged her. No one really *ever* hugged her. Certainly not friends. The group that she hung with...they weren't exactly huggers.

But it was...nice. Unexpected, but nice. Still...

"I came in here an hour ago. You were standing in the same spot."

Cassidy glanced at Tanya and shook her head. "No. I was over there," she said, pointing toward the opposite wall.

"Do you need me to find you something to do?"

Cassidy went around her desk and sat down. "I have plenty to do, I just don't feel like doing it."

"So what's her name? You haven't mentioned anyone lately and you've said only a few words about your pool party."

"I wasn't in the party mood, it turns out. Everyone else seemed to have a good time, though."

Tanya sat down across from her. "So? Who's the flavor of the month?"

"No one. I was actually single at the party."

"Really? That's a first, isn't it?"

Cassidy leaned back in her chair and folded her hands together. "I'm in a rut, I guess. No one seems to interest me right now."

"I'm sure that will pass. I've known you twenty years. You're never lacking for company."

"I have made a new friend," she said, the thought of Laura bringing a smile to her face. "She's my neighbor. She does my yard, borrows my pool." She leaned closer to the desk and rested her elbows on it. "She's like…real."

"Real? You mean compared to your usual friends?"

"Yes. Normal. Down to earth. What you see is what you get. There's no pretense with her."

"Ah. I bet that's refreshing. I've met a few of your friends, remember."

Cassidy laughed. "I know. That was a bad dinner party mix, wasn't it?"

"Yes, the worst. So when do I warrant an invite out to the country?"

She very nearly offered an invitation for this weekend, then remembered her plans with Laura. "How about next week Saturday? I'll do an early dinner."

"I'll check with Derrick. An afternoon relaxing by the pool sounds wonderful."

"Great. Let's plan on it then. I've been waiting on an excuse to try out that new smoker." She rubbed her hands together. "Ribs. Maybe some chicken too."

"I make an excellent potato salad. I'd be happy to bring some."

"Good. I'm looking forward to you seeing the house. And all my flowers. I actually helped build a flowerbed over the weekend."

"Well, that I've got to see." She stood up. "I did come in here for a reason. The monthly reports from Hub Six are going to be late."

"Again? What's the deal?"

"They're the busiest hub. She needs more help."

"At times she needs more help, like when reports are due. Give her permission to hire someone part-time. A college student."

"Okay. She'll be happy about that." Tanya turned to leave, but Cassidy called after her.

"I want to meet them before she hires."

"As always."

She'd been thinking about splitting up Hub Six, but that would entail purchasing another building, stocking it, and hiring licensed technicians to man it. For that kind of expense, she wanted to wait at least another year.

With a sigh, she opened up her laptop. Time to get to work.

CHAPTER TWENTY-EIGHT

It was entirely too hot to be traipsing through the woods, but Laura had thought Tuesday—when the pool boys came—was the perfect time to resume her search for the leaning tree. Afterward, she'd try to coax her mother into the pool for some water therapy. She had done some Google searches that morning and had found a few exercises that she thought her mother could handle. Even if she couldn't, just being out in the pool would break up the routine that her days had become—a routine that mostly involved her recliner and the TV.

She worried about her mother. Some days she seemed to be filled with motivation, wanting to get outside and mess with her flowers. Other days, she showed no inclination to do anything other than sit and watch TV. But the hot, dry weather of summer was fast approaching. The occasional watering that she gave their flowers would become a daily thing. And as much as Laura enjoyed planting the flowers, watering them was a chore. Her mother, on the other hand, used to enjoy walking around the yard with a water hose, tending to the flowers. She wondered if her mother could manage a walker and a hose at the same time.

She shook her head. No, she'd probably get tangled and fall and that would be the end of Laura's attempts at getting her outside. Baby steps. She needed to take baby steps. Like hand watering the flowers and plants on the patio. Her mother needed some purpose, even if it was as mundane as that.

Laura ducked under a low hanging limb of a post oak, then moved the branches aside from a rather large cedar. With a little imagination, she could almost convince herself that she was following the old trails she'd made years and years ago. She paused to take a drink from her water bottle, then slowly lowered it, her eyes wide.

The leaning tree. Right there. *The freaking leaning tree.*

"I'll be damned," she muttered as her face broke out into a smile.

It looked smaller than she remembered, but of course she'd been a kid back then. It had been huge as she'd scrambled along its bark. She walked closer, inspecting the brush that had grown up around it, trying to find a path to the trunk. It was an oak of some kind. She remembered taking her tree identification book out once and had settled on the Mexican White Oak, but she had no idea if that was actually the tree or not. It didn't matter, really. Even in its gnarly state, it was still magnificent.

The trunk sloped upward at a forty-five degree angle, perfect for climbing. It had been blown over as a young tree, no doubt, but its roots had held. It was now thick and hardy, the branches that reached skyward were as big around as some of the smaller trees that grew nearby.

She pulled some of the brush away, making sure there weren't any creepy crawly things there—like a snake slithering by or a nest of spiders.

It appeared safe, and she pulled herself up, the rough bark of the tree digging into her palms. She stood on the trunk, holding on to one of the thick branches to balance herself. She walked higher along the trunk, although quite a bit more cautiously than she had as a kid. As she got as high up as she dared to go, she finally took a look at the view. And…

"Wow."

It was still there…the clearing, the open space of a hay meadow or valley that sloped down and out of sight, leaving her with a perfect, unobstructed view of a summer sunset. Of course, it was still hours before the setting sun would creep into this window. It was pretty now, nonetheless.

She sat down on the trunk and leaned against a branch, enjoying the view. She had been lost in thought on her hike out here, and she had no idea where she was or if she could find the tree again on another day.

She closed her eyes, listening to the sounds of the woods; the leaves rustling in the breeze, the chatter of a squirrel, the sound of a male wren as he sang from a nearby tree, the sharp call of cardinals, and the thundering sound of a woodpecker as he hammered his beak into a tree. She opened her eyes slowly, letting the peacefulness wash over her. She looked skyward, seeing only a handful of puffy white clouds dancing across the blue.

Another glorious day—yet she was feeling like a bit of a slug. How long was she going to take a break from writing? Or was this permanent? She had to admit that since she'd stopped trying to force words onto the page, her stress level had decreased significantly. But still, she was a writer. Writers wrote. Writers didn't mow lawns, tend to flowers, hike the woods…and play in a crystal clear pool as if they hadn't a care in the world.

She sighed quietly. Was she a writer? Was it a fluke that she'd managed to actually write a novel that got published? It must have been. She hadn't been able to produce anything since. Her publisher had long ago given up on her.

Was she a writer? Growing up, she was never much of a reader but she did like to write silly stories, stories that she'd read at the dinner table to groans and eye rolls from Carla. In high school, she dabbled in poetry. Poetry that was so bad, she rarely shared her creations with anyone. It wasn't until her first year of college that she discovered Kay Scarpetta. She devoured every novel featuring the famed medical examiner. Admittedly, she became somewhat obsessed with her, so much so that she wanted to create her *own* Kay Scarpetta. *Murder by Day* was born with dreams of *Murder by Knight* to follow. Unfortunately, her heroine—Claire McDonald—wasn't interesting enough. No matter how many times she tried for a second book, Claire fell flat. Hell, even *she* didn't like Claire all that much at this point.

Was she a writer? She blew out a heavy breath. No. She wasn't. She was thirty-eight years old. She had no job. She lived with her mother.

How depressing. She liked it better when she could at least *pretend* she was a writer. Maybe she should think seriously about starting up a lawn business in the area. God knows she had time on her hands and she did really enjoy the work. If she could pick up five or six yards, that would at least give her some income. She had all of the equipment. She had Frankie's old truck. All she'd need was a trailer to haul the mower and her tools on.

Yeah…maybe that's what she'd do. Yeah, she'd think about it more tomorrow.

She stood up, a smile on her face again. It was time for some pool therapy.

CHAPTER TWENTY-NINE

Cassidy was humming quietly to the song on the radio as she headed out of the city. She needed to stop at a grocery store along the way, but she still hoped to make it home by three. She'd actually intended on heading to the country yesterday, but a glitch—again—with their online appointment scheduling had kept her at the office. Instead of being at the house in the country—and in the pool—on an early Thursday afternoon, she was at the office, brow-beating the two so-called geniuses she'd hired to handle all of their computer needs. She'd threatened them both with unemployment if the system went down again. Not that she'd really fire them. She liked them both, nerdy as they were.

But she'd slipped away today at noon, feeling the urge to get out to the country. She was actually looking forward to a weekend alone. Well, not really alone. Laura would be around. Their dinner plans for jerk chicken were Saturday, but she thought she could talk her into dinner tonight as well. She wouldn't mind having another steak on the grill. Of course, there was her mother to consider. Laura may not want to leave her two nights in a row.

That thought made her wonder if Laura had managed to get her mother into the pool for some exercise. She'd almost called her a couple of times during the week, but, really, she didn't have a reason to. Then again, they were friends. Did she need a reason?

The truth was, Laura crossed her mind far too often as it was. If she didn't know better, she'd think she had a little crush on her. Then she shook her head. Laura was so not her type. Laura had a little too much tomboy in her for that. No… Claudia, Larson…women like that were her type. Women who dressed up, wore makeup. Women who were a little on the skinny side. Not that Laura was fat. She had a very nice body… curvy, athletic. But dressed up? Wearing makeup? No. She'd seen Laura in cutoff jeans, a swimsuit, and khaki shorts. She smiled. And in a sleep shirt with no bra. But man, those cutoff jeans sure fit her good. She shook her head again.

No, Laura wasn't the type of woman she'd date. Actually, Laura really wasn't the type she usually made friends with either. Wonder why that was? Why *did* she hang with the group she did?

* * *

Cassidy's face broke out into a smile when she found Laura in her front yard, a garden hose in her hand as she watered flowers. Did she even own a garden hose? She buzzed her window down, still smiling as she eyed Laura in her cutoff jeans.

"Sorry," Laura said. "But if you want me out of here when you get home, you need to let me know that you're coming early."

"No problem." She arched an eyebrow. "Where did you find a garden hose? I didn't even know I had one."

"You don't." She grinned. "Well, now you do."

"I see. So are you about done?"

"Yes. I'll be out of your hair in a second."

"No, no. I meant, if you're about done, come up for a beer," she offered.

"You sure?"

"Of course. I've had a stressful week. I'm ready to relax and get in the pool."

"Is that an invitation?"

"It is."

"Good. Because I happen to have the weekend to myself."

"What a coincidence. So do I."

She was still smiling as she unpacked the groceries she'd bought. Three steaks—in case Laura's mother wanted to join them, which now seemed like she wouldn't. Potatoes for baking. Wild rice for the pilaf she'd make for tomorrow. Broccoli and cauliflower, which she'd steam for tonight's dinner. Chicken— drumsticks and thighs—and the makings for the jerk sauce, which she'd get Laura to help her with tomorrow. Two bottles of wine, even though her wine rack was already fully stocked. And…a bottle of Crown, just because.

She turned the AC down a little to cool off the house, then went upstairs to change into a swimsuit. She owned four suits, but gravitated to the black one-piece most often. The bikini was only for those occasions when she planned to take it off quickly, like when Claudia was still in the picture. She tossed the bikini back down and picked up the black one-piece instead. Not a romantic weekend, she reminded herself. It would be nice to have a stress-free few days where she didn't have to entertain anyone—day and night. It would just be Laura and she'd found Laura didn't need entertaining. That—as Tanya had suggested— was refreshing.

When she went downstairs and back into the kitchen, she heard a splash. Looking through the window, she found Laura already in the pool, struggling to get onto one of the two floats that she'd apparently tossed in. Cassidy laughed as the float flipped over, dunking Laura. She opened the kitchen door.

"Need some help?"

"This damn thing always fights me," Laura said as she grabbed it again, this time plopping across it sideways, then squirming onto it properly.

Cassidy took the small bucket and put four beers in it and then filled it with ice. She brought two koozies and a couple of towels, then she walked into the pool using the steps, forgoing the diving board. She ducked under the water and swam toward the float, then paused to slick the hair back from her face before climbing onto it.

"Okay, how is it that you can get on the thing so gracefully and I flop around like a beached whale?"

Cassidy laughed. "Lots of practice. My college years were spent either in a pool or out in a lake. My parents have a pool. My brother has a pool." She grasped Laura's float and turned it a little to face her. "I see that your farmer's tan is disappearing."

"That's because I've started to wear this thing when I mow." Laura grinned. "Much more convenient when I'm sneaking into your pool afterward."

"Speaking of that, did you get your mother in?"

"I did. Two times. The first time was not very productive—she was convinced I was trying to drown her. Yesterday she did much better."

"And how is it that you have the weekend to yourself?"

"My sister came about noon and picked her up. The twins—my sister's kids—have some school program tonight that she wanted to go to. Then Carla—my sister—is taking Mom into the city for a day of shopping on Saturday. They asked me to go...I told them I'd be way too busy enjoying a root canal instead."

Cassidy laughed again. "Shopping isn't your thing, huh?"

"I love grocery shopping. It's relaxing to me. But a mall? Clothes shopping? God...just shoot me."

"I know what you mean. I buy most of my things online now."

"Do you have to dress up? I hated wearing business suits at my old job."

"Yes, we dress up. Corporate office and all. We have clients that come in. Builders, contractors, and the like."

"So what do you wear? I guess I can picture you in a power suit. A skirt? No way."

"No skirts. No dresses. But yes, power suits. I've got a closet full of them."

"Here too?"

"No. As long as I keep my apartment—which is only about fifteen minutes from the office—I don't really need them here."

"Do you plan to live here full time someday?"

"I imagine so. In fact, I could work from here on some days. I just haven't initiated that yet. Why?"

"Just wondering when I'm going to lose my private pool." Laura put her float in motion and drifted over to the side where the beer bucket was. "You ready for one?"

"Please."

Cassidy watched as Laura put a bottle in each koozie, then shoved both between her legs as she paddled back over to her. Cassidy's eyes were drawn to the beer cradled between Laura's thighs and she had only one thought...a thought that surprised her.

Lucky beer.

Damn...where did that come from? This was Laura, for God's sake! Not one of her skinny blondes. Not Claudia. Not Larson. Not Becki. Not even Ashly. But *Laura*.

"Here you go."

"Thanks."

Laura smiled at her as she took a drink. "No...thank *you*."

Cassidy looked around, finally taking note of the manicured lawn. "The yard looks nice. The flowers are filling out."

"Thank you. Yes, the flowers are coming along. I turn the planters every couple of days so the flowers don't grow one-sided."

"So you're enjoying your part-time job?"

"I am. So much so that I think I'm going to hit up some of the elderly neighbors and see if I can pick up a few more yards."

"Won't that cut into your writing time?"

Laura snorted. "Writing? I think I've given that up."

"Really?"

"I decided the first book was a fluke. Or else I was so intimidated by the whole process that I've unconsciously created this writer's block so that I don't have to go through it all again."

"Fear of failure?"

"Maybe. Or maybe I really just don't have a second book in me." Laura stared past her for a moment, then met her gaze. "I'm not a writer. It took me eight years to admit it, but that's the truth. And honestly, since I've been taking a break from writing, my temperament has changed." She grinned. "You probably can't notice since I've always been so nice to you, but I feel like I have no more stress."

Cassidy laughed. "Yeah, right. You were Miss Sunshine when we first met."

"I know. I may have been a little moody with the whole mowing thing."

"I called you a bitch."

Laura laughed. "That pissed me off."

"Sorry."

"So, anyway, I was thinking that I'm little more than a slug... living with my mother, no job."

"You take care of your mother, that's a job."

"It's a job with no pay and no benefits. But my mother can't live alone and we can't afford care for her. I mean, realistically, she could probably handle things at night okay. They have services that will come during the day, cook meals, do light housework, that sort of thing," she explained. "If I was working again—and I gave up a really nice salary when I quit—we could swing it."

"Or if you got a job close by, you could still live here and be here for her at night."

"Yes. But there are no jobs close by so I'd end up working in the Metroplex somewhere and no way am I making that commute every day."

"So yard maintenance it is."

Laura smiled. "Like I said...I've decided I'm not a writer. I'm a yard girl. I had that revelation while sitting in the leaning tree."

"You found it?" Then she smiled. "Trespassing again, huh?"

"Yes. And I literally stumbled upon it. It had grown up around there, but I could still climb the tree. I sat there for a while, absorbing the quiet, the sounds of the woods." Laura's voice took on a faraway tone and Cassidy knew she was going back there in her mind. Then Laura sighed and looked at her. "Anyway, I need to do something. I'm going to get fat and lazy if I don't."

"I've seen you work. There's nothing lazy about it."

"Now that the flowerbeds are built, there's nothing to sitting on a riding lawn mower. Weed trimming takes the most effort, that's it."

"I don't think you give yourself enough credit. And you're not anywhere near fat."

"Compared to your skinny model types, I'm huge!"

Cassidy couldn't help but let her gaze linger on Laura's body. The odd tan lines were mostly merged now. Her legs were firm, well-muscled, evidence that she worked outside and didn't sit behind a desk. Her feet were slender, her toes manicured, but there was no trace of nail polish. There was nothing huge on her at all, although her breasts were full...nice. Laura cleared her throat dramatically, and Cassidy finally met her eyes, smiling somewhat sheepishly for blatantly staring her up and down.

"Not huge in the least," she murmured around her smile as she paddled over to the beer bucket. "Another?"

"Sure."

"Oh...I've got steaks. For dinner. You interested?"

"I'll never turn down a steak," Laura said. "But we're still on for jerk chicken, right?"

"Absolutely."

CHAPTER THIRTY

Laura didn't quite know what to make of the weekend thus far. Last night had been so relaxing and fun—the impromptu steak dinner. And this morning, as she was sitting on the patio having coffee, she had heard the now familiar "hey, you out there?" from across the fence again. Cassidy had come over and they'd had three cups each while chatting and watching the birds at the feeder. And now, when she should be doing laundry—which she'd put off for the last two days—she was slipping into her swimsuit to join Cassidy out at the pool. Again.

Not that she was complaining…no. But it did puzzle her somewhat. Did Cassidy really want her company or was it a need on her part to have somebody around? To have somebody around so she wouldn't be alone?

Again, not that she was complaining. A day at the pool beat laundry by a wide margin. She looked at herself in the mirror, the one-piece clinging to her curves. Curves, yes. Not skin and bones. Not by a long shot. But at least her tan was more universal now.

She met her reflection. Did it matter? She wasn't trying to impress anyone—Cassidy. She couldn't compete with the skinny, blond models that had been paraded through here. She arched an eyebrow at herself in the mirror. *Compete?* Where did that come from? She had a little crush on Cassidy, that was all. And who could blame her? She was cute—attractive. She was nice. She was charming. She was playful. She was...*cute!*

"Oh, Laura...she's so out of your league," she murmured. Yes, she was. Because Cassidy had given no indication—not even a tiny hint—that she found Laura attractive or viewed her as anything other than a friend. Well...there was the full body perusal that Cassidy had done yesterday in the pool. When their eyes had met, she would have sworn Cassidy's brown ones were a little darker than normal, but that hardly meant anything.

So she vowed she would simply enjoy the weekend—and the pool—and Cassidy's company and her cooking. Laura was going to help—mostly watch—Cassidy make the sauce for the green jerk chicken. Then playtime in the pool...all afternoon if they wanted. Then dinner, which again, Laura had volunteered to help with. Cassidy said she had a Jamaican rice dish she wanted to try, a pilaf of some sort. It would be another full day, and she knew she'd be scrambling tomorrow to get the house in order and laundry done before her mother came back. But for the time being, she was going to enjoy her free weekend...and not worry about the chores that were being pushed aside so she could play. Her mother would understand.

* * *

"Wow, that smells hot! I love it!"

Cassidy grinned. "I suspected you liked things hot," she said with a teasing wiggle of her eyebrows.

Laura wasn't afraid to meet her gaze. "Are you flirting with me?"

Cassidy's smile didn't falter. "Flirting? I don't flirt."

"No, I don't suppose you have to, do you? Those women flock to you like a moth to a flame."

Cassidy made a show of looking around the kitchen. "I don't see anyone flocking." She held the spoon up. "You want to taste it?"

"Dare I? I saw how many jalapenos you put in." She watched as Cassidy's tongue came out, grabbing a taste of the green sauce.

"Good stuff," she said as she reached for her water bottle. "Nice and hot."

"Okay, give it here."

Instead of handing her the spoon, Cassidy held it up for her, close to her mouth. Their eyes held as Laura licked a little from the bottom of the spoon. Cassidy smiled at her as Laura's eyes widened.

"Wow! That is so spicy. And *so* good!"

"Thanks. When the chicken grills, the sauce gets a little smoky flavor to it. It's not quite as sharp, but still plenty spicy."

Laura stood back as Cassidy coated the chicken—thighs and drumsticks—liberally with the sauce. It was a thick, green goo, and she didn't remember all of the ingredients, but it smelled oh so good and dinner was still *hours* away.

They cleaned up the mess together, easily working around one another in the spacious kitchen. After the Vitamix had been dried and put away, Cassidy announced that it was pool time… and beer time.

"I'm glad you like beer," Cassidy told her as she added ice to the bucket with four bottles in it. "Some women don't care for it."

"You mean all your pretty model types?" she asked as she pulled their two floats from the closet.

"Yeah, them."

"My dad was a beer drinker. When my mother wasn't looking, he'd let me sneak a swallow or two." She grinned. "Or three," she added, remembering the fun conspiracy between them.

"Yeah, my dad too. Back in the day when he not only ran the company but went out on calls too, I remember him coming home, usually at dark. My mother would meet him at the door with a can of beer and a kiss."

"Did your mother work?"

"Yes. She's a nurse. Well, retired now. Yours?"

"No. Stay-at-home mom. Which was great when we were young. She was always here when we got home from school. At least once a week we'd come in to the smell of cookies baking."

"Did you have a lot of friends in school?"

Laura frowned, wondering at the question. She shrugged. "I guess. Normal. Why?"

"You never mention any that you've reconnected with, now that you've moved back."

"Oh. Well, honestly, when I left home, those friendships kinda fizzled. I had an inkling I was gay back in high school, I just didn't want it to be true. And I had my share of crushes. When I finally gave up on the whole straight thing, I think I was embarrassed to let them find out…so I mostly avoided old high school friends."

"Why embarrassed?"

"I didn't want them thinking about gym class and how many of them I'd seen naked." She laughed. "Oh, but there was one girl—Monica Russell—that I had such a crush on. I'm sure she knew it. I *always* stared at her breasts."

"Why didn't you want it to be true?"

"Oh, the usual reasons. Turns out I had nothing to be afraid of. My parents were great when I came out to them."

"I came out in high school," Cassidy said. "My mother cried."

"Oh, I'm sorry. Were you devastated?"

"Not really. She was hugging me and telling me she loved me while she cried, so it wasn't so bad."

"And your father? Brother?"

"Dave claimed he knew it by the time I was ten. Tomboy to the max. My dad took the news with a shrug. In fact, to this day, we've never talked about it."

"Dads are like that, I think. My mother, on the other hand, wanted to know *all* the details."

Cassidy laughed. "Thankfully, my mother wasn't quite as curious."

Laura tilted her head, watching Cassidy. "Why so many women?"

Cassidy raised her eyebrows. "Me?"

"Yes."

"Still looking for that…that *one*. Definition of insanity, remember?"

"Still looking in the same places." Laura splashed water on her legs, cooling them. "What's the longest you've dated someone?"

"Oh…a month, maybe."

"Claudia?"

"Yes."

"Yet you knew she wasn't the one, but you kept dating."

"Are you accusing me of using her?"

"No. You must have more patience than I do. If after the second date I know it's not going anywhere, I feel like I'm wasting my time if I continue to go out with them."

"I don't know about patience. It's easier, I guess."

"Easier to go through the motions than to hurt their feelings?"

Cassidy smiled. "Is it arrogant of me to assume by ending it, that it's hurting feelings?"

"No. I imagine you know which ones are more invested in it than you are. Ashly? The model? She was straight, wasn't she?"

Cassidy laughed. "She likes to play both sides, yes." She held up her hand. "And for the record, I did not sleep with her."

"I saw her naked in your pool," she blurted out.

"Doesn't mean I slept with her. She *wanted* to, don't get me wrong."

"But?"

"I wasn't in the mood to pretend, I guess."

"You invited her out for the weekend with that intention, though."

"Yes, I did." Cassidy took a scoop of water with her hand and splashed Laura. "Why all the questions?"

"I've never met anyone as attractive, as nice, as successful," she said, motioning to the house, "who is perpetually single."

"You're attractive, you're nice…you're single."

Laura laughed and threw two handfuls of water at her. "Left out successful, huh?"

"Well, your yard business isn't up and going yet."

Laura sighed. "My mother says I'm too picky and that I'm looking for perfection. She also says that person doesn't exist."

Cassidy nodded. "My mother tells me the same thing. Maybe they're right."

"I see no need to lower my standards. I'm fine being alone. You, on the other hand…" she said with a smile.

"I'm alone this weekend."

"So you are. Are you enjoying it?"

"Yes. I was thinking earlier how great I slept last night. And…I've enjoyed spending time with you."

"Me too. It's been a rather lazy weekend. I haven't even had to cook!"

"You can help me with the rice dish."

"I will. I can't wait to try that chicken."

"We can eat earlier than normal, if you want."

Laura grinned. "You don't have to offer twice."

CHAPTER THIRTY-ONE

"It's huge."

"I know it's huge. But if I ever live here permanently, I want a stocked pantry. And I also want to be able to walk around in there and find whatever I need."

"It's as big as my bedroom."

"Oh, it is not."

Laura arched an eyebrow. "You haven't seen my bedroom."

"Are you offering?"

Laura smiled into her eyes, then patted Cassidy's stomach as she walked past her, causing Cassidy to catch her breath. She dropped her gaze to Laura's hips, then quickly averted her eyes as Laura turned around.

"How many mushrooms for the rice?"

"A good handful. Slice, then quarter."

It occurred to her then that this was the first time someone had shared her kitchen while she cooked. While *they* cooked. Laura obviously knew her way around a kitchen, and she made quick work of the mushrooms. Before long, they were back outside, wineglasses in hand while the amazing aroma of green jerk chicken filled the air.

"I can't wait to try that," Laura said when Cassidy closed the lid on the grill. "How long?"

"It's got to cook slow. A good thirty minutes, at least."

They sat under the shade of the outdoor kitchen, the ceiling fan stirring the air around them. The sky was darkening to the south and she wondered if they might have rain later.

"It's been a really good weekend," Laura offered.

"I've enjoyed it too. Thanks for helping cook. I normally do that alone."

"I didn't realize I enjoy cooking as much as I do. When I lived alone, it was something I seldom did. Now, with Mom, I cook nearly every day."

"During the week, I don't cook much."

"Dinner dates?"

Cassidy shook her head. "Not every night, no." She smiled. "What? Do you think I have an unlimited number of women to choose from?"

"Don't you?"

"Not really. I mean, I know a lot of people—women—but I don't date all of them."

"You have couple friends too, I guess. I mean—"

"The ones you've seen out at the pool?" At Laura's blush, she laughed. "Just how well can you see from the windows up there?"

"From my bedroom, the pool is all but blocked by the maple tree. From my writing room, there's a perfect view of the pool."

"I see." She leaned forward. "So…I do remember stripping one day. Were you watching then?"

Again, a very cute blush covered Laura's face. "I, of course, was looking at the blonde and not you, smarty-pants."

Cassidy laughed, knowing Laura was lying. She had made no secret that the women Cassidy had brought over did nothing for her.

"You have the worst taste in women."
She sighed. Yeah, she did.

* * *

"Oh, my goodness! This is amazing," Laura said as she licked at the green sauce at the corner of her mouth. "Just spicy enough. Tender. Juicy."

"Glad you like it. And glad that you know how to eat a chicken drumstick properly—with your fingers."

"Growing up, I used to fight Carla for the drumsticks. She was quick, but I had longer arms." Laura paused. "So when you made this the last time...who was it?"

"Ashly."

"Right. Ashly...the model you didn't sleep with. When you made it then, what?"

"Knife and fork."

"Oh my God! To eat a drumstick? What's the point?"

"Exactly."

Laura put her chicken down and licked her fingers before wiping them on her napkin. "I'm sorry. I guess I must seem a little simple to you after dining with women like that."

Cassidy frowned. "Simple? What do you mean?"

"The opposite of sophisticated."

"Oh, Laura...no," she said with a wave of her hand. "You're...you're real. That's how I described you to Tanya. Real. No pretense."

"Who's Tanya?"

"My assistant. She and her husband are coming next Saturday, actually. You should join us. Ribs and chicken on the smoker."

Laura smiled. "Why do you keep enticing me with food?"

Cassidy smiled. "Because you're not shy about eating."

Laura picked up her chicken again. "I'm going to get fat."

"I don't believe it for a minute." She took a bite of her own chicken. "So does that mean yes?" she asked as she chewed.

Their eyes met across the table, the candle flickering between them. "Will you have weekend company?"

"Like a date? No."

Laura nodded. "Okay. Then I'll join you."

* * *

It started innocently enough. Laura was helping load the outdoor dishwasher when the wineglass hit the granite countertop. She tried to catch it before it shattered. The next thing Cassidy saw was red. Laura's hand was covered in blood and she held it up, her eyes frightened. Cassidy grabbed a towel.

"Let me see."

There were two cuts and Laura winced as Cassidy pressed the towel against the biggest cut at the base of her palm.

"I'm sorry," she said gently.

Laura shook her head. "No. I'm sorry. It slipped and—"

"Don't worry about the wineglass." She lifted the towel, only to see blood still seeping from the cut and she covered it again. "It looks deep. Here…sit down." She walked her over to the table, still holding the towel in place.

"You've got blood on you," Laura said.

Indeed, Cassidy had blood on both of her hands. "What? Should I be worried I'm going to catch something from you?"

Laura smiled. "I've been practically a saint my whole life. I'm certain I'm clean." She raised an eyebrow. "You, on the other hand, have been with more women in the short time I've known you than I have in my whole life."

Cassidy peeked again at the wound. "Just because I have female company doesn't mean I always sleep with them."

"No?"

"No. Ashly, for instance."

"The model? The naked model who was floating in your pool?" Laura smiled. "So you keep saying."

"Really. And I'm very careful. I get tested. And I've given up on oral sex. I absolutely don't do it anymore. Those dental dams are a big turnoff, in my opinion."

"I've only used a dental dam once, and yeah, it was kinda weird. It was kinda like...well, it defeated the purpose. But no oral sex? Wow...that's got to suck." Then Laura laughed. "Sorry."

"What? Oral sex? Is that at the top of your list?" Their eyes met and Cassidy felt a jolt in her midsection, imagining oral sex...with Laura.

"We're not having this discussion. No way."

Cassidy smiled. "You're blushing."

"No doubt."

Cassidy stood. "Let me get something to bandage this with."

"It's probably fine." Laura lifted the towel. "Oh." She met Cassidy's gaze again. "Yes, maybe you should."

"Does it hurt?"

"Now that I've looked at it, yes."

"Okay. I'll be right back."

She hurried into the house, trying to remember where she'd stashed the first aid kit. Her bathroom? The main bathroom downstairs? The kitchen? She paused in her search, her eyes staring at nothing. So Laura liked oral sex. Judging by her blush, she liked it a lot.

Cassidy blinked her eyes several times, then shook her head. *Don't go there*, she warned herself. There was just enough attraction between them to be dangerous. And this was Laura. Her friend. Not some blond model type she'd invited to dinner to...to what? To date? To have sex with? She shook her head again. No. This was Laura. Best to get the image of Laura...and oral sex...out of her mind.

"The utility room," she said out loud, remembering where she'd put the first aid kit.

Laura was still sitting when she came out. "Sorry. I couldn't remember where I put it. Come up here, let's wash it."

Laura grimaced. "That's going to hurt."

"I'll be as gentle as I can." Laura still tried to jerk her hand away when the water hit the deepest cut. "Sorry."

"Stings."

The other cut, slightly below her little finger, wasn't deep at all and had already stopped bleeding. The cut on her palm, at the heel of her hand, was deeper and nearly an inch long. As soon as the water washed the blood away, more appeared, but it was slowing.

"You might need stitches."

"Oh, no. No, no, no. Just slap something on it, it'll be fine."

Cassidy dried her hand, then put a gauze patch on the wound, pressing down gently, holding it there. Blood seeped through and she discarded it, getting another one. She went through three of them before she was satisfied.

"Hold that there." She got two bandages out—one for the small cut and a butterfly for her palm—then another piece of gauze and some tape. "Okay, take it off." She quickly put the butterfly bandage on, then covered it with the gauze before securing it in place with the tape.

"You're very good at this," Laura said quietly.

Cassidy looked up from her task, meeting Laura's gaze. Darkness surrounded them yet they were in the light. Laura's hand was still cradled in her own. Again, a sense of…of *something* hit her. She swallowed, trying to push it away.

"My mother was a nurse, you know. And as a kid, I had my share of scrapes that I watched her tend to." Laura still held her gaze but said nothing. Cassidy wasn't able to look away this time. "I'm…I'm attracted to you."

The words were out before she could stop them, and Laura slowly moved her head back and forth.

"I'm…I'm not your type. I've seen the women you've brought here…and I'm not your type."

Cassidy let Laura pull her hand away, but she held firm to her gaze. "You're attracted to me too."

There was a moment of silence, then Laura smiled and took a step away from her. "God…damn that sixth sense of yours," she said in a teasing tone. Then her smile faded. "That doesn't matter though, does it? I've seen the women you bring here. I'm not one of those women, Cassidy." She shook her head. "I don't *want* to be one of those women."

Cassidy had no reply to that. Laura didn't want to be one of those women? Those women who came around for a weekend, sometimes two? Or like Claudia, a month before Cassidy tired of them, ending whatever semblance of a relationship they had. No, she didn't blame Laura in the least. So she nodded.

"You're right. You're not one of those women." She smiled apologetically. "Not my type at all."

CHAPTER THIRTY-TWO

Laura rolled to her side, silently pleading for sleep to come. As had been the case for the last two hours, it eluded her.

"*I'm attracted to you.*"

God, what was she supposed to do with that? Shocking, yes. And as she'd told Cassidy, judging by the women she kept parading through here, she wasn't her type. She wasn't even *close* to her type.

Then why?

And how could she possibly know that Laura was attracted to her? She'd been so careful, hadn't she? What had given it away?

Oh, God…now what? Now what were they supposed to do?

She rolled onto her back again and pulled her hands out from under the sheet. She touched the bandage on her right hand, remembering Cassidy's soft touch, her gentle fingers… remembering the way her stomach had flipped over—like a damn teenager's—when Cassidy had been holding her hand. Remembering the look in her eyes…remembering her words.

"I'm attracted to you."

Laura took a deep breath and closed her eyes. What if…what if she *was* Cassidy's type, yet Cassidy didn't know it? Cassidy had ended up waving her words away, apologizing for saying them in the first place. However…the other part of the equation was still out there; Laura was attracted to her, and Cassidy knew it. Laura had made no attempt to deny it.

Now what were they going to do?

CHAPTER THIRTY-THREE

Cassidy intentionally stayed late at work, making up some excuse to Tanya. She'd pushed her out the door with a "see you tomorrow" and a wave, then had closed her office door and leaned against it. No, there was no urgent work she had to tend to. Tanya most likely knew it too. Tanya knew everything that went on at the office. No…she was simply delaying her trip home, her trip to the country. She tilted her head thoughtfully. Home? Yes, it was starting to feel like home, wasn't it? And she was afraid to go there.

Because of Laura. Because she was afraid to see her.

"*I'm attracted to you.*"

"Jesus, you're so stupid sometimes," she whispered.

She pushed off the door and went to sit down at her desk. She spun the chair around, facing the window and city beyond it. Downtown. Five o'clock traffic on a Friday. The fifteen-minute drive to her apartment would take over thirty, at least. She decided she'd wait until six to leave the office. She had a few things to pack. She wouldn't hurry. She had a stop at the grocery store to make too. If she was lucky, it would be nine or later when she got there. Much too late for Laura to be outside.

But what was she going to do? Avoid her from now on? For what reason? They'd each said their part. It was over and done with. They were friends and that's what they would remain. No, Laura wasn't the type of woman she dated. And hell, for all she knew, *she* wasn't the type that Laura dated.

It was a damn stupid thing to blurt out, and she wished she could take it back. But she couldn't. She couldn't that night and she couldn't now. And God, when was the last time she'd told someone she was attracted to them? She frowned. Surely she had, but no names or faces would come to her.

And tomorrow, Tanya and Derrick were coming over. Laura had said she'd join them. Cassidy had half a mind to invite someone along...anyone. But it would be awkward enough. No sense in adding to it. Besides, she'd already told Laura that she wasn't bringing a date.

She blew out a deep breath. She was a grown woman. Forty-four years old, for God's sake. And here she sat, afraid to go, afraid to see Laura. What exactly was she afraid of?

"It's just Laura," she murmured.

With that, she spun around and closed her laptop. She couldn't possibly sit around here until six...thinking. She'd rather fight five o'clock traffic.

* * *

Laura sat on the patio sipping iced tea. Friday night and she was drinking sweet iced tea. She had beer, but she wasn't in the mood for it. She had bourbon, but that too wasn't appealing.

Where was she? Was she even coming this weekend? Since Laura had moved there—what was it? Over two months now?—Cassidy always came early on Fridays, even a few times on Thursday. But today? No. Here it was, nearly nine and there had been no sign of her. Laura knew why, of course.

"*I'm attracted to you.*"

Yeah...that was it. That was *still* it. She'd almost called her this week, just to clear the air a bit between them. She didn't want there to be awkwardness. She didn't want Cassidy to feel uncomfortable around her. But in the end, she didn't. And now Friday had rolled around again and the weekend was here. Was she even coming? Didn't she say she was having a Saturday barbeque? Had that been canceled? Was Laura even still invited?

She saw lights flash across the trees, and she turned, listening. Sure enough, she heard Cassidy's gate opening. She was surprised by the nervousness she felt, surprised that her heart rate kicked up a notch or two...surprised by how thankful she was that Cassidy had come home after all.

CHAPTER THIRTY-FOUR

Cassidy leaned against the island, a steaming cup of coffee in her hand. It was barely daybreak. Was she out there on her patio? Was she already sitting, having coffee, watching the birds?

She walked to the double doors and stared out at the pool, her gaze drawn to the fence as if she could see through it. Yes. Laura was out there. She could almost feel her.

Damn.

She'd busied herself in the kitchen last night, seasoning the ribs and chicken. She wanted to get the ribs on the smoker about nine this morning. She'd busied herself with unpacking, with tidying the house for company. She'd busied herself, yes, but that didn't mean that Laura wasn't on her mind. She had been, just as she'd been on the drive home. Just as she was now.

Well, she was being ridiculous, she told herself. She couldn't avoid her forever. Best to get it over with now than to wait until Tanya and Derrick were here. Get it over with, talk about it if they needed to, then get back to normal. Because normal was what she wanted.

So she opened the doors, pleased by the coolness of the morning after such a hot day yesterday. She strode purposefully around the pool and into the grass, taking note of the good job Laura had done with the lawn. She walked over to her spot by the fence and paused, taking a deep breath before speaking.

"Hey…you out there?" There was only a slight pause before she heard Laura answer.

"I am."

"Feel like company?"

"Sure. Come on over."

Cassidy smiled. That all seemed normal. Laura sounded the same as always. Maybe there wasn't anything to talk about after all. She made her away around the shrubs at the side of the house and onto the driveway in the front, walking up to the gate. She punched in the code and waited while it opened, then went out onto the road and over to the Morrisons' place. As was the norm, the lawn here was perfectly manicured, the flowers bright and vibrant…reminding her that she'd not even taken a glance at her own flowerbeds, the ones that Laura had worked so hard on.

Laura gave her a welcoming smile. Cassidy returned it, wishing now that she hadn't avoided her yesterday—last night.

"Hey."

"Good morning." Cassidy sat down. "I see your bird feeders are active."

"You just missed me throwing a stick at a squirrel," Laura said with a grin. "He was chasing off my cardinals."

"Wonder why I haven't put a feeder up?"

"Because your yard girl would be in charge of filling it during the week and your yard girl has enough to do."

"Speaking of that, the yard looks nice…as always."

"Thank you." Laura took a sip of her coffee, eyeing Cassidy over the top. "You got home late last night."

"You saw me?"

Laura nodded. "I was out here. I saw your lights."

"Yeah…I had some work I needed to finish up," she lied. "Then grocery store on the way here."

"You came alone?"

She was sure Laura meant the question to be indifferent or at least sound that way. But her tone was a little guarded, almost as if she was afraid of the answer. Cassidy was so glad that she hadn't given into her insecurities and invited someone along. She met Laura's gaze, surprised by the uncertainty she saw there, surprised that she couldn't pull away from that gaze.

"I'm alone, yes." Laura turned away quickly but not before Cassidy saw a flash of relief in her eyes. She leaned forward, resting her arms on her thighs, her gaze on the feeders and not Laura. "You still coming over today? Pool?"

"Ribs and chicken."

Cassidy laughed. "I see where your priorities are." She leaned back. "How's your hand, by the way?"

Laura held it up. "It's fine. Healing." Laura rubbed a finger across the bandage. "I keep this waterproof bandage on it so it's fine."

"Good. Did you get your mother in the pool this week?"

"I did. Twice. Thank you."

"Are you still trying to drown her?"

"After her exercises, I actually got her up on a float, but she made me keep her in the shallow end. She's doing really well in the water. I can't thank you enough for letting me use your pool as therapy."

"It's no problem. I'm glad it's helping."

"You want another cup?"

Cassidy hesitated. She had a ton of things to do before Tanya got there at noon. But the prospect of spending a few more minutes with Laura was too tempting.

"Yeah, that'd be good. Then I'll need to go. They're coming over about noon or so. I need to get the beans on."

"Is there something I can bring? An appetizer or something?"

"I picked up a couple of dips at the store."

"Deviled eggs?"

"Sure, that'd be great. I love deviled eggs."

Laura reached out to take her cup and as she handed it over, their fingers touched. Their fingers touched, their eyes locked together, and damn…just like that, it was back. Laura looked like she wanted to say something, but she didn't. She turned and went into the house. Cassidy let out a breath and closed her eyes.

I'm attracted to her. And on the heels of that…*Laura's attracted to me.*

CHAPTER THIRTY-FIVE

Laura felt a tad guilty for leaving her mother alone, but as her mother had told her, Saturday was just like any other day. Except, she'd added, that she would be having leftovers for dinner. Laura had promised to make it up to her tomorrow by roasting a chicken in the oven. In turn, her mother had promised to make the gravy for their mashed potatoes. It was a win-win in Laura's opinion.

And despite the little bit of awkwardness between them that morning, she was looking forward to spending the afternoon with Cassidy and her friends. Well, mostly with Cassidy, which was turning more dangerous with each encounter. Because…

I'm attracted to her.

So much for spending the week trying to forget about it. All it had taken was a few minutes together…a few minutes, an innocent touch, and Laura had fallen into her eyes and couldn't get back out.

But she needed to, she told herself. She needed to push this aside—push it away and keep it away—and forget about it. Because there was only one way this could end...badly. She would lose the friendship she and Cassidy had, yes. But she would also lose her heart and she was too damn old for a broken heart.

She wasn't one of Cassidy's "women." She was a simple yard girl who barely knew which fork to use at dinner. She rolled her eyes. Okay, so that was an exaggeration but still...as she'd told Cassidy last weekend, she wasn't sophisticated, she wasn't worldly. She ran in a whole different circle from the women—and friends—that Cassidy surrounded herself with. Laura simply didn't fit in. She didn't *want* to fit in.

So, in order to maintain the friendship she and Cassidy had between them, she would dismiss this silly attraction—for both of them—and hopefully, it would go away—for both of them.

She stood now on the patio, the plate of deviled eggs in her hand. Should she go over already? She could hear voices at the pool, but if Cassidy's company had just gotten there, should she wait a respectable amount of time before joining them. What was a respectable amount of time?

"You're being ridiculous," she murmured.

She stepped off the patio, then paused. What if she was dressed wrong? Was walking over in her swimsuit and a cover-up too little? She had her bag over her shoulder with dry clothes for later...should she wear them now and change into the swimsuit later?

"Hey...you out there?"

She smiled at the fence. "Yes."

"Well, come on over already."

She walked closer to the fence. "I don't know if I'm dressed properly."

She heard Cassidy walk closer too. "I'm in a swimsuit, shorts, and flip-flops."

"Bikini?" she asked hopefully, the question out before she could stop it.

A pause. "No," she said slowly. "Would you like me to be in one?"

Damn. Laura cleared her throat. "Never mind. I'll be right over."

She heard Cassidy's quiet laugh as she turned away.

"Idiot!" she muttered as she rolled her eyes. Yeah, she was doing a great job of pushing her attraction away. A great job.

When she walked around the back to the pool, Cassidy was chatting with an attractive dark-haired man, so she went directly to the outdoor kitchen and fridge, putting her eggs inside.

"You must be Laura."

She turned, finding a petite woman with sandy brown hair coming out of the house. Laura nodded. "Yes, Laura Fry."

The woman held her hand out with a smile. "I'm Tanya Grayson. Good to meet you. I've heard a lot about you."

Laura's eyebrows shot up. "Oh?"

Tanya smiled. "All good, I assure you. I'm Cassidy's assistant, but we're also friends." She motioned to where Cassidy was. "That's my husband, Derrick. Cassidy actually introduced us. She knew Derrick from college."

"Oh, so you go way back then."

"Yes, twenty years or more. We've been married seventeen." She leaned closer. "Cassidy was in our wedding, if you can picture that."

Laura laughed. "Bridesmaid dress? Oh, I've got to see a picture of that."

"Consider it done!"

"What are you two laughing about?" Cassidy asked as she came over. She smiled at Laura. "Hey."

"Hi."

"She wants a picture of you."

Cassidy grinned. "You told her about the wedding, didn't you?"

"I did." Tanya turned back to her, still smiling. "They were lilac-colored, shoes to match." Then she laughed. "And a big, floppy hat. The look on Cassidy's face is so like 'I'm going to kill you when this is over with' that I break into a fit of giggles every time I see it."

Laura laughed again, surprised at the blush on Cassidy's face.

"You will so not share that picture with Laura."

"I so will."

"And you wonder why I haven't invited you over before."

"Oh, please. I'm just thankful you were able to squeeze us into your busy social schedule." Tanya touched Laura's arm. "I hope you have a swimsuit on under that. I'm ready to get in."

"You two go ahead," Cassidy offered. "I'm going to show Derrick my gym."

"Have you had a tour yet?" Laura asked Tanya.

"Not yet. I think Cassidy is stalling. It's huge."

"Yes, it is. I'm surprised she doesn't get lost in it." Laura pulled off her top and kicked her flip-flops to the side of the table where a familiar bucket of beer sat.

"A lot of it the designer added on his own. I think she got tired of fighting him," Tanya said. "He called daily."

"I love the kitchen, though. And have you seen the pantry? It's as big as a bedroom."

Tanya laughed. "Yes, she did open the door so I could see. Cassidy loves to cook."

They walked down the steps in the shallow end of the pool. The cool water felt good as the hot sun beat down on Laura's shoulders.

"I understand you're responsible for these lovely flowers."

Laura nodded. "I went a bit overboard, I think."

"They look great. Cassidy is very proud of them. Especially the flowerbed that she claims she helped build. Is it true?"

"It's true. I made her do the hard part—hauling stone."

"Well, everything looks great. I'm envious. I have a brown thumb. As Derrick told me once, I'd probably kill a plastic plant!"

"I get it from my mother. She's always had a green thumb."

"She lives next door too, right?"

Laura nodded, wondering just how much Cassidy *did* tell Tanya about her. "Technically, I'm living with her, not the other way around. When her husband died, she needed help here. She's partially disabled," Laura explained.

Cassidy and Derrick came out and Derrick's eyes were wide. "Man, you should see that gym. I want one!"

"Sure, honey. As soon as you start using that treadmill you just *had* to have," she said with a laugh. "This is Laura. Laura… my husband, Derrick."

"Nice to meet you," Derrick said with a nod.

Laura smiled, then slid her glance to Cassidy. "Coming in?"

"Yep. Let me get some floats." She pointed at the bucket of beer. "Want one?"

"If everyone else does, I will."

"Count me in," Derrick said as he dove in off the side.

It turned out to be one of those relaxing, stress-free days that Laura loved. As Cassidy had promised, Tanya and Derrick were "normal" and Laura enjoyed both of them. They made her feel as if she were old friends like they were, including her in the conversation as they told stories of when they'd first met. Laura got a glimpse of the younger Cassidy and judging by the tales she heard, she had been quite a handful back then. Cassidy, in turn, seemed almost embarrassed and tried to shift the conversation away from herself as often as she could.

All in all, it was a fun afternoon in the water and by the time six rolled around, she was feeling quite relaxed, having had three beers. The deviled egg tray had been mostly devoured, leaving only a few left on the plate. The dips and chips that Cassidy had put out were nearly gone too, but Laura still found herself ravenous as she smelled the delectable aroma coming from the smoker.

"That smells delicious."

"That's the third time you've said that."

Laura smiled at Cassidy. "So?"

"Are you hungry?"

"Starving."

Cassidy smiled and shook her head. "You can't possibly be." She reached out and teasingly rubbed Laura's stomach. "There's room for one more egg in there, I think."

She didn't take her hand away immediately, and as their eyes held, Laura wished she was brave enough to wear a bikini. If she was, then Cassidy's hand would be resting on her skin instead of her swimsuit. She finally found her voice when Cassidy slowly removed her hand.

"No. I'm saving every bit of room for ribs and chicken. I may even skip the potato salad."

"I made dessert."

Laura arched an eyebrow. "Something decadent?"

"It involves chocolate."

Laura's mouth watered. "I love chocolate," she said quietly.

Cassidy leaned closer. "I guessed that about you. Glad I was right."

Laura found her gaze lowering to Cassidy's lips as she smiled, then she forced them back up, immediately being captured by Cassidy's. God, she was doing a horrible job of pushing this attraction away, wasn't she?

Cassidy leaned closer, her voice little more than a whisper. "I'm still attracted to you."

Laura's heart jumped into her throat, and she didn't dare take a breath until Cassidy had turned away, heading over to the smoker, presumably to check on the progress of dinner. She spun around, trying to collect her thoughts when she found Tanya watching her with a bit of an amused expression. She felt a blush light her face, but she returned Tanya's smile and walked over to her.

"Where's Derrick?"

"He went to change into dry clothes."

"I guess it's time, isn't it?"

"I suppose we have to. It's been such a fun afternoon," Tanya said. "You are *so* different from Cassidy's usual friends, and I mean that in a very good way."

"I haven't actually met any of her friends."

"Consider yourself lucky."

"Well, there was the one woman she brought out here… Ashly, I believe. I was out working in the flowerbed and Cassidy came home early. I was a filthy mess."

Tanya glanced over to where Cassidy was, then looked back at Laura. "I hope I'm not out of line for saying this, but you and Cassidy…you have this energy between you. It's very noticeable." She smiled. "Also very cute."

Laura felt another blush threaten, and she hoped she managed to stave it off. "An…an energy?" She laughed. "No, no. I've seen the women Cassidy's been with. Trust me, I am not her type."

Tanya again looked at Cassidy. "That's the problem with my hardheaded friend there. She thinks she knows who her type is, but she has no clue." She looked back at Laura, holding her gaze. "You like her, don't you?"

Laura could blow off the question if she wanted to. She could dismiss it. She could lie. "Yes." She turned her gaze to Cassidy, watching her. "I wish I didn't."

"Cassidy is hard not to like."

"And no doubt she's left a string of broken hearts behind."

"No doubt. She's looking for the love of her life. Looking in all the wrong places, as the old song goes." Tanya tilted her head. "And what about you? Single, too, I'm assuming?"

Laura nodded. "Yes. We seem to be looking for the same thing."

Tanya surprised her by reaching over and squeezing her forearm gently. "Don't give up. It's worth waiting for."

CHAPTER THIRTY-SIX

Laura was barely able to stop herself from snatching a rib off the platter while Cassidy cut them with the electric knife. Cassidy laughed at her.

"I know what you're thinking. Don't do it."

Laura knew she was playing with fire, but she simply couldn't resist. She moved closer, moving her eyebrows teasingly.

"You have *no* idea what I'm thinking."

Cassidy paused in mid-cut, a smile on her face. "You're coveting my ribs…among other body parts."

Laura laughed. "Oh, I love your modesty!" Laura met her gaze. "You're right. I can't wait…to taste…your ribs."

Cassidy leaned closer. "Are you flirting with me?"

"Of course not. I don't flirt."

"Because I think you are."

"You're delusional," Laura said with a smile as she swiped a rib. "I was simply distracting you." She took a bite and moaned. "Oh my God. It's like…melts in your mouth."

"I see someone couldn't wait," Tanya said as she came out of the house, dressed in dry clothes. She, too, took a rib off the platter.

"Hey...both of you, stay away from my ribs!" Cassidy said with a laugh as she slid the platter away from them.

"Wow," Tanya murmured as she chewed. "Fabulous. You're pretty good at this."

Cassidy grinned as she met Laura's eyes. "I'm *very* good."

Laura laughed. "Again...your modesty—you're far too humble."

Tanya laughed too. "I don't think you're going to win with this one, Cassidy."

"Met my match, huh?"

"I believe you have."

Laura felt her heart flutter as Cassidy stared into her eyes. A slow—sweet—smile appeared on Cassidy's face, but she said nothing else. Laura finally broke the contact and took a step away, only to have her eyes collide with Tanya's. She gave Laura a very subtle wink.

"Let's set the table," Tanya offered. "Eat out here, right?"

"Unless you think it's too warm," Cassidy said. "We can eat inside then."

"This is fine by me," Laura said, looking to Tanya for confirmation.

"Yes. It's cool enough with the ceiling fan."

Within twenty minutes, the four of them were seated, and they all held their wineglasses up in a toast.

"To good friends," Cassidy said. "It's been an awesome day."

"Yes, it has," Tanya agreed. "Cheers."

"Cheers," Laura echoed, her gaze drifting across the table to Cassidy. Yes, it had been an awesome day. She was so thankful to have been included. Cassidy smiled at her.

"Okay...*now* you can have a rib."

Laura took not only another rib but also a piece of chicken—a thigh. Tanya's potato salad looked delicious and creamy and Cassidy had a pot of beans that she'd been slow cooking all day. Her plate was full, but she managed to squeeze in a spoonful of broccoli florets, just because she felt she needed to. That, of course, didn't mean that she would eat them. She had to save room for dessert...something chocolate and decadent.

However, when she finally pushed her plate away—her stomach full to the brim—she thought she would surely burst if she attempted dessert. The first thing Cassidy put on the table was ice cream...vanilla. Tempting, but Laura would politely refuse. But then here it came...a plate full of chocolate squares. Creamy chocolate squares.

"Double chocolate coconut fudge brownies," Cassidy announced. "I won't tell you how much butter and cream cheese is in there, but after one bite, you won't care."

"They look sinful," Tanya said. "I'm going to want the recipe, aren't I?"

"You are."

"I should skip the ice cream," Laura said. She pointed her finger at Cassidy. "You're going to make me fat!"

"So you keep saying." Cassidy scooped ice cream on her piece anyway, smiling as she slid it to her. "Enjoy it and don't worry about the calories."

Tanya was the first to take a bite, and her mumbled "oh my God" made Laura snatch up her fork too. Oh my God indeed. She closed her eyes as she savored the taste. Judging by her moan, she would have sworn her mouth just had an orgasm. When she opened her eyes, Cassidy was watching her.

"I have no words," she murmured as she took another bite. "You should be ashamed of yourself for making this!"

Cassidy laughed. "Consider me reprimanded."

* * *

Despite telling them that they didn't have to help with the cleanup, both Tanya and Laura helped load the outdoor dishwasher while she put the leftovers away. Not a single rib remained and only two pieces of chicken were left. She had to admit, it was fun cooking for people who actually liked to eat. Like Laura. She wasn't shy in the least about taking second helpings.

"You can give me the recipe on Monday, but I'm taking two brownies home with me now."

"Take some for the boys too," she offered. She glanced over at Laura. "Your mother would probably like one too."

"Trust me, if one of those made it into the house, my mother wouldn't be the one eating it."

Tanya laughed. "I feel the same way. I'll probably hide them from the boys." Tanya walked over to her and hugged her. "I like her. A lot," she whispered into her ear before pulling away. "Thank you for a great day, Cassidy."

"Glad you came."

Tanya then walked over to Laura and hugged her too. "So nice getting to know you, Laura. I hope we get to see you again."

"Thank you. I enjoyed your company. It was a fun day."

Tanya looked over at Derrick, who was patiently waiting. "Ready?"

"I should go too," Laura said. "It's getting late."

"Stay," Cassidy said without thinking. "I mean...have a nightcap with me."

"Yes, stay," Tanya said. "Don't leave on our account." She linked arms with Derrick. "See you Monday."

"Be careful," she called as they walked around the side of the house and disappeared.

She turned to Laura, suddenly feeling nervous. They'd spent the entire day together, yet they'd only had a few moments alone. They'd chatted like friends, they'd teased and played... and they'd flirted. And now here they were—alone—and she felt a little out of her element. She was used to being in control. With Laura, she never felt in control.

"I like them," Laura said, breaking the silence. "Tanya is very nice."

"She is."

"She said you introduced her to Derrick."

Cassidy nodded. "Derrick and I were buddies in college." She walked over toward the pool, feeling Laura following her. The shadows were heavier here, the pool lights softer now as she'd switched from dark blue to red and yellow, giving the water a mild orange tint. It was...romantic. She turned to Laura, searching her eyes in the muted light. Yes, Laura was nervous too. What was she thinking? Was she thinking—like Cassidy was—that this was a dangerous situation they found themselves in? Was she wishing she'd gone home when Cassidy had asked her to stay? Or was she ready to explore this attraction that had sprung up between them? No. She'd already told Cassidy—in so many words—that she wasn't interested. Yet...sometimes, Cassidy didn't get that feeling at all. Sometimes, when Laura looked at her, Cassidy got a completely different feeling.

Like now.

She took a step closer. They were surrounded by the night and she could almost feel it touching her, touching them. She imagined she could hear Laura's heartbeat, *see* her heart beat. The air around them seemed to sizzle as she took another step closer.

"Don't...don't do it," Laura whispered.

Cassidy held her gaze steady. "Do what?"

"Don't you dare kiss me."

"No? I've thought of little else all day." All week, really, if she was being honest with herself. "You have too."

Laura shook her head. "No."

Cassidy smiled. "Liar," she whispered, seeing Laura's answering smile.

Both of their smiles faded, however, as their eyes held. Again, Laura tried to protest.

"We can't do this. We both know we...we shouldn't do this."

"We both know we're going to do this," she murmured as her gaze lowered to Laura's mouth.

She didn't know who moved first. She assumed it was her, but then Laura's mouth was meeting hers with a gentle urgency, a gentle desperation. Twin moans broke the silence around them, and Cassidy felt her knees tremble. She felt weak. She felt light-headed. God...she felt *faint*. She deepened the kiss, moving closer to Laura. Her head began to spin and she was afraid she'd fall.

But Laura stepped away from her, her eyes wide. She backed up slowly, her own legs appearing a bit wobbly as she took several steps away before turning and hurrying past the shrubs and around the house.

Cassidy reached out a shaking hand and grasped the back of a chair before lowering herself into it. She still stared at the spot where Laura had been. Where Laura had been kissing her.

"What the hell just happened?" she whispered to the night.

CHAPTER THIRTY-SEVEN

Laura intentionally stayed in bed longer than usual. An hour longer and even then, she was afraid to get up. Afraid that she'd hear Cassidy's familiar morning greeting at the fence.

"Hey, you out there?"

Of course, she could always just take her coffee inside. That would prevent her from having to answer. That would prevent her from having to *see* Cassidy. Because, right now, she simply couldn't see her. She was afraid to see her.

She rolled over and faced the window. She wanted to tell herself that it was just a kiss…a little, silly nothing kiss. That's what she wanted to tell herself. That's what she wanted to believe. But it would do no good to lie to herself. Because never in her life had a kiss made her dizzy before. Never before had she feared her knees would buckle. *Never* had she felt a kiss all the way down to her toes.

She closed her eyes, once again reliving the kiss in her mind. And once again feeling butterflies fluttering in her stomach.

"Oh, God," she whispered. What was she going to do now? How could she possibly face Cassidy after that?

She tried to muster up some anger toward Cassidy. It was her fault. She'd asked her not to kiss her. She'd told her it wasn't a good idea. But no. Cassidy hadn't heeded her warning. She kissed her anyway. So Laura wanted to be angry with Cassidy.

If only those damn butterflies would get out of her stomach.

CHAPTER THIRTY-EIGHT

"If you don't jump on this one, you're out of your mind," Tanya announced after ignoring Cassidy's closed office door and barging inside.

Cassidy feigned ignorance. "What are you talking about?"

"Laura. I'm talking about Laura."

Cassidy shook her head. "Don't read anything into it. We're just friends."

"Just friends, my ass."

Cassidy sighed and leaned back in her chair. "Tanya, she's… she's not my type."

Tanya sat down across from her, her head shaking disapprovingly. "She's exactly your type. It's all these other women who keep waltzing through your life who aren't your type. Don't you know that by now?"

Cassidy met her gaze. "Laura…Laura scares me."

Tanya's expression softened. "You're attracted to her and that scares you?"

Cassidy nodded. "Yes. I don't feel like I'm in control when I'm around her."

"And we all know you like to be in control," she stated. "You should see your face when you look at her, Cassidy. It's like you're glowing or something."

Cassidy snorted. "Oh, please. I don't glow."

"Believe what you want. I just hope you don't run and hide because what you're feeling scares you."

"Well…I kinda did run," she admitted. "We…we kissed. After you left, we kissed. And I thought I was going to faint." She laughed nervously. "From a damn kiss." She shook her head. "I was in shock. I couldn't speak. We didn't say a word. Laura left and the next morning, bright and early, I ran. I came back here."

"So you kissed and you didn't say a word to each other?"

"No."

It was Tanya's turn to shake her head. "You're going to screw this up, aren't you?"

Cassidy stared at her. "There's not really anything to screw up. I told you—"

"She's not your type. You're just friends." Tanya stood up. "You felt faint from a kiss. I don't think you're going to be able to outrun this, my friend."

After Tanya left, Cassidy got up and paced across her office floor. Yes, she'd run. Like a coward, she admitted. But she couldn't see Laura. She didn't know what she'd say to her. Was an apology warranted? No. While she was the one to initiate the kiss, she certainly wasn't the only one participating in it.

God, Laura's lips were so soft. Soft and responsive and… and she wanted to taste them again. Because the truth was, the kiss didn't last nearly long enough. No. Laura had pulled away. Laura's eyes had been filled with wonder, shock…and something else. It was that "something else" that scared her.

She'd been with more women than she could remember, but that look in Laura's eyes…Cassidy was certain she'd never seen it before. She was afraid. She was afraid that when she saw Laura, she might see that look again.

Or maybe she was afraid that she *wouldn't* see it again.

CHAPTER THIRTY-NINE

Laura had a good week, she admitted. It hadn't started out that way, but by Thursday, while she was mowing Cassidy's yard, she'd finally gotten to the point where the damn kiss wasn't at the forefront of her mind.

On Sunday, even after she'd realized that Cassidy had left—without saying goodbye—she hadn't wandered outside of the house. If her mother was curious about her being underfoot, she didn't mention it. A brief rain shower and the ensuing humidity was as good an excuse as any to stay inside. She'd roasted the chicken early and after dinner, she'd joined her mother in the den to watch TV. A mindless activity but at least it kept Cassidy—and the kiss—at bay.

Monday and Wednesday were water therapy days and she found her mother was actually looking forward to their sessions now. She also noticed that her mother was getting stronger. After they got out of the pool, her suggested walk was not met with rejection, and both days they'd made it to the end of the road and back without any missteps. And they'd finally agreed on a paint color for the house—a light brown with beige trim.

So yes, it had been a good week. Things were back to normal. She was the yard girl and she kept busy. The lawns were manicured to perfection, the flowers were watered and blooming beautifully. A good week.

But now that Friday had rolled around, she wondered if the good week would be followed by a good weekend. Would Cassidy avoid her? Would *she* avoid Cassidy? She supposed, really, there was no reason for them to even see each other. They had no plans for dinner. It wasn't like they had to hang out at the pool together. And anyway, Cassidy was probably bringing company with her. Female company. Some skinny blonde.

She refused to acknowledge the stab of jealousy she felt at that thought. Jealousy, of all things! They kissed. A tiny, little, quick kiss. It was nothing. It meant absolutely nothing.

But it wasn't tiny and it wasn't quick, and when she closed her eyes, she could still feel Cassidy's mouth on hers. She could still taste her...taste the lingering sweetness of her lips.

Damn.

No. She hoped she didn't see Cassidy. She hoped that Cassidy brought company. Yes, that's what she hoped. Cassidy and one of her women, hanging out at the pool...probably naked.

No! That's not what she wanted. She didn't want a skinny, blond woman—naked—out with Cassidy.

What she wanted was...

The ringing of her phone interrupted her, and she didn't have to glance at it to know who it was. She'd changed the ringtone weeks ago. But why was she calling? Maybe she wasn't coming this weekend after all. Maybe all this worrying was for nothing.

She swallowed down her nervousness before answering. "Hi," she said, hoping her voice sounded normal.

"Hey. What are you doing?"

Laura bit her lip. "Thinking about you and that damn kiss" didn't seem like the proper thing to say. She pushed open the back door and went out onto the patio.

"Nothing really," she said. "Where are you?"

"Here."

She raised her eyebrows. "Here here?"

Cassidy laughed. "Yes. So why don't you come over? Pool?"

Bad idea, she thought. Very bad idea. But it was hot, she reasoned. The cool water would feel good. *Damn.* But no. She shook her head. Bad idea. Very, very bad idea.

"Please."

Oh, God. "Okay. When?"

"Now?"

"Are you...are you alone?"

"Does that make a difference?"

"If there's a skinny, blond model there with you, I'd just as soon not join you," she said bluntly.

"Laura...I'm alone. Come over."

She sighed. "This is a bad idea."

"I promise I'll behave."

Laura grabbed the bridge of her nose and squeezed. "We should...we should talk."

"I think we are talking...right?"

Laura smiled. Well, apparently Cassidy wanted to pretend that the kiss never happened. She also wondered if she was going to pretend that she didn't leave extra early last Sunday to avoid her. But she was here early, Laura noted. Extra early on a Friday. Oh, it didn't matter. None of it mattered.

"Okay. Let me change. I'll be right over."

* * *

Cassidy wasn't sure what it was about Laura that made her question her own self-assurance, but as soon as the call ended, she felt a little apprehensive...a bit nervous. She, who prided herself on her confidence, was feeling nervous, of all things... because Laura was coming over.

Maybe she shouldn't have called her. Maybe she should have waited until tomorrow. But no. Erica and Amber were coming tomorrow. They were spending the night. And for once, Cassidy hadn't been the one to extend the invitation. Erica had called on Thursday, saying they were free for the weekend and would she mind guests. What was she supposed to say? No? No, she couldn't have guests because she was all mixed up inside because she and Laura kissed. Wouldn't Erica find that amusing? Cassidy—who could date any woman she wanted—was feeling insecure because she and Laura kissed.

You've kissed *lots* of women, she reminded herself. Tons. Why was Laura's kiss different? She swallowed, glancing to the spot where they'd been. It was different because she hadn't been in control. No…she'd felt light-headed. She'd felt faint, for God's sake.

"Are you okay?"

She jumped, finding the woman who had been invading her thoughts for the last week. She looked at Laura. Not just the last week, no. Much longer than that.

"Cassidy?"

She finally shook her thoughts away and smiled. "Hey."

Laura came closer, a frown on her face. "A million miles away?"

Cassidy nodded. "Lost in thought, yes." She took a step away from Laura. "Beer?"

Laura eyed her suspiciously. "You're acting weird."

"That's because I don't know how to act."

"I thought you said that we didn't need to talk."

"I never said that."

Laura pulled off her shirt and Cassidy's breath held. Laura pointed at her. "Get in the pool. I'll get the floats. I'll bring the beer."

Cassidy stood there mutely as Laura walked away. She had her cutoff jeans on…and all Cassidy could think of at that moment was slipping *off* those cutoff jeans. She shook her head quickly, then yanked her own shorts off and practically fell into the pool. She ducked under the water and swam down to the deep end where it was cooler. She surfaced under the shade of the diving board and held onto the side, turning to watch as Laura made her way back over. Two floats were tossed into the pool and Laura—like Cassidy always did—covered the beer bucket with a towel.

And then…those cutoff jeans were unbuttoned, the zipper lowered…and Cassidy felt her heart hammering in her chest, felt her breathing increase, felt her losing her grip on the side of the pool. She held on, her gaze locked on Laura's hands as they shoved the cutoff jeans down her legs, past her thighs and knees to her ankles. When she stepped out of them, Cassidy lost her grip on the side and slipped under the water. She came up sputtering and coughing, finding Laura staring at her.

"What in the world is wrong with you, Cassidy?"

Laura was across the pool on the other side, not even in waist-deep water. There were no longer any oddly placed tan lines to be seen. It was the same swimsuit she normally wore—the one with shades of purple and black. She also had a solid black one, but that was a little more sporty than this one and didn't show quite so much cleavage. Of course she was staring, and she certainly didn't need to be staring at Laura's breasts… she was liable to drown.

She cleared her throat. "Do you think we should talk?"

Laura raised her eyebrows.

"Because I think we should probably talk," Cassidy continued.

"About the kiss?"

"Yes."

"Okay."

Laura stayed where she was, the water lapping just above her thighs. Cassidy stayed where she was, holding on the side of the pool for dear life. They stared at each other for a long—quiet—moment. Then Cassidy smiled and Laura did the same. Cassidy finally looked away, laughing a little at how ridiculous the situation was. Laura laughed too.

"Okay, then…glad we got that out of the way."

"Will you just relax," Laura said as she shoved a float toward her.

"I thought you wanted to talk."

"I changed my mind."

"Good. Because I didn't really want to talk about it either."

Laura got on her float, fighting with it as she usually did, making Cassidy laugh.

"I hate this damn thing."

Cassidy got onto her own float on the first try. "You have all week to practice; I don't know what the problem is."

"If you think all I do is lounge in your pool all week, you obviously have not inspected your yard."

"You're right. It was dark when I got here. My apologies."

Laura spun her float around to look at her. "You got here last night? Why did it take you so long to call me?"

"I...I had things...to do. Then—"

Laura met her gaze. "You left early last Sunday, you got here late yesterday—a Thursday. So..."

Cassidy sighed. "You know why."

"You were avoiding me."

"Yes. And don't ask me why. You know why."

"Because you kissed me."

"Look, it wasn't only me kissing you. *You* kissed me too, you know."

"Against my will!"

"Oh, please!"

Laura smiled. "I thought we weren't going to talk about it?"

"Yeah...let's don't." She paddled over to the beer bucket. "Did you have a good week?"

"I did. I stayed busy. I hardly gave you a thought at all."

"Good. Me too." She put two beers into koozies. "See? We kissed. We didn't give it another thought. It's over with. See how easy that was?"

Laura met her gaze. "I'm lying, you know."

Cassidy nodded. "Yeah...me too."

Laura took the beer from her. "So we won't ever do that again, right?"

Cassidy tried to read her eyes. "Is that what you want?"

"Yes," she answered quickly.

Yes, that was probably the best way to handle this. Just don't do it again. That's what Laura wanted. But no. That's what Laura was *saying* she wanted. Her eyes, however, said something else entirely. But Cassidy would play along with her. For now.

"Okay. We won't ever do that again."

Laura smiled. "See? Now we can forget about it and get back to normal."

"Normal? Like me bringing women here on the weekends? Normal like that?"

"Yes. If that's what you consider *normal*," she said a bit tersely.

Cassidy went to great pains to hide her smile and keep her expression even. "Wish I had known that before I came down. I've got some friends coming tomorrow—Erica and Amber. I would have made arrangements for them to bring someone. You know, for me."

Laura simply stared at her but made no comment.

"Of course, if you're free, you might want to join us."

"I don't think so."

"I've known Erica ten years or so. Amber's been around the last two, I think. They've been out here before a couple of times."

Laura shook her head. "No."

"Steaks," she said with a teasing smile. "Cooked to perfection."

"Must you?"

"What? Tempt you with food?"

"Yes."

Cassidy smiled. "So join us. It won't be nearly as much fun as it was with Tanya and Derrick but…" But what? It would give them time together? It was probably a mistake. Erica and Amber were so different than Laura. She couldn't imagine them having anything in common and even less to talk about. Why would she even suggest it? Because she was being selfish, she admitted. She wanted Laura around. Even if she had to tolerate Erica and Amber for a few hours, she wanted Laura's presence there.

"So you're already telling me that I won't have a good time, but you still want me to come."

"Yes."

Laura tilted her head. "Why?"

Cassidy met her gaze and held it. "Because."

Laura stared at her for a long moment, then she simply smiled. "Okay."

"Thank you." Then she grinned and splashed water at her. "See? Normal stuff."

"I'm only coming for the steak, you know."

"Sure. You can believe that if you want."

"It's the truth."

"It's so not the truth."

Laura dove off her float, tipping Cassidy—beer bottle and all—into the water. She came up laughing, only to have Laura dunk her under again. A water fight ensued and Cassidy had to admit, it had been years and years since she'd engaged in such adolescent fun in the pool.

Or maybe it wasn't so adolescent, despite the tickling. When Laura's hand accidently grazed her breast—her nipple—their eyes flew together, both of them bobbing there in the water. Then Laura smiled, then laughed.

"Sorry."

"Nothing to be sorry about. Really. Feel free to do it again... anytime. As much as you want."

Laura jumped on top of her, taking them both under water. Cassidy was still smiling when Laura finally released her.

"Okay...truce," Laura said breathlessly. "I'm too old for this."

Cassidy nodded. "Truce." She got back on her float. "You owe me a beer."

CHAPTER FORTY

"If you want to go over there for pizza, I won't mind."

"Mom...I was over there this afternoon. I'm going over tomorrow for dinner. So no. We'll eat here."

"I'm just saying, if you want—"

"I know what you're saying." Laura pointed her finger at her. "Do *not* play matchmaker. It's not going to work."

"You sure spend a lot of time together," her mother said, playing innocent.

"We're friends," she said, dismissing her mother's comment. But she couldn't keep the smile from her face. It had been a fun afternoon and she hadn't seen the need to ruin that by having a huge, serious discussion about...the kiss. Far easier to simply ignore it and pretend it never happened. Of course, they didn't really do that either. Whether they were playing or floating idly or chatting...it was always there. The kiss.

And now Cassidy was coming over for pizza. Pizza and wine. Or maybe a cocktail with Coke. At least her mother would be there as a buffer. That is, if her mother would behave.

"Don't make any innuendos, either."

"I don't know what you're talking about."

"And it goes without saying…*never* mention the binoculars."

"You should come clean on that in case I slip."

"I will not come clean on that! And she's having two friends over tomorrow for dinner. I just hope it's not any that I've seen naked."

"Laura Sue, when would you have seen them naked?"

Laura rolled her eyes. "Through the binoculars, Mother."

"You've spied on them when they've been *naked*?" Her voice lowered. "Have you seen Cassidy naked?"

Laura blushed head to toe and spun away from her mother's laugh.

"Does she know you've seen her naked?"

"I only saw her breasts when she took her bra off. At least I had the good sense to not use the binoculars." She rubbed her head. "Please…not a word. You're stressing me out."

"You have a crush on her. You should just tell her."

"I'm thirty-eight years old. I do not have a crush!"

"Then what do you call it?"

"I don't call it anything. We're friends." She held a chair out for her mother and moved the walker out of the way. "What would you like to drink?"

"I'll take a Coke with a splash of bourbon in it."

Laura stared at her. "I don't think so."

"Why not?"

"Loose lips sink ships."

"Oh, for God's sake, Laura Sue. I won't say anything to her. Although I don't know what the big secret is. She can probably tell you have a crush on her."

"I swear, Mom! You're going to push me over the edge," she threatened.

Her mother shook her head. "Kids nowadays."

"I'm not a kid."

"Well, you're certainly acting like one."

Laura blew out her breath. "I walked right into that one, didn't I?"

Her mother smiled teasingly. "Oh, I'm just having some fun with you. We've got to stay on Cassidy's good side. I'm enjoying my water therapy too much. We don't want her to ban us from the pool or anything."

"She wouldn't dare. I'll let all her flowers die." She poured a smidgeon of bourbon over ice, then smiled and added a little more before dousing it with Coke. "Here you go."

"What are you having?"

"I'll wait for Cassidy," she said. "Pizza should be here in about ten minutes." A knock on the back door made her heart jump a little wildly in her chest. "And she's here now." She walked past her mother and squeezed her shoulder. "Behave," she murmured.

Cassidy was dressed in khaki shorts and a navy tank top, sandals instead of flip-flops. She looked so fresh and clean and… and cute that Laura had a hard time taking her eyes off her. She finally stepped back, holding the door opened.

"Come in."

"You're wearing my favorite shorts," she said with a smile before looking over at her mother. "Hello, Maggie. I hope you don't mind me sharing dinner with you."

"Not at all, Cassidy." Her mother patted the seat beside her. "Here, sit. We'll make Laura Sue wait on us. I already have a cocktail, which she made way too strong for me."

Cassidy glanced at her, a smile on her face. "Laura Sue? I like it."

Laura shook her head. "My mother is the only one who is allowed to call me that. So don't get any ideas." She motioned to the make-do bar on the counter. "A drink? Wine?"

"Whatever you're having is fine."

She nodded. "Easy on the Coke then?"

Cassidy nodded, then turned her attention to her mother. "How's the water therapy going?"

"I'm enjoying it immensely. Thank you for letting us use your pool."

"Of course. It's no problem."

"I used to be so afraid of the water," her mother continued. "I like it now. Well, after I got over the fear of Laura drowning me."

Cassidy laughed. "Yeah. She tried to drown me today too. Maybe we shouldn't turn our backs on her."

"I'll say."

Laura was smiling as she placed a drink in front of Cassidy. "I did not try to drown either of you, although I did come close with you," she teased, pointing at Cassidy.

"But it was the prospect of a steak tomorrow that held you back, huh?"

Laura met her gaze, a smile still playing on her lips. "It was the prospect of *something*, yes."

Oh, the look in Cassidy's eyes made her stomach roll, and Laura mentally chastised herself for flirting with her. Wasn't it hard enough being around her without adding to it?

"You can have whatever you want, you know."

The front doorbell saved her. She pulled her eyes away from Cassidy, hurrying out of the kitchen. She could swear she heard her mother's quiet laughter as she fled.

When she returned with the pizza, she paused outside of the kitchen, trying to eavesdrop on their conversation. She heard her name and more laughter, and God, she'd *kill* her mother if she was telling Cassidy anything inappropriate! Like tales of binoculars and the like.

She cleared her throat when she walked in, her gaze—her glare—going to her mother, not Cassidy. Her mother smiled sweetly at her, and Laura pinched her arm as she walked by, causing her mother to burst out in laughter.

"What did you do that for?"

"As if you don't know," she murmured.

"So...Laura Sue, your mother tells me you play the piano."

Laura whipped her head around. "I do not play the piano. I hated piano lessons." She pointed at her mother. "She tortured me with them for seven years. And she wonders why I try to drown her."

Her mother and Cassidy both laughed. "She was quite good," her mother continued.

"I was not. I embarrassed you at recitals."

"I think you did that on purpose so that I'd let you quit the lessons."

She put three plates on the table and opened the box, revealing the large, loaded pizza. "What about you?" she asked Cassidy. "Did your mother torture you with anything?"

"Believe it or not, she tortured me with dance lessons… ballet, the whole works."

"Oh my God. How long did that last?"

"Two long years."

She turned to her mother. "See? Only two years. Why did I get seven?"

"You played lovely, Laura Sue. I hate that you gave it up."

She glanced at Cassidy. "I think I would have rather taken dance lessons than piano."

Cassidy smiled as she bit into her pizza. "You'd probably look cute in a tutu."

Her mother nearly snorted. "I couldn't keep her in a dress to save my life! I can only imagine the fit she would have thrown if I'd put her in dance classes."

"Too much tomboy, huh?"

"The worst," her mother said.

Laura shook her head. "I wasn't that much of a tomboy."

"You still are," her mother corrected. "But it's you. I wouldn't change it for the world."

She stared at her mother, feeling a lump forming in her throat. Not that she needed reassurance, but her mother did indeed love her.

"My mother faced the same issues," Cassidy admitted. "I think she got tired of me showing up for dance class with skinned knees."

"Do you have brothers or did you tag after your father like Laura did?"

"One older brother. I drove him nuts chasing after him and his friends."

Her mother seemed genuinely interested in Cassidy and Cassidy didn't seem to mind the many questions directed her way. Laura didn't mind either, as she was learning a few things about Cassidy—she hated Brussels sprouts but loved broccoli and cauliflower. However, Laura nearly spit her pizza out when her mother asked Cassidy about being gay.

"Mother!"

"What? Too personal?"

"You think?"

Cassidy laughed. "It's okay. I knew I was gay probably before I was even in high school. I came out to my family when I was in the tenth grade. But I didn't...well, I didn't act on it until college."

"You didn't have sex until college?"

"Mother!"

Her mother turned to her. "What about you?"

"No. No, no, no," Laura said firmly. "Next topic."

"I was just—"

Laura held her hand up. "No."

Cassidy was still grinning. "I don't mind personal questions."

"I do. Eat your pizza." She turned to her mother. "You too."

Her mother was quiet for a moment, eating silently. Then she looked up. "Laura Sue didn't come out to us until she was in college."

"Oh, for God's sake!"

* * *

Cassidy helped Laura clean up the kitchen, all the while still chatting with her mother. Thankfully, the conversation had drifted to less personal topics and Laura had finally relaxed. It had been a fun end to the day and as before, not even a crust was left of the large pizza.

"I can't believe we ate the whole thing again."

"I know. I'm stuffed." Cassidy broke the pizza box down and put it in the trash. "I'm going to get fat hanging around you."

"Oh, funny."

Cassidy smiled at her. "I had a good time. Thank you." She turned to her mother who was still nursing her drink. "Enjoyed the evening, Maggie. I'll have to have you over to my place soon."

"Thank you, Cassidy. Glad you came over. And thank you again for letting me use your pool."

"It's not a problem at all. Good night."

"I'll walk you out," Laura said.

Once out on the patio, Cassidy pointed through the trees. "Full moon tonight."

It was dark and still, no breeze to speak of. Frogs were peeping in the woods and nighttime sounds seemed almost deafening when Laura turned to face Cassidy. She tried to think of something witty to say, but nothing would come.

"You probably shouldn't wear those cutoff jeans tomorrow."

Laura looked down at her shorts, then shook her head. "No. I know they're not dressy enough for a party."

Cassidy took a step closer. "That's not what I mean at all. I find them...you...incredibly sexy."

Laura sucked in her breath, her heart hammering in her chest at Cassidy's words. *Say something*, she thought. *Do something. Turn and walk away. Bid her good night. Run back into the house where it's safe.*

But no. Cassidy's eyes held her captive. She wouldn't swear to it, but she was the first to move. Move closer, that is. Like magnets, their mouths met. Laura didn't even try to stop it. She felt Cassidy's body press against hers, heard the moan that hung in the air—hers?—tasted the lips that parted against hers. She opened her mouth, letting Cassidy's tongue inside. Mistake, of course. Big mistake. Cassidy's moan drowned out hers and strong arms pulled her tight. Every part of their bodies seemed to be touching and her legs began to quiver. The incessant throbbing between her thighs made her press even closer and she feared they were going too far, too fast. No, what she really feared was that she'd have an orgasm right there on the patio.

With a strength she didn't know she had, she pulled away from Cassidy, ending their heated kiss. They stared at each other, their breathing ragged through parted lips. Cassidy took a step away and so did Laura. Then Cassidy backed up off the patio, nearly stumbling off the edge before she turned and hurried away.

Laura licked her lips, then steadied herself on the chair before falling down into it.

"Sweet Jesus," she murmured. "Can that woman kiss or what?"

She sat there several minutes, trying to get her body under control...her breathing under control. How did that happen? One minute, they're talking...the next, kissing like there was no tomorrow. Kissing like it was going to lead to something else. Her eyes widened a bit. If kissing was like that...what would making love be like? She slammed her eyes shut. Oh, don't go there, she warned herself. Do *not* go there!

She smiled. So Cassidy liked her cutoff jeans, huh? Cassidy thought they were sexy. She had four or five pair. She practically lived in them. And apparently they were sexy. Who knew?

When she felt in control again, she stood and went back inside the kitchen. Her mother, still seated, was smiling. No, she was grinning.

"What?"

Her mother's smile got broader. "Nothing...it's just so cute to see you like this."

Laura felt a red-hot blush cover her face. "There is nothing going on."

"Right."

"Really."

"Okay." Her mother pushed herself up from the table. "Whatever you say." But she was still smiling as she shuffled out of the kitchen with her walker.

Yes, Laura Sue...just what in the world *is* going on? She shook her head. Nothing. There was absolutely *nothing* going on.

Liar.

CHAPTER FORTY-ONE

Cassidy was going to be brave and pop over to Laura's for coffee like normal. Except Laura wasn't out there...like normal. No, she wasn't. Because of the kiss. Again.

So instead of calling her, instead of making a big deal about it, she spent the morning changing the sheets in one of the guest bedrooms for Erica and Amber. She even cleaned the downstairs bathrooms, a chore that reminded her she was going to hire a cleaning service but had yet to get around to it. She took time for a workout in the gym. She did laundry—last weekend's clothes that she'd forgotten when she'd escaped early.

She smiled at that. Escaped? From Laura? No...she feared there was no escaping Laura. Damn...that kiss. If she'd been butter, she would have melted on the spot. Laura apparently wasn't happy with her, though. In all fairness, Laura was the one who started this kiss, of that she was certain.

And she'd almost made a fool of herself by falling off the patio step when she'd attempted to run...run from the kiss—and Laura.

But enough of this already. No, Laura wasn't the kind of woman who Cassidy normally dated. Perhaps Tanya was right. She'd been dating the wrong women. She not only liked Laura as a friend, she was extremely attracted to her. Not only that, Laura was everything she'd been looking for. Someone who could make her laugh, someone she wanted to be around—constantly. Someone who could take her breath away. Someone whose kisses made her weak. Someone who could be both best friend and lover. That person she'd been looking for her whole adult life...that person was Laura. Laura...that person she tried to run from because she scared her. Scared her because her knees got weak when they kissed. Scared her because she took her breath away. Scared her because she wasn't in control. Scared her because...because she could lose her heart.

And she'd never lost her heart before.

She looked out at the pool, at the water glistening in the bright sunshine. She could imagine Laura out there, fighting with her float. Or jumping off her float to tip Cassidy off hers. She could picture her out there—naked—the sunlight dancing across her skin. She could picture Laura coming to her, touching her. And she could see Laura out there at night, the moonlight a halo around her as she beckoned Cassidy closer. And Cassidy would go. She wouldn't run. Not anymore.

Now if she could just convince Laura not to run.

* * *

Laura stood at the window in the bedroom, looking at Cassidy's backyard and the tiny corner of the pool that she could see from there. It was empty now, but she expected Cassidy's friends at any moment. If she had any sense whatsoever, she wouldn't go over there. She apparently couldn't be trusted in Cassidy's presence. Because yes, she was the one who started the kiss last night. And she was the one who had ended it. She remembered the shocked look in Cassidy's eyes as she'd backed away...and run.

Laura hadn't dared go down for coffee. She wasn't ready to see Cassidy. The kiss was still too fresh. But as the morning drifted past lunchtime, she wondered if she should call Cassidy, if they should talk. She didn't want to just pop over there with her friends around and act like nothing was going on between them. Of course, maybe she didn't need to go over at all. Maybe she should cancel. Maybe she should—

The phone halted her thoughts and the ringtone made her heart leap in her throat. She took a deep breath, then answered with a quick "hello."

"Quit hiding, Laura Sue."

"What makes you think I'm hiding?"

"Because you kissed me and now you don't know what to do about it."

"I kissed *you*? I think it was mutual."

She heard Cassidy's quiet laugh. "Yeah, it was. Only you started it, not me."

"You did too start it! Telling me my cutoff jeans were sexy!"

"That's all I have to say to make you kiss me?" Her voice lowered. "Please wear those again today and we'll test that theory."

Laura smiled. "You're a troublemaker."

"Come over."

"Are your friends there?"

"Not yet."

She swallowed. "Then don't you think I should wait?"

"Afraid to be alone with me?"

"Actually, yes."

"Afraid you'll be tempted to kiss me again."

Laura closed her eyes. "Yes."

She heard Cassidy sigh. "Laura...let's stop this game we're playing. I'm attracted to you. You're attracted to me. Let's stop pretending we're not."

"I'm...I'm afraid."

"Of me?"

"Yes. I don't want to be another in a long line of women who've paraded through your bedroom, Cassidy."

There was another long sigh before Cassidy spoke. "I'm sorry, Laura. I can't undo my past. I was looking for someone and when I didn't find her, I kept looking. But these past few months, it's like I did stop looking. The last few times when I did bring company along, I didn't sleep with them, Laura. And I really didn't know why at the time." She paused. "Now I do. It was because of you. You were the one on my mind, not them. You were the one I wanted to be with, not them."

Laura sat down on the bed. "What am I supposed to say to that?" she whispered.

"Tell me you're attracted to me. Tell me you think about me during the week when I'm not here. Tell me you've imagined us in bed together. Tell me you want to be with me like I want to be with you."

Laura lay down on the bed and closed her eyes. "Yes. To all of those things...yes."

"Then come over already, Laura Sue. Come over."

Laura smiled. "You don't get to call me Laura Sue."

"Too late. Get up. Put your suit on. Come over."

Laura let out her breath. "Okay." She paused. "Maybe you could wear your bikini today."

Cassidy chuckled in her ear. "As you wish."

Laura was still smiling long after they ended the call. Yes, Cassidy did that to her. She made her smile. Then her smile faltered a little. She was going to fall in love with her. And then she'd most likely get her heart broken.

She sat up and rubbed her face with both hands. Yes, she'd probably end up with a broken heart, but that wasn't going to stop this from happening. Because everything Cassidy said was true. She was attracted to her. She did miss her during the week. She did imagine them in bed together. And yes, Cassidy was the one she wanted to be with. All true. They'd said it, it was out there in the open...and there was no going back.

No, there was no going back. That didn't mean she wasn't scared of going forward.

CHAPTER FORTY-TWO

Cassidy was out by the pool, getting the beer bucket ready for her and Laura. She knew Erica and Amber would prefer margaritas; she already had the stuff for that sitting out on the outdoor bar. She found herself whistling and had to stop and smile, conscious of her good mood. Laura was coming over. They'd talked. No one was freaking out about the kiss…and what it meant. They'd talked. Everything was good. And part of her wished she wasn't having company this weekend—more time with Laura. But a part of her was glad she was—she didn't want to rush things with Laura and if they were alone this weekend, judging by the kisses they'd shared…well, if they were alone, she knew how it would end. She stared off into space, imagining that very thing, imagining Laura in her bed. She closed her eyes for a moment, recognizing the turn her stomach had just taken.

A car honked its horn down at the gate, and she hurried over to the keypad on the back wall, quickly punching in the code to let them in. She was a bit disappointed that Laura hadn't beaten them over. She wouldn't have minded a few minutes alone with her. A few minutes to kiss.

She went back inside, through the kitchen and past the informal sitting area to the formal living room, finally to the front entry. She had the door opened before they rang the bell. The smile on her face faltered, however, as she stood face-to-face with Claudia...of all people.

"Well, hello again," Claudia nearly purred. "I hope you don't mind me crashing."

Cassidy was at a loss for words, and she jerked her attention to Erica, raising her eyebrows questioningly.

"We had dinner with Claudia last night," Erica explained. "I knew you wouldn't mind if we invited her. Foursomes are so much better than three," she said with a smile.

"Of course," she said politely. "It's no problem." She opened the door wider. "Come in."

They each carried an overnight bag, and she led them through the house and into the long hallway where the guestrooms were. She put Erica and Amber in their normal room, then moved down the hallway to open another door. As Claudia brushed by, she smiled seductively at her.

"If you want company upstairs tonight, I do remember the way to your bedroom."

So that's how it was going to be, huh? Well, she wouldn't be rude to her but...

"I don't think so," she said with a smile. "There really wasn't much going on with us anyway, you know."

"No? I beg to differ. There was a *lot* going on between the sheets." She stepped closer to Cassidy. "No lover has ever come close to you."

Cassidy took a step away from her. "If your sole purpose for coming here this weekend was to get into my bed...it's a wasted trip, Claudia. I'm sorry."

"Oh, Cassidy...you're alone. We all know that you don't do well alone. I'm just letting you know that I'm available." She started unbuttoning her blouse. "I bought a new bikini for the weekend. Red. It's a little bit of nothing but hey, you've seen it all already anyway."

Cassidy turned away when Claudia dropped her blouse on the floor. She closed the door to the bedroom, then went back down the hallway. She could be angry with Erica—in fact, she *was* angry with her—but it would do no good. Claudia was here now. She couldn't exactly ask her to leave.

At least she'd picked up an extra steak. She had planned on cooking it for Maggie. She doubted she would want to join them for dinner, but she thought maybe Laura could take her a plate. Speaking of Laura…how was she ever going to explain Claudia being here? Well, she had no time to prepare. Laura was already out by the pool.

She went out onto the patio, smiling as their eyes met. Yeah…she wished they were alone.

"Am I early?"

"No. They just got here. They're changing." She walked closer. "There…there is something, though."

Laura raised her eyebrows. "You're fidgeting and nervous. What's wrong?"

"How can you know that?"

"I can read you like a book." Then she smiled. "I just can't write a book."

Cassidy laughed. "You need to give me a copy of your first one. Is it still in print?"

"No. I happen to have like ten or twelve copies, though." Laura looked her up and down. "Is there a bikini on under that?"

"There is. I see you forgot your cutoff jeans."

"I didn't think they were appropriate. Your friends probably don't even know what cutoff jeans are." Laura put her hands on her hips. "So what's wrong?"

Before Cassidy could answer, Laura's eyes were drawn to the double doors. Cassidy could tell by her expression that she'd seen Claudia. Laura slowly brought her gaze back to Cassidy.

"Seriously?"

"I didn't know she was coming," Cassidy whispered. "She's friends with Erica. Apparently, they thought it would be a good idea, you know, for me…"

Laura nodded. "Erica thinks…what was her name again?"

"Claudia."

"Right. She thinks Claudia—the very thin, beautiful blonde—is perfect for you."

"Something like that."

"So…would you like for me to leave so you can have time with her?"

"God, no! I want—"

"Oh, the pool looks lovely, Cassidy. The flowers are gorgeous."

Erica, with Amber and Claudia at her heels, descended onto the patio. She felt Laura stiffen beside her, and she plastered a smile on her face, turning to her friends.

"I have Laura to thank for the flowers. She's my neighbor… and friend," she added quickly. "Laura, this is Erica, Amber, and Claudia."

To Laura's credit, she showed no outward signs that she was miffed in any way. She smiled pleasantly at them.

"Nice to meet you all," she said. "I hope you don't mind if I join you."

Erica's eyes widened. "Oh. Well…if Cassidy doesn't mind, I certainly don't."

Cassidy laughed. "I invited her, Erica. She's not crashing the party."

"Weren't you telling us one time that your neighbor did your yardwork?" Amber asked. "Is she the one?"

"I am," Laura answered.

Claudia came up close beside Cassidy, brushing her shoulder. "You do her…*yard*? What does that entail exactly?"

Cassidy took a step away from her. "She mows the lawn, Claudia. Trims the weeds. Tends to the flowers. That sort of thing."

Claudia gave a condescending laugh. "Why on earth would you do that?"

Laura remained undaunted as she smiled at Claudia. "It pays well and I've got some pretty good perks." At Claudia's blank stare, Laura motioned to the pool. "I have permission to use the pool. That way I don't have to sneak over and…you know, trespass."

"Sneak over to your neighbor's property? Trespass? But—"

"How about instead of talking about the pool, we actually get in it?" Cassidy asked, trying to end this vein of conversation. "Shall I make a pitcher of margaritas?"

"Oh, that sounds wonderful," Claudia said. "Can I help?"

"No, no. I got it." She looked over at Laura. "Do you mind getting some floats?"

"Happy to."

Cassidy smiled, relieved to see an amused expression on Laura's face rather than annoyed. As she added ice to the blender, she glanced over at the pool. Claudia was indeed in a tiny—skimpy—bikini. As thin as she was, it wasn't at all flattering on her. Claudia's gaze was on Laura and Cassidy followed it. Laura looked healthy and vibrant, her tan natural, her hair color natural. And despite the situation, she sported a rather easy smile on her face. Claudia, on the other hand, looked anything but healthy—listless and frail. Her hair had been dyed so many times, it appeared dull and lifeless. The smile on her face was forced, and Cassidy imagined she was a bit perturbed by Laura's presence. As she looked at the two of them she wondered what she'd ever seen in Claudia.

Nothing, really. She was a friend of Erica's—that's how they'd met. And like most of the women she went out with, she knew after the first date that there was nothing there. There shouldn't have been a second date. There certainly shouldn't have been a fourth and fifth. But at the time, it was easier to continue than to stop. But Claudia was starting to talk long-term, and Cassidy had finally broken things off. Claudia had been hurt; she'd said as much. Not so hurt, though, that she wasn't willing to come for the weekend uninvited…and offer to share a bed.

"You need some help?"

Cassidy hadn't even seen Erica come over. She shook her head. "No. Sorry. Lost in thought."

"I hope you're not mad about Claudia being here."

She shrugged. "As long as she realizes that she's not sleeping in my bed tonight."

"Well, I figured you were on good enough terms with her since she'd been invited to your pool party." Erica leaned closer and smiled. "I thought you might even want to give it another try. It would be fun to hang out with you two again."

Cassidy put the lid on the blender. "No, Erica. It's not happening." She turned the blender on, stopping any further conversation. Mad? No, she wasn't really mad that Claudia was there. Actually, she wished none of them were there. She wanted to be with Laura. She didn't want to have to make small talk with them and entertain them...she just wanted to be with Laura. She wanted to play with Laura and tease with Laura and laugh with Laura and *be* with Laura.

She poured the margarita mix into three glasses, then put the pitcher in the fridge. Erica took two of the glasses.

"Just three?"

"Laura will have beer," she said, perhaps a bit presumptuously. But she looked over and Laura was already taking two out of the ice bucket and putting them in koozies.

"I didn't realize you were on such friendly terms with her... your yard girl. Friendly enough that you'd invite her over to mingle with your real friends."

Real friends? Cassidy shrugged. "She's nice. I enjoy her company."

"So you hang out?"

"What's with all the questions?"

"Well, if I didn't know better, I'd say you were interested in her." Erica laughed. "Certainly not your type, though."

Cassidy didn't feel the need to discuss Laura with Erica so she didn't bother with a reply. She walked over to the pool and handed Claudia—who was sitting with Amber under an umbrella—the margarita. Laura was standing out in the sun, looking longingly at the pool. Cassidy went over to her and took one of the beer bottles out of her hand.

"Jump in. I'm right behind you," she whispered.

"Thanks. I didn't know what the protocol was."

"No protocol. Grab a float."

Laura groaned. "There's no way I'm going to fight with that damn float in front of your friends," she whispered.

Cassidy laughed. "Don't worry about them. I like watching you fight with it."

"Yes, I know you do. And if any of them laugh at me, I'll tip them off their floats when they're least expecting it," she threatened with a grin.

Cassidy felt quite giddy as she stared at her. "I really want to kiss you," she whispered.

Laura held her gaze. "Probably not a good idea. Your friend Claudia has been shooting me daggers. She may attack."

"I'll help you flip her off the float later."

Laura smiled into her eyes. "Then I'll let you kiss me later."

Laura set her beer bottle at the edge, then jumped into the pool, splashing her with water. Cassidy watched her for a second as she went to retrieve a float, then turned to her friends, finding them all watching Laura as well. Erica turned to her first, her eyebrows raised questioningly. It wasn't any of their business, she decided, so she felt no need to explain Laura's presence there. Besides, what would she say? Would she tell them how badly she wanted to kiss her? Being attracted to Laura was one thing…but being *insanely* attracted to her was something else entirely.

She plastered a smile on her face and moved closer. "You guys getting in the pool or can I get you another margarita?"

"I'm getting in," Claudia said. "I want to visit with your yard girl a little." Then she smiled. "She looks like she's having trouble with the float. Perhaps I'll help her."

She turned, seeing Laura struggling to get the float under her. As Claudia made her way over to her, Laura righted herself finally.

"She has a hard time getting it to hold still for her," Cassidy explained with a laugh. "It's quite amusing."

"Just how often does she come over?"

Again, it really wasn't any of Erica's business, but she wasn't going to hide her friendship with Laura.

"She uses the pool during the week whenever she wants. And when I'm here on the weekends, she usually comes over and we share the pool…and dinner."

"Dinner? Yes, the rumor floating around the group is that you've been coming out here alone lately. Even your big party, I don't recall you stealing someone and whisking them away to your bedroom." Erica put her drink glass down. "Dry spell or…"

"Dry spell?" Amber asked with a laugh. "I can name six women off the top of my head who would kill to be here with her. Claudia included. I wouldn't call that a dry spell."

"There's not anyone in the so-called group that I'm interested in dating," she said.

"What about Melissa?"

"Melissa?"

"Melissa Hurst. The blonde. She's thirty-three, I think."

Cassidy laughed. "They're all blond, Erica."

"True. But—"

Cassidy held up her hand. "No, thanks. I'm fine." She glanced into the pool, seeing Laura's brows draw together from something Claudia said. "I think I'll join them."

CHAPTER FORTY-THREE

"Whatever your plan is with Cassidy, it's never going to work. She is so far out of your league, it's not even funny."

"Excuse me?"

"Cassidy doesn't date yard girls," Claudia said, her expression and her voice both condescending. "In fact, you don't stand a chance."

"What makes you think I want to date her?"

"Oh, honey...everyone wants to date her. And why not? She knows how to wine and dine a lady. I should know." Her voice lowered. "She's also really good in bed and she doesn't even use toys."

"You don't say?"

Laura shook her head, once again wondering what it was that Cassidy saw in this woman.

"I'm sharing her bed tonight, of course," Claudia continued.

"Really?"

"And I imagine I'll be over again next weekend." Claudia's smile was downright patronizing. "Trust me, you won't be invited."

Laura silently counted to ten, anything to prevent her from hurling herself at Claudia and tipping her into the pool. Tipping her into the pool and holding her head under water. Although drowning one of Cassidy's friends probably wouldn't go over too well, she supposed. Thankfully, Cassidy was getting in and coming toward them, saving Claudia a dunking. She gave Claudia an evil grin, then looked at Cassidy as she approached.

"So you don't use sex toys, huh?"

Cassidy's eyes widened. "What?"

"Claudia said you were *really* good in bed and you didn't even need toys."

A wonderful, bright red blush covered Claudia's thin face, and Laura continued. "After tonight—after she shares your bed and you have sex—you can tell me all about it tomorrow. Can't wait for the details. I doubt I'll even be able to sleep thinking about it."

Laura could tell Cassidy was trying very hard not to laugh, but she couldn't hide the amusement in her eyes.

"What in the world brought on *that* conversation?"

"She thinks I have designs on you. She was warning me to stay away." She glanced over at Claudia, who was still blushing. "Right?" She looked back at Cassidy. "She says I'm not your type, though. She says you don't date women like me. You know, just a lowly yard girl and all. She says I am *far* out of your league."

A smile finally broke on Cassidy's face. "She said all of that, huh? And...let me guess. You want to tip her off her float?"

"I want to dunk her under the water. Can I? Please?"

They both turned to look at a still blushing Claudia, who was apparently stunned speechless. Her gaze went between the two of them several times before settling on Cassidy.

"So...I was...I was just telling her...well, I didn't mean to imply...anything. I mean—"

"I didn't invite you here, Claudia. I *did* invite Laura. Maybe that should tell you something," Cassidy said bluntly.

Laura stared past her to Erica and Amber, who were coming over, both holding on to the same float.

"What did we miss?" Erica asked innocently.

"Nothing," Claudia said quickly. She moved her float away. "I think I'm going to get another margarita."

* * *

The afternoon was endless and several times Laura had to talk herself out of leaving, steak or not...rude or not. After the exchange with Claudia, the woman hadn't said another word to her. Laura couldn't really blame her. She tried her best to carry on a conversation with Erica and Amber, but she found that not only did she have little—nothing—in common with them, they were rather boorish. In fact, it seemed as if Erica was intentionally leaving Laura out of the conversation, focusing instead on mutual friends that they had with Cassidy. And Claudia, of course. The situation was becoming uncomfortable, not only for her but for Cassidy as well. Cassidy contributed little to the conversation, seemingly a bit irritated by Erica's attempts to monopolize the conversation and blatantly ignore Laura.

When Erica launched into yet another story about one of their friends, Laura simply stood and walked away. She went into the kitchen, the coolness of the air welcome after being outside all afternoon. There was a bathroom outside that she could have used but she went down the hallway, finding one of the two guest baths instead.

She sighed as she looked at herself in the mirror. This day had to rank as one of the worst she'd ever endured. Not only had the anorexic blonde tried to put her in her place—*yard girl*—but Cassidy's other two friends acted like she wasn't even there. She really didn't know what she'd been expecting. Well, she hadn't expected Claudia to be there, that was for sure. But Erica and Amber? She'd expected them to be nice, normal...like Tanya had been. But no. That was the furthest thing from the truth.

She brushed at the hair over her ears, feeling the dampness from the pool. She wasn't bad looking, she supposed. Not beautiful, certainly. Nothing like Cassidy's usual dates. What did Cassidy see in her? She was practically the complete opposite of who Cassidy dated. She frowned. *Did* Cassidy want to date her? What, exactly, would that mean? They were already spending the weekends together. They'd played in the pool. They'd had dinner. They'd kissed. Would dating mean Cassidy would introduce Laura to her friends? Would she be forced to endure more days like today?

"No, thanks," she murmured.

She sighed again. Well, she couldn't hide in the bathroom until dinner. She wondered if Cassidy would mind if she raided her liquor cabinet. She had a feeling she would need something much stronger than beer to get her through until dinner.

When she went back into the kitchen, she was surprised to find Cassidy there—alone. She took out a platter of rib eyes from the fridge and placed them on the island.

"There you are. I was wondering where you'd escaped to."

"Just taking a break," she said. "And that steak you promised me better be worth it."

Cassidy came closer. "I'm sorry. I'd like to say that they're not usually this rude but…" she said with a shrug.

"I'm an outsider."

"That's no reason to exclude you from every conversation."

"You noticed that, huh?"

Cassidy met her gaze and held it. "I wish we were alone."

"God, me too."

Cassidy smiled. "Were you really going to tip her off her float?"

"Of course. I wanted to drown her!"

Cassidy's smile got bigger. "I could tell." She took a step closer. "You know what I want? I want to kiss you."

"Why do you always say that when you know we can't?"

"Why can't we?"

"Because we're not alone."

Cassidy took her hand and tugged her along, opening the pantry door and pulling her inside. "Now we're alone."

"You're kinda sneaky."

"I'm kinda attracted to you."

Laura took a step away from her. "Maybe…maybe we should rethink this."

"This? That we're attracted to each other and we want to kiss? Rethink that?"

Laura pointed out the door. "Claudia was right. That's who you date, Cassidy. Beautiful women like her. Not…not me."

"I would never call Claudia beautiful. And women like her… their kisses never once made my knees weak. Never once, Laura. You? I just look at you and I get light-headed." She took a step toward her. "I kiss you and I feel like I'm melting."

Laura looked into her eyes. "Do I really make your knees weak?"

"Really." Then Cassidy gave her a soft smile. "Should I show you?"

Laura swallowed. "Yeah…maybe you should."

As soon as their mouths met, however, she realized that it probably wasn't such a good idea. She found herself against the door, Cassidy's body pressed impossibly close to her own. Her hands wound their way up Cassidy's shoulders and behind her neck, her moan mixed with Cassidy's as their tongues brushed each other's. She felt her stomach flip over as Cassidy's hips moved against her.

Yes, her knees were weak. No, she couldn't open her eyes. Yes, her body was on fire and no…she couldn't catch her breath. All of that paled in comparison to her heart jumping into her throat when Cassidy's hand settled on her breast, her thumb rubbing circles around her nipple. The thin material of her swimsuit was barely a barrier and she had half a mind to lower the straps and guide Cassidy's hot mouth to her breast.

Cassidy's mouth left hers and moved to her neck, nibbling at the hollow of her throat. Laura leaned her head back, giving Cassidy more room. She moaned again as Cassidy's mouth moved to her ear, her tongue bathing it, making Laura nearly delirious.

"If you don't stop, I'm going to rip my suit off," she whispered. "And yours."

Both of Cassidy's hands cupped her breasts, and Laura whimpered as Cassidy's tongue continued to snake in and out of her ear. The throbbing between her legs was nearly unbearable and she spread them, desperately trying to find purchase on

Cassidy's thigh. Cassidy moved her hands to her butt, cupping her and pulling her hard against her.

"Oh, dear God," Laura breathed as she held on to Cassidy, fearing she would fall. She could feel her legs trembling; she could feel her orgasm building. She was gasping for breath as Cassidy's thigh bucked against her center, pressing into her clit.

"Cassidy? Are you in here?"

Laura banged her head against the door. "Oh, God...*no*," she groaned.

Cassidy's eyes were clouded with desire as she stepped away from Laura. She ran a hand through her hair. "Jesus Christ, Laura Sue," she murmured with a shaky breath. "How can you do that to me? I don't think I've ever wanted anybody as much as I want you right now."

Their eyes held and Laura watched as Cassidy's chest heaved with each breath she sucked, much as her own was doing. Yes. She should repeat Cassidy's words back to her. Because she knew with complete certainty that she'd *never* wanted like this before.

"Cassidy?" the voice called again.

"Whoever that is, I *hate* them," Laura whispered.

Cassidy laughed quietly. "I'm sorry. It's Erica." Cassidy took another step away from her, still holding her eyes captive. "That was like the best kiss ever."

Laura smiled. "No. It was about ten seconds from being the best kiss ever."

* * *

Cassidy opened the pantry door as Erica came fully into the kitchen. Cassidy knew she was flushed. Hell, she still hadn't caught her breath yet. She didn't dare look at Laura. Knowing Laura, she was probably blushing. Erica stared first at her, then at Laura before bringing her gaze back to her again, one eyebrow arching.

"So...umm, I'll just...take the...the..." Laura stammered.

"Fridge," Cassidy said without thinking. "Umm...the cheese tray...in the fridge." Their eyes met for a second, but it was long enough for her to see the smoldering desire still evident in Laura's. Oh, yeah…ten more seconds.

"Right. Cheese tray. Got it."

Laura hurried to the fridge, leaving Cassidy and Erica staring at each other. Neither spoke until Laura left the kitchen.

"Really? You're all flustered, Cassidy. The *yard* girl?" she asked incredulously.

Cassidy played dumb. She wasn't sure she was ready to bring her feelings for Laura out into the open yet. She'd barely had time to reconcile them herself.

"I don't know what you're talking about."

Erica pointed at the closed door. "Weren't you just having a make-out session in a closet?"

At that, Cassidy smiled. "It's actually the pantry. And yes, we were."

"Oh my God! The yard girl? Have you lost your mind? She's…she's so…so *butch*."

Cassidy laughed. "Butch? *Laura*?" She shook her head. "No. She's just a tomboy. But butch? No. Not even close."

"Well, she's cute, I'll give you that. But Cassidy, she's not *you*. She doesn't fit." She leaned closer. "You and Claudia are perfect together. She fits. This woman? Never."

"There was nothing perfect about me and Claudia. Nothing. I'm not attracted to her, Erica. I was never attracted to her. You set us up on a date and…well, my fault. There should have never been a second date."

Erica pointed out the door where Laura had gone. "And that woman? You're attracted to *her*?"

Cassidy looked out the double doors, finding Claudia and Amber sitting under an umbrella. Laura was in the pool, fighting with her float again. Her hair was wet and Cassidy imagined her jumping into the pool, trying to cool off and douse the flames that had been consuming them only minutes earlier. *Ten more seconds.*

She smiled and looked at Erica. "I could fall in love with that woman."

CHAPTER FORTY-FOUR

Laura paused at the back door, trying to collect her thoughts before going inside. The others were still out by the pool. She could hear voices from across the fence. The steak, as usual, had been cooked to perfection, as promised. The vegetable medley—lightly sautéed—was crisp and flavorful. The baked potato was soft and fluffy. In defiance—after seeing Claudia cut hers in half and skip the butter and sour cream—Laura had lathered hers with so many additional calories, including cheese, that she was almost afraid to eat it. And now, after having dinner with her, she knew why Claudia was so skinny. She barely touched the little half of the potato and only cut three small bites from the steak, eating two. It was a damn shame.

But the mostly silent dinner was enough to make her want to end the evening early. She'd helped clean up but gave a rather hasty goodbye to everyone, including Cassidy. Cassidy had offered to walk her home, but she'd declined. One look into her eyes had told her that Cassidy hadn't forgotten their encounter in the pantry. And of course, neither had she.

She leaned her forehead against the doorjamb. Ten seconds away from an orgasm. Good God...in the *pantry*! When she jumped in the pool, she wouldn't have been surprised if the water had started boiling. Never in her life had someone's kisses affected her that way. Of course, they were doing a little more than kissing, weren't they? She closed her eyes, swearing she could still feel Cassidy's hands on her breasts, her fingers rubbing her nipples...her tongue doing all sorts of wonderful things to her.

"Jesus..."

She stood up straight, feeling her pulse racing again. Perhaps it was good that Cassidy had company. If she didn't...they'd be in bed right now. And Laura wasn't sure she was ready.

"Oh, please," she muttered, knowing she was lying. She'd been ready in the pantry, for God's sake! Ready and willing.

But now what? She didn't think they could take baby steps with this, not after what happened earlier. Did she even want to take baby steps? No. But Cassidy had company. And her company usually didn't leave until well after noon. Cassidy would no doubt be leaving then too. They would have no time alone. To talk. Or...whatever.

She finally pushed open the back door and went into the kitchen. She heard the TV on and was actually glad that her mother was still up. She looked around the kitchen, noticing that her mother had cleaned up the dishes from her solitary dinner—leftovers that Laura had assembled for her to microwave. She felt a twinge of guilt. She would have rather been here with her mother than suffer through dinner with Cassidy's friends. Of course, she wouldn't have missed the pantry episode for anything.

She went into the living room, finding her mother in her recliner. She turned her head when Laura walked in.

"You're home already?"

"Yes. I couldn't take it any longer."

Her mother muted the show she'd been watching. "What's wrong?"

"They weren't very nice to me—her friends."

"Oh, that's too bad. You had such a good time with Cassidy's other friends."

"Very different than Tanya and her husband. There were three of them. They brought a woman who Cassidy used to date…hoping to set them up again."

"Oh, I see. And how did that go?"

Laura sat down in the other recliner and popped the footrest out. "I wanted to drown her," she admitted with a laugh. She looked at her mother, her smile fading a little. "I…I really like Cassidy. We…we kissed."

"Again?"

"*Again?*"

"Well, I saw you last night."

Laura felt a blush on her face. "You *saw* us? You could have turned away!"

"I could have, yes, but it occurred to me that I've never seen you kiss anyone before."

Laura shook her head, dismissing her mother's comments. "I'm very attracted to her."

"I would hope so. I saw that there were tongues involved."

"*Mother!* Oh my God!"

"What? I'm just saying…"

Laura held her hand up. "Don't. Just don't."

"Tongues, Laura Sue. It's not like we're talking about sex or anything. Are we?"

"We most certainly are not!"

"Well, then…go on. You're attracted to her."

"Yes. But I'm not anything like the women she dates. They're all girlie-girls. Thin. Fashionable. Lots of makeup. They barely eat enough to sustain a bug."

"Well, we know how you like to eat."

Laura raised her eyebrows. "You think I'm fat, don't you?" She patted her full stomach. "I just ate a huge steak and a thousand-calorie baked potato. It's like she's *trying* to make me fat."

"Did you ever think that maybe that's one of the things she likes about you? You say she loves to cook. What fun is it to cook for someone if they're going to eat like a bird?"

"I'm not sure that's a compliment."

"Laura Sue, you're not fat. You get too much exercise to worry about that."

"That's another thing. I don't even have a job. These women? They appear to be successful, competent, professional women."

"You have a job. And I thought you were interested in expanding your business."

Laura laughed. "Expanding my lawn service business? I know. I just haven't gotten around to it."

"Well, we do let things go, don't we? I still haven't set up a date for the painters yet."

Laura let out a deep breath. "I'm going to get hurt."

"You think so?"

"Yes. She's going to break my heart. Then it'll be awkward living here next door. I'll lose my one yard job. Your pool therapy will come to an end." She sighed again. "All because she's like the best kisser ever."

Her mother laughed. "That's how it's going to play out? What about the alternative?"

"What alternative?"

"She falls madly in love with you. You move in with her and I still get my pool therapy."

Laura smiled. "Got us getting married, do you?"

"Wouldn't that be wonderful, Laura Sue?" her mother asked wistfully. "I always worried about you being alone."

"I'm only thirty-eight, Mom."

"And how old is Cassidy? I'd guess early forties."

"Forty-four. Young enough to still look really good in a bikini."

"So you kissed again? In front of her friends?'

"God, no! In the pantry, of all places."

"The pantry. How on earth?"

"It's as big as my bedroom."

"Oh. So up against the canned goods then?" her mother teased.

"It was a *really* good kiss. Let's just say that if her friends hadn't been there…"

Her mother grinned. "So are we going to talk about sex now?"

Laura pointed her finger at her. "You have a one-track mind."

"I'm a widow. And for your information, Frankie and I had a very active sex life."

"Ew...I don't want to know."

"Your father and I did too," she continued.

Laura stared at her. "I'm sorry, Mom. I'm sorry that I...that I disappeared from your life. That was selfish of me."

Her mother nodded. "Yes, it was. I know you didn't understand...I know you disliked Frankie." She waved her hand in the air. "I...I just wasn't good alone. I was used to your father taking care of things. And yes, Frankie had his faults...but he loved me."

Laura leaned her head back. "I'm sorry," she said again. "Those are years we won't get back and I'm sorry."

"You're here now, Laura Sue. You're here now."

CHAPTER FORTY-FIVE

Cassidy punched at her pillows again. It had been a long, stressful day, yet sleep wouldn't come. She still felt restless. Restless because—besides the few stolen moments in the pantry—she hadn't had a single second alone with Laura. And Laura had left so quickly after dinner, Cassidy hardly had time to say goodbye...a very public goodbye which consisted of nothing more than a smile and a nod. Of course, she had offered to walk Laura out, but Laura had politely declined. And why? Because they both knew that if they were alone...in the dark... with the full moon filtering through the trees...

Cassidy closed her eyes, remembering the scene in the pantry. God, Laura had been so...so *ready*. Cassidy could feel the wetness between her thighs. She could still hear the quiet moans, the almost desperate hold Laura had on her. Cassidy never meant to take it that far. She had simply been craving a kiss, a touch. She never expected it to turn into all that. Not that quickly.

But it had. And she wanted more of it. Much more.

She rolled over and picked up her phone. It was 12:48. Laura would be asleep. She pictured her in bed, curled on her side, her eyelids fluttering while she dreamed. She held the phone to her chest. She was forty-four years old. How was it that Laura could make her feel like a teenager? So, despite her better judgment, she called her. After three rings, she very nearly hung up but before the fourth, she heard a very sexy, sleepy voice in her ear.

"You better be calling because you miss me. I was in the middle of a *very* good dream."

Cassidy grinned. "Was I in your dream?"

"Yes. We were very naked. And we weren't in the pantry," Laura murmured.

Cassidy heard the muffled sound of the sheets, and she imagined Laura shifting, perhaps sitting up against pillows. She found herself doing the same.

"Yes…I missed you," she said. "You left in a hurry."

"I'm sorry. I couldn't take it anymore. Your friends hate me."

"Hate is not the right word, Laura. It's just that Claudia is their friend, and they wanted a nice, tidy foursome. I think Erica was trying to highlight the differences between all of them and you."

"And she succeeded."

"Yeah, she did. She made me see just how shallow they all are. Laura, when I first told Tanya about you, when we were first becoming friends, I told her how different you were from my usual group. Good different. I told you were…real. Genuine. You don't hide behind anything. There aren't any pretenses with you." She gripped the phone tighter. "I'm a little out of my comfort zone here," she admitted. "I'm used to being in control. I'm not used to this…the way you make me feel. I'm not used to wanting someone this badly."

"I want to make love with you."

Cassidy felt her stomach clench into a tight knot, felt her heart jump into her throat. "You scare me," she whispered.

"You're afraid I'm going to steal your heart?"

Cassidy swallowed. "I'm afraid you already have."

Laura was quiet for a moment, and all Cassidy heard was the sound of her breath. "I'm afraid…I'm afraid I'm going to fall in love with you."

"I'm afraid that you won't."

Again, there was only a slight pause before Laura spoke. "Can you call in sick to work on Monday?"

Cassidy smiled. "Is that what you want?"

"As soon as your friends leave tomorrow, I want to come over. I want to spend the day with you." A pause. "I want to spend the night with you."

Cassidy felt her heart hammering in her chest. "Yes."

"Good. Now get some sleep. You're going to need your strength."

And just like that, Cassidy sank back under the covers, a smile plastered on her face. Laura wanted her to stay home tomorrow. Laura wanted to make love with her. She closed her eyes, letting her imagination take her there.

CHAPTER FORTY-SIX

"God…will they *ever* leave?"

"Why are you so anxious? It's not even noon."

Laura stared at her mother. Should she tell her? Should she tell her she was anxious for Cassidy's friends to leave so that she could go over? Go over and…

"I probably won't be home tonight. At all."

Her mother's eyes widened. "Oh?"

"I know since I wasn't here yesterday to cook for you that I probably should today…but…well…"

"You're going to have sex?"

"Oh my God! What is it with you and sex?"

"Still blushing at thirty-eight. That's so cute!" She waved Laura's protest away. "Don't worry about me. There are still some of those frozen dinners in the freezer."

"You will not eat a frozen dinner. I can make a casserole or something, then all you'll have to do is heat it," she offered. "Or I can make—"

"Laura Sue, we just had breakfast. I can't even think about dinner yet. Quit worrying."

"I just feel guilty leaving you alone again."

"You have a budding romance to enjoy. Do not worry about your mother."

"She...she called me. Last night. Well, this morning, really." Laura twisted her hands together. "Remember when I said that I was afraid she was going to break my heart? Well...she's kinda afraid of the same thing."

Her mother reached out and grasped Laura's clenched hands, tugging her down into the chair beside her. "Falling in love is a scary thing. It's wonderful and scary at the same time." She smiled. "Like being on a roller coaster...you're at the very top, you crest the highest peak, then you plunge down into God knows where...so fast, you're screaming and laughing at the same time. Falling in love is like that. You're afraid of what you're feeling. You question it. You doubt it." Her mother squeezed her hands tightly. "Laura...I saw the two of you together Friday night. The way you look at each other, the way you tease each other...I don't think either of you has to worry about a broken heart. Go spend the day with her. Spend the night with her. Explore this love that you're starting to feel for her."

"Oh, Mom...I love you. I don't say it nearly enough."

"I know you do, honey. I love you too."

Laura wiped at the corner of her eye where a tear had escaped. Then she smiled. "I'm still scared, though."

Her mother smiled too. "It's just like a roller coaster, Laura Sue. Enjoy the ride."

"Thank you, Mom. You're the best."

A moment later, the front doorbell rang, then knocking was heard. They looked at each other.

"You think that's Cassidy?" her mother asked.

"No. She would come back here to the patio."

Laura got up and went through the house to the front, peeking out before opening the door.

"What are you doing here?"

"Hey, sis." Carla smiled and kissed her on the cheek. "I had a free day. Thought I'd come visit." She walked into the house. "Where's Mom?"

"Kitchen."

Laura stared at her retreating back, then leaned against the door with her eyes closed. Of all the days for Carla to pop over. She pushed off the door and followed her, forcing a smile to her face when she joined them in the kitchen.

"I haven't seen you in a while, but you look great," Carla was saying to her mother.

"I feel darn good too. I never thought I'd enjoy the pool so much."

Carla's eyes widened. "You don't swim!"

"Water therapy," Laura corrected. "Cassidy's pool next door."

"You're afraid of the water," Carla reminded their mother.

"Oh, Laura Sue tried to drown me at first, but we're over that now."

Laura rolled her eyes. "I think it was you who tried to drown me the other day." She looked at Carla. "She flipped me off my float."

"It wasn't on purpose. I couldn't touch bottom. I may have panicked."

"You think?"

Carla sat down at the table. "It's so nice that you two are getting along. At first…I was worried."

"You want something to drink?"

"Oh, a Coke, if you've got it."

Laura looked at the clock, wondering if Cassidy's company had left yet. "So…you had a free day?"

"Yes. Movie day for the kids so I thought I'd drive down." She took the Coke from Laura. "Thanks. Anyway, I thought maybe you two might like to take in a movie too. Then we could grab a late lunch or an early dinner. You want to?"

Laura and her mother exchanged glances. No, she wanted to do no such thing! But she couldn't very well tell her sister that she had tentative plans to…to have sex this afternoon! She looked away from her mother, feeling a blush trying to sneak up to her face.

"Well?" Carla asked again.

"I would love to," her mother said in a cheerful voice. "But I think Laura Sue has plans."

She turned her gaze to Laura. "What kind of plans?"

She swallowed. "Well, Cassidy has invited me over…to…to…"

"Laura Sue is in the pool all week, but when Cassidy is here, she likes the company," her mother supplied, a smile playing on her lips. "And dinner too, so it would be nice to take in a meal with you, Carla."

Carla eyed her suspiciously. "It's Sunday. Doesn't she go back to Dallas on Sundays?"

"She's not working tomorrow," Laura said quickly. "So…what movie are you going to see?"

"I don't even know what's playing. Are you sure you don't want to go? As Mom said, you can get in the pool any day of the week. Of which I am very jealous," she added.

"No…I already promised her. But you two have fun."

"Okay…what's going on? You're acting weird."

"I am not acting weird."

"Mom is about to break out into a fit of giggles and you're blushing!"

"Oh…*God*," she murmured.

"She's having sex," her mother blurted out.

"Mother!"

"*What?*" Carla asked with wide eyes. "With the *neighbor*? Since when?"

"Since this afternoon," her mother supplied with a smile.

"Oh my God! Laura's got a sex date?"

The blush she'd been trying to keep at bay had to be lighting up her face like a Christmas tree. But she ignored it the best she could "You two are *really* ruining the mood."

Carla laughed. "But that's good, sis. I mean, it's been a while, hasn't it?"

Laura held her hand up. "I will not discuss my sex life—or lack of—with you and Mother. Ever. Not ever, ever, ever!"

"I really like Cassidy," her mother said. "She's so nice. And pretty."

"When did you meet her?"

"She's been over for dinner a couple of times. Usually when she keeps Laura over in the pool drinking beer...they come over here for pizza afterward."

"Really? How long has this been going on?"

Laura gave up and plopped down in the chair, joining them at the table. Her mother reached over and patted her leg.

"Laura Sue's way past the crush stage."

Laura groaned.

"Cassidy is too," her mother continued. "Laura's over there every weekend."

"But they haven't slept together yet?"

"Well, they've kissed."

Laura dropped her head to the table in defeat, banging it slowly, as hard as she dared.

"In the pantry," her mother continued in a whisper.

"First thing tomorrow morning, I'm moving you into a nursing home," Laura mumbled.

"Oh, honey, first thing tomorrow morning, you'll still be in the afterglow of sex."

Carla laughed loudly, and Laura finally lifted her head off of the table, staring at them. "Really?"

"I can't believe you have a sex date! That's so cool, Laura!"

"Don't you have a movie to get to?"

CHAPTER FORTY-SEVEN

Cassidy tried not to seem impatient as they lingered over brunch. Brunch that she intended to be breakfast as she'd started it as soon as she'd heard movement in the guestrooms. But no. Ten thirty was creeping toward eleven, and they were still lounging at the table, second cups of coffee turning to three. Yes, they'd lingered over brunch, but there was still so much food left. She glanced at Claudia's plate, seeing the food pushed around, nothing more. Erica and Amber had barely eaten half of theirs. A quick glance at her own plate showed it bare, except for the remains of syrup from the pancakes and a little egg that she'd missed. She was, after all, trying to keep her strength up. She had—she hoped—a very busy day ahead of her. That is…if they would leave already.

"I heard that Macie and Karon are on shaky ground."

"No way," Amber said to Claudia.

"Macie is supposedly having an affair with one of their friends…Ashly." Claudia leaned closer to the table with a smile. "She's straight too, you know."

"Oh my God! And Karon found out?"

Barely containing her sigh, Cassidy got up and began clearing the table. The others didn't seem to notice. She ignored their conversation. That is, until she heard her name mentioned.

"Didn't you, Cassidy?"

She turned away from the sink. "What?"

"Ashly? She's one of your castoffs, isn't she?" Claudia asked, a smirk on her face.

Cassidy shook her head. "No."

"I heard she spent the weekend here," Amber said. "Friday alone, then with Macie and Karon." The others laughed. "No secrets in the group, you know!"

Cassidy shrugged. "Doesn't mean I slept with her."

"According to Karon, Ashley said you were 'fabulous,'" Erica contributed. "They all say that about you, Cassidy. You must really be something under the sheets," she teased.

"I can vouch for that," Claudia drawled, as again Erica and Amber laughed.

Cassidy simply stared at them, wondering if they recognized the bored expression on her face. She wondered how many breakfasts, brunches, lunches she'd spent with friends like this, gossiping about other friends in the group. And in turn, how many of her friends gossiped about her? She hated to think that she was a topic of conversation, but apparently she was. And she hated to think that the so-called friendships she'd maintained all these years were really as shallow as they seemed to her now. No wonder she couldn't name a one of them as a best friend.

She went to the island, about to toss out the leftovers, then paused. If Laura came over and spent the day—and night—this would probably make for quick nourishment in the morning. That was still on, right? Was Laura waiting next door? Waiting on them to leave? She smiled as she pictured her pacing in her kitchen.

"Are you okay?"

She looked up, finding Erica watching her. She lost the smile and nodded. "Yeah. Why?"

"You've been a little...I don't know, off your game."

"My game? What game is that?"

"She means you've been a little stick in the mud," Claudia supplied.

"Wow," she murmured. "I supplied you with drinks, with a pool, with dinner…with breakfast…and I've been a stick in the mud?"

"You just haven't been your usual fun self," Erica explained.

"Maybe making out with the yard girl will do that to you! I know that would bring me down."

Amber and Erica laughed at Claudia's words, and Cassidy had finally had enough. She tossed down the dish towel that she had slung over her shoulder earlier.

"I think we need to call an end to the weekend. You're right. I'm not myself. Hopefully, I won't ever be that person again." She went to the table and took the plates away, piling them on top of each other. "I'm shocked by your attitude, but I guess I really shouldn't be. For the first time in…in forever," she said with a shrug. "For the first time, I feel happy inside. Happy by being with another person. Laura. The yard girl. Not someone who a friend has set me up with," she said, looking at Erica. "Not someone who doesn't care about me but only cares about what I can give her." She looked pointedly at Claudia, who had the grace to look away. "Not a straight woman who wants to play games. Not someone looking for a boost in their social status."

She let the plates clank down loudly in the sink. "If you were truly my friends, you would be happy for me. I'm forty-four years old. It's taken me all these years to find someone who… who makes me smile, makes me laugh. Makes me damn crazy. You should be happy for me. But instead…you're being petty. You're being childish. Selfish." She tapped her chest. "This is about me. This isn't about you. So…I'd like for you to leave." The three of them looked at her quizzically, yet no one moved. "Now," she clarified. "I'd like you to leave *now*."

CHAPTER FORTY-EIGHT

After Erica tried to apologize—and after Claudia told her she was making a big mistake—it still took nearly an hour before they finally drove down the driveway. Cassidy stood there for several minutes, long after the gate had closed behind them. Their goodbyes were said curtly, if at all. She wondered crazily if she would ever see them again. And…if she would miss them.

She hadn't realized how selfish her friends were. Had it always been that way? Were they only concerned with what they were getting out of the relationship? Even before the house, she always entertained at her apartment. She supplied the booze and the food—always. Friday and Saturday nights, there was constantly someone around. Two or four people. Six. Sometimes more. Mini-parties, every weekend. And it was a very rare occasion that she went to bed alone. Once the house was built, the parties continued. Sometimes four people. Sometimes six. Then parties got bigger. And again, it was rare that she went to bed alone.

Until she had a fight with the neighbor over the yard-mowing schedule. She smiled, remembering that day she'd met Laura. She's been hot and sweaty, a baseball cap covering her hair, those damn sexy cutoff jeans showing off tanned legs. She didn't know it at the time, of course, but her world started changing that very day. Changing for the better.

She took a deep breath, then quickly blew it out before turning and going back inside. The house was quiet, but it didn't feel empty. Maybe she really was starting to think of it as home. She went into the kitchen, looking out at the glistening water of the pool. Then movement caught her eye and she saw Laura heading toward the closet where the floats were kept. But Laura wasn't wearing her swimsuit. Cutoff jeans. A tank top. She raised an eyebrow. No bra?

She opened the door and Laura turned to look at her. Cassidy returned her smile.

"Time for a swim?"

Laura nodded. "Yes. You won't need your suit."

Cassidy felt her stomach turn over, felt her heart flutter in her chest, felt the blood rush into her ears…felt a smile light on her face. As usual, Laura seemed to be the one in control, not her. Never her.

Laura tossed the floats into the water, then came closer, studying her. She tilted her head, her eyebrows raised.

"What's wrong?" she asked quietly.

Cassidy shook her head. "Nothing."

Laura took another step toward her, then reached out and touched her cheek lightly, her brown eyes gentle.

"Tell me."

"How is it you can read me so well?"

Laura stepped closer still, finally pulling her into a hug. "I know they don't like me. I'm sorry."

Cassidy shook her head when Laura pulled away from her. "It's not that. Well, no, they don't like you. But it's not that. I don't care if they like you or not." Cassidy took her hand and squeezed it. "I'm crazy about you, Laura. Crazy. My friends…

well, I realized they don't really want me to be happy. At least not with you. They want things to stay the same. They want *me* to stay the same."

Laura met her gaze, but she didn't say anything. Cassidy let her hand drop and walked a few steps away, trying to gather her thoughts, trying to find the words to explain to Laura how she was feeling.

"It occurred to me that I'm not lonely anymore." She turned back around to Laura. "All these years, I've been so lonely. Whether there was one person with me or thirty, it didn't matter. I felt lonely."

"The night of your party…when you looked so sad?"

"Yes. You came over. You hugged me. I wanted the party to be over with so that the day would be over and then it would be morning. And I could take my coffee and go over and see you. I never felt lonely around you. Quite the opposite." She shoved her hands into her pockets. "I have a lot of friends, Laura." She shook her head. "But they're not *really* friends. Not the way it should be. And it took this weekend for me to see that." She shrugged. "So—I don't have a lot of friends, I guess. But I don't feel lonely anymore. I don't feel…empty anymore."

Laura held her gaze. "I'm kinda crazy about you too. I won't break your heart."

Cassidy nodded. "That would be really nice."

Laura smiled. "You're supposed to say that you won't break mine either."

Cassidy smiled then. "Oh, that's what I'm supposed to say?"

"Uh-huh."

Cassidy's expression turned serious. "I wouldn't dare break your heart."

"That would be really nice," Laura whispered. "And…I'm sorry about your friends. It's because of me…"

"No. It's them. It's me. I've…I've changed. And it feels good. I feel good. *You* make me feel good. Happy." She tapped her chest. "Inside. Deep inside…I feel happy." Cassidy turned and motioned to the pool. "So…enough of that. They're gone. Pool time now?"

"Pool time now." Laura wiggled her eyebrows. "Naked pool time."

But when Laura's hand went to the button of her shorts, Cassidy stopped her. "I...I want to take them off." Laura raised an eyebrow and Cassidy nearly blushed. "It's been...kind of a..."

"Fantasy?" Laura teased. "My cutoff jeans?"

Instead of reaching for the shorts, though, Cassidy ran her fingers along the hem of Laura's tank top. Their eyes held, then Cassidy pulled it up—slowly—revealing a surprisingly tan stomach. She paused only a second before lifting it higher and over her head. Her breath caught as Laura stood there, her breasts bare, the nipples rock hard. They, too, had been touched by the sun.

"You've been skinny dipping in my pool," Cassidy accused in a whisper.

A small smile played on Laura's mouth. "I have."

Cassidy met her eyes again. "You're so beautiful, Laura." When she would have protested, Cassidy held a finger to her lips. "Beautiful. Natural. There's nothing fake. There are no pretenses. I love that about you."

Laura smiled. "Thank you. And now I would love it if you would take some clothes off."

"As you wish."

But Laura stopped her. "No. Let me."

As was usually the case, Laura was now in control, not Cassidy. Laura gave her a flirty smile, then tugged the T-shirt over her head. Cassidy stood still as Laura's eyes flitted across her black bra. Then Laura looked up, meeting her gaze.

"I...I don't think I want to get in the pool anymore," Laura said quietly.

Cassidy frowned. God...had she changed her mind? Why? She swallowed with difficulty. "What's wrong? Are you not ready?"

"I...I think...I think I want to go inside." She met her eyes again. "Not the pool."

Cassidy sighed with relief. "I see. Bedroom?"

"Yes. Bedroom." Laura smiled then. "Any bedroom...I don't care at this point."

They didn't make it to her bedroom, however. Not right away, anyway. Halfway up the stairs, she paused to look at Laura. Laura's eyes were full of wonder, excitement...desire. Cassidy stopped, meeting her gaze. Laura was the one to pull her closer, the one to close the gap between them. Their lips met and—like their previous kisses—it caused her heart to race, her knees to wobble. Laura's bare breasts smashed against her own and she felt hands tugging at her bra. Cassidy pulled away far enough to rip the thing off, then found Laura's mouth again, swallowing the loud moan from Laura as they pressed together. Her hands slid to Laura's hips, pulling her closer, feeling Laura arch against her.

"I can't stand up any longer," Laura whispered against her mouth. "I'm going to fall down."

Cassidy smiled as she pictured them tumbling down the stairs in a heap, their mouths still locked together.

"You think I'm kidding?" Laura asked with a smile of her own. Then Laura kissed her again, her tongue teasing Cassidy's. Cassidy put a hand against the wall, steadying herself. Yeah... they were going to fall down the damn stairs. When Laura's fingers moved between them, touching her breast, her nipple, Cassidy gasped.

"Bedroom," Laura murmured. "Now. Please."

Cassidy nodded and stumbled up the stairs as fast as her shaky legs would allow. She was as nervous as a virgin bride and she wasn't entirely sure why. She had taken women to her bed more times than she could count. But none of them were Laura. None of them ever meant anything to her. Sex. Physical. Never emotional. Never like this.

She looked at Laura now, remembering a conversation of theirs. Laura had a rule. If she wasn't emotionally invested, she didn't have sex. Sex was too personal, she'd said. Cassidy hadn't really understood that at the time. Sex was just an act, a game. A game she played well. It wasn't personal.

Now? Now she was trembling at the thought of touching Laura...of Laura touching her. Not a game. Not an act. Everything that was about to happen wasn't hers to control, to orchestrate. No. Because Laura was in control.

It was Laura's hands at the button of her shorts, Laura's fingers sliding the zipper down. But she didn't push the shorts off Cassidy's hips. No. Those same fingers slid back up her body, pausing at her breasts, making circles around each nipple. She closed her eyes with a quiet moan, letting Laura do as she pleased. Seconds later, she felt a wet tongue brush her nipple and she jerked as Laura had intuitively found her most sensitive spot. Laura's tongue bathed both nipples, then she raised her head, her mouth finding Cassidy's, kissing her softly, slowly... almost excruciatingly so. When Laura pulled back, Cassidy was breathless...and still trembling. The look in Laura's eyes made her knees shake and she finally reached out, grasping Laura's waist, steadying herself.

"Are you nervous?" Laura whispered in awe.

"As if it's my first time, yes."

"Why?"

"Because...because it is my first time."

Laura seemed to understand what she was trying to say, and she moved closer, letting their bodies touch.

"Then we should go slow. Take our time," Laura murmured into her ear.

"Is that what you want?"

"No. I want you to take these damn cutoff jeans off me already so we can get naked."

Cassidy laughed lightly, feeling some of the tension leave her body. But she sobered quickly as Laura took her hands and guided them to her shorts.

"Please, take them off," Laura whispered. "Or I will."

Cassidy gave in to the fantasy that she'd had for weeks now, lowering the zipper slowly, her hands slipping inside as she shoved the cutoff jeans—and the black panties—down Laura's legs. Laura kicked them away, then tugged at Cassidy's shorts, insistent hands making quick work of them.

Cassidy jerked the covers back on the bed and pulled Laura down with her. She spread her thighs and felt Laura press against her as their mouths met in a fiery kiss. So fiery, in fact, that Cassidy felt like she was melting into the bed. She cupped Laura's hips, pulling her even closer, feeling her wetness as Laura strained to touch her.

Cassidy rolled them over, taking control. Her mouth covered Laura's nipple and her tongue twirled around it before sucking it inside. Laura moaned and ran her fingers through Cassidy's hair as she held her tightly at her breast. She wanted to go slow, she wanted to savor this time, but Laura's body was trembling beneath hers, Laura's quiet sighs and moans were echoing in her ears.

With her knee, she spread Laura's thighs, letting her body sink against her wetness. Laura arched up to meet her, rocking against Cassidy. Cassidy shifted, her hand going between them, delving into the wet arousal, exposing Laura's swollen clit. She did the same to herself, then pressed hard against Laura, their wet centers meeting.

Cassidy moved to Laura's other breast as she rubbed against her. Laura gasped—moaned—with each thrust of her hips. Cassidy was shaking so badly, though, that she couldn't maintain her position. Laura groaned in frustration when Cassidy pulled away from her.

"Oh my God…are you *kidding* me?"

Cassidy smiled as she kissed Laura again. "Sorry. But I'm very aroused. I'm shaking, for God's sake."

Laura ran her hands across Cassidy's back. "That felt really, really good," she whispered. "Ten more seconds."

"Ten seconds, huh. How about I take care of that then?" She kissed Laura, long and slow, drawing out a deep moan from her. "With my mouth."

Their eyes met. "But…but you said you don't—"

"I want to do everything with you, Laura. Everything."

She felt Laura trembling again as she kissed her skin, moving down her body slowly, pausing to nibble at the curve of her hip.

Laura's breath was coming in short, quiet gasps as she gently pushed Cassidy down.

"I'm going to pass out," she whispered.

Cassidy smiled against her skin. "I'll go slow."

"Trust me, you can go as slow as you want...it's going to happen very fast."

CHAPTER FORTY-NINE

Cassidy took forever as she thoroughly kissed her stomach, her hips, her legs…making Laura squirm with anticipation. She was on the verge of begging when Cassidy finally moved between her thighs. She barely had time to register Cassidy's mouth on her, feel her tongue as it grazed her clit. One simple brush of her tongue had her orgasm screaming through her. She arched up hard, her hands holding Cassidy tight against her.

"Oh my God," Laura breathed. "That is so not fair."

"I'll say. I barely got started," Cassidy mumbled as she rested her head on Laura's stomach.

Laura ran her fingers through Cassidy's hair. "We've got all night, you know." She gently pulled Cassidy up her body, squeezing her arms around her tightly, then deftly rolled them over. "But right now…I want to have my way with you."

Cassidy looked at her oddly. Laura frowned, then lowered her head and kissed her softly. "What?"

"I'm not sure anyone's said that to me before."

Laura looked at her quizzically. "All those beautiful women in your life and none of them wanted to simply devour you?"

"Is that what you want to do?"

Laura kissed her again, letting her tongue trace Cassidy's lower lip. "I want my mouth on every inch of your body." She leaned up on her elbow, watching Cassidy. She finally understood what Cassidy was trying to say. "They were more interested in you pleasing them?"

"That was partially my fault. I usually took control and never relinquished it."

"Don't you dare try that with me." Laura dipped her head, kissing lightly around Cassidy's nipple, teasing her. "Because I want to do everything with you," she said, repeating Cassidy's words.

She straddled her thigh, then pressed her own against Cassidy's hot, wet center. Cassidy moaned and grasped Laura's hips, pulling her closer. Laura's mouth settled over Cassidy's breast, licking and sucking at her nipple, feeling Cassidy squirm beneath her. Ah...so she had sensitive nipples. Laura smiled as she moved to her other breast and Cassidy again sighed with pleasure. But Cassidy's hips pressing up told her what Cassidy really wanted and Laura moved her hand between them, sinking her fingers into Cassidy's wetness.

It was Laura's turn to moan and she kissed Cassidy passionately. "God...you're so wet." She held her fingers inside Cassidy, moving her mouth to her ear. "It's been a while since I've been with anyone. Forgive me if I want to take my time."

Cassidy brought Laura's mouth back to hers. "Take your time...*next* time."

Laura moved her fingers, causing Cassidy to arch her hips against her hand. She smiled wickedly as she pulled them out, rubbing against her clit instead.

"I like that too," Cassidy murmured with a shaky breath.

Laura went back to her breast, then slipped her fingers inside her once more. Yes, it had been a while. But she was *inside* Cassidy and she decided that no, she didn't want to go slow.

She'd go slow next time.

CHAPTER FIFTY

Laura was fairly certain she'd never taken a midnight swim before. Certainly not naked. The pool's lights—both red and yellow—gave the water an amber color and Cassidy looked like a goddess as she was bathed in liquid fire. Laura let go of the side and moved toward her. The water rippled gently around her and she watched Cassidy watching her.

She paused, just out of arm's reach. The water was barely above their waists, and Laura let her gaze travel to Cassidy's breasts…breasts that she now knew intimately. She'd discovered that Cassidy had very sensitive nipples, and she'd tormented her for what seemed like hours. Tormented her so that Cassidy actually had an orgasm just from Laura's mouth at her breast. That had been…incredible.

She raised her eyes again, meeting Cassidy's. "You look like a goddess," she said, expressing her earlier thoughts.

"I was about to say that very thing."

Laura shook her head. "I'm not a—"

"You have no idea how lovely you are, Laura. You take my breath away." Laura stood still as Cassidy came closer. "How many hours have you been here?" She smiled slightly. "I've had my world rocked more times than I can count."

Laura smiled too. "Rocked your world, huh? Well...must have been the oral sex."

"I thought I was going to pass out when you first touched me," Cassidy said quietly. "I liked that very much."

"Yes, I could tell. I happen to like it too." She moved closer. "You know what I love?" she asked in a whisper.

"What?"

"You have extremely sensitive nipples." By the lights of the pool, Laura couldn't tell if Cassidy was blushing or not, but her facial expression changed to one of embarrassment. "I loved it."

"That's never happened to me before."

"No?"

"No one's ever taken the time."

"I could have spent hours."

Cassidy smiled again. "I think you did." Then she arched an eyebrow. "Are you...are you still aroused?"

"Are you still naked?"

"I thought...maybe..."

"You've had an active sex life," Laura countered. "I have not. I have a *lot* of making up to do."

"Well...lucky me."

She finally slid into Cassidy's arms, but before she kissed her, she pulled her mouth an inch away. "I've never made love in a pool before."

CHAPTER FIFTY-ONE

Cassidy stood at her office window, looking out, seeing the shimmering heat bouncing off the sidewalks and streets down below and it wasn't even noon yet. She let out a rather bored breath, then went back to her desk. She should be at home. She should be with Laura.

She smiled. She wasn't certain she had the stamina to be with Laura today. But God, what an awesome two days it had been. Not only had she taken off work on Monday, she'd stayed Monday night and driven into work early this morning. Laura had still been in her bed, sleeping, when she'd crawled out. Yesterday was actually a blur, she admitted. Really, everything past their midnight swim was a blur. Yes, they'd made love in the water. They'd made love on a chaise lounge. They'd made love on the kitchen floor—God, she had nearly ravished Laura. They made love on the stairs, in the gym, and in her office. And they cooked together and ate together and she hardly had a recollection of either of those things.

She had no recollection of much except Laura's beautiful, naked body…and the honest, pure reflection of desire that had been in Laura's eyes. Desire, yes, and so much more. But they hadn't really talked. They'd chatted and played in the pool like normal, but there had been no serious discussion about how they'd spent the last two days...and what it meant.

And what did it mean? They were lovers, obviously. She closed her eyes for a moment, remembering Laura's mouth at her breast...and elsewhere. God...Laura was so damn good. But where did they go from here? How do you date someone who lives next door to you? How do you date someone who you've been seeing for months now?

No. She didn't want to date. She'd spent a lifetime dating. She simply wanted...to love.

She was smiling as she picked up her phone. What was Laura doing? Was she making lunch for her mother? Was she out tending to flowers? Was she still passed out in bed? Or was she in the pool, recuperating?

The phone was answered on the third ring, and then Laura's voice was in her ear.

"I can't walk. You've ruined me."

Cassidy burst out laughing. "Where are you?"

"I'm in the pool. Water therapy."

"Maybe you should ask your mother for pointers."

"Very funny." A pause. "I miss you."

Cassidy couldn't keep the smile from her face. "Oh, yeah?"

"Yeah. You know, I may need help getting out of the pool later."

Cassidy laughed quietly. "I wish I was there. Are you naked?"

"No. The pool boys were here. I didn't want to shock them."

Cassidy leaned back in her chair. "Do we...need to talk?"

"I don't know. Do we?"

Cassidy smiled. "Will you be my girlfriend?"

Laura laughed. "You're so cute. You'd give up your beautiful, skinny models for me?"

"In a heartbeat."

There were several seconds of silence, but when Laura spoke, her voice was no longer teasing. "When you come home, we'll talk."

Cassidy had a moment of panic. What did that mean? Her heart was pounding nervously in her ears and she couldn't even offer a reply. But as usual, Laura seemed to be able to read her mind, even over the phone.

"Cassidy...you must know that I'm in love with you."

Cassidy squeezed her eyes shut in relief. "Okay. So when I come home...we'll talk." She opened her eyes and smiled. "I'm in love with you too."

"I know you are. See you Friday?"

"No. Thursday. I'll sneak away early. Meet you out in the pool."

"It's a date."

She put her phone down, still unable to get the silly smile off her face. And why should she? Laura was in love with her. Her heart felt like it flipped over in her chest at the thought. All these years...all these many, many years and finally, she'd found her love. And all she wanted to do was bask in it for a while. Maybe next week she'd ask Tanya to clear her calendar. She had that contractor's meeting tomorrow, but other than that, there was nothing pressing. She could take a week off. And she could work from home some. She could set up her office for real.

She paused. Home? No, her apartment wasn't home anymore, was it? Her home was an hour's drive away...where Laura was. Laura was home.

* * *

"You want me to what?" Tanya asked with raised eyebrows.

"Clear my schedule," she said again, this time more slowly. "All week."

Tanya stared at her. "All week? You never take vacation."

Cassidy stared back at her. "Problem?"

Tanya put her hands on her hips. "You're acting weird."

Cassidy smiled. "I just need some time off, that's all."

Tanya studied her. "What's going on? Is it Laura?"

Cassidy shrugged. "What makes you think it's got anything to do with Laura?"

"Because you didn't come to work yesterday, for one. And two...now that I'm looking at you, you're all glowing and stuff." She grinned. "So I guess this means you didn't screw it up, huh?"

"I'm in love with her," Cassidy said simply.

Tanya rolled her eyes. "I could have told you that a month ago. So I take it you've been...getting to know her better," she teased with a wink.

Cassidy actually felt a blush on her face. "Must you?"

"Oh my God...you're so cute when you blush! I can't wait to tell Derrick." Tanya walked around her desk and bent down to hug her. "Seriously, I'm so happy for you. Laura is perfect."

"Yeah...she's pretty awesome. So...can I have a week?"

"You can have a week off, yes."

"Gee, thanks, boss."

Tanya surprised her by leaning down again and kissing her cheek. "You did good."

"Thank you. Oh...and I'm leaving early on Thursday. And I may start working from home a few days a week too."

"Good. Then I can really be the boss here in the office." She laughed as she walked out. "Don't stay in bed the whole week. You're getting old. You need to pace yourself."

CHAPTER FIFTY-TWO

"Pace yourself?" Laura smiled contentedly as she pulled Cassidy into her arms. "She's so funny," she murmured, kissing Cassidy lazily, still coming down from the high she'd been on only seconds ago. "You have a very talented tongue." Cassidy laughed quietly and Laura nuzzled her face into Cassidy's neck. "I could get used to this."

"This what?"

"Making love on Thursday afternoons." She bit playfully on Cassidy's chin. "It sure beats yard work."

Cassidy rolled to her side, her hand still rubbing lightly across Laura's hip. "I could get used to it too."

Laura rolled her head to look at Cassidy. "You want to talk?" Laura wasn't sure why, but Cassidy seemed a bit insecure, as if she wasn't certain of Laura's intentions. "We've been talking without words. Do you want to talk *with* words?"

"There's not much to say. You already know I'm crazy about you. You already know I'm…I'm in love with you."

Laura met her gaze. "Yet you're afraid?" Laura touched just above Cassidy's breast. "Afraid of a broken heart?"

"This is all kinda new to me. I don't know if we should slow down or speed up. I don't know if we should say we're dating or going steady," she said with a smile.

Laura nodded. "I was thinking about that too, actually. I've come to the conclusion that we've already been kinda dating, we just didn't call it that." She leaned closer and kissed her. "I don't want to slow down or speed up. I like the pace we have. Playing with you in the pool is fun. I enjoy cooking meals with you. We never lack for conversation. I just want to be with you for a while, alone. Like we've been doing. Getting to know one another, spending time together." She kissed her again. "Making love. Getting to know each other this way." She leaned back, still holding her gaze. "But what do *you* want?"

"You fill all these empty spaces that I've had for so long now. I want to wrap you up in my arms and never let you go. I want to sleep with you and wake up with you and share my life with you." Cassidy looked away for a moment, then met her eyes again. "And maybe that is moving too fast, but I feel like I've been searching for you my whole damn life. Now that I've found you, I don't want to miss out on even a second of it."

Laura touched her cheek lightly, then rubbed a finger across her lips. "Okay. We can go steady and I'll be your girlfriend."

Cassidy laughed. "That's it? Easy as that?"

"Yes." Laura sat up and pulled Cassidy up too. "But be warned. If you're here during the week, I'll put you to work." She wiggled her eyebrows teasingly. "Because I got another job."

"Oh?"

"Uh-huh. Mr. Hamilton, who lives two lots down past us, is in need of a yard gal."

"You don't say. How much is he paying you?"

"Not as much as you are. He does his own flowers." She got out of bed and stood there, seeing Cassidy's eyes roving over her body. She shook her finger. "No, no, no. We're going out to the pool to play." She took Cassidy's hand and pulled her out of the bed.

"Do we have to dress?"

"Yes. I seasoned some hamburger meat earlier. You can grill burgers for us. I invited Mom to join us."

"Okay," she said easily. "I like Maggie."

Laura wrapped her arms around Cassidy's neck and pressed their bodies together. "Thank you."

"For?"

"For the day, for the afternoon. For being who you are. For liking my mother," she whispered before kissing her. "For loving me."

"And thank you for stealing my heart."

"Mmm. I'm not giving it back, you know."

"That's only fair. I've got yours locked up tight."

Laura smiled at her. "I love you, Cassidy."

Cassidy's expression turned serious and she nodded. "I love you too."

Laura nodded back at her. "We're going to have so much fun together." She took her hand and tugged on it. "Come on. Pool."

CHAPTER FIFTY-THREE

"Why am I doing all the work, Laura Sue?"

"I'm helping," she said as she kicked her legs in the water.

"You are not! You're weighing me down!" her mother complained.

"Well, this is your therapy, not mine. I'm just along for the ride."

"I'll say."

Laura laughed. They were draped across the float on their stomachs, using their legs to propel them over the water and to the other side of the pool. Well, mostly her mother was.

"You've gotten so much better, Mom. You hardly use the walker at all anymore. Doesn't it feel great?"

"Yes, it does. Thank you for talking me into this all those months ago."

"You're welcome."

"Now that you've given me my independence back, does that mean you're ready to move on? Leave me on my own?"

"If I moved on anywhere, it would be over here, you know. I'd still be here for you every day."

"You practically live here now."

Yes, Cassidy had taken to working from home on most Mondays and nearly every Friday. And yes, Laura stayed with her when she was here. But she still saw her mother every day and still cooked some meals for her. Of course, since she was getting along better and could make it to Cassidy's without the walker now, she joined them for dinner a lot of nights…unless it was one of her TV nights. Despite her newfound independence, she was still hooked on her TV shows.

"I'm a little nervous about meeting her parents," Laura admitted.

"Why?"

"Maybe they won't think I'm good enough."

"Oh, Laura Sue…that's ridiculous. Cassidy is head over heels in love with you. Anyone can see that. They'll love you just as much."

"You're still coming, right?" she asked, referring to the Labor Day party Cassidy was having. Tanya and Derrick would be there, as well as Dave, Cassidy's brother. Laura had met him once, when his family came out to see Cassidy's house. He was much like Cassidy in personality although perhaps a little more serious and a little less playful. Still, he had been very friendly to her. His wife was down-to-earth and so like Tanya that Laura had taken an instant liking to her. She was looking forward to seeing them again. And of course Tanya too. They'd become friends and she and Derrick had been out on several Saturdays over the summer.

"You don't think I'll get in the way."

"Of course not. Cassidy would be hurt if you didn't come. And besides, if it's not to your liking…just complain of being tired and you can limp badly and I'll help you back home."

Her mother laughed. "Escape plan, huh?"

"Yes. I just hope I won't need one."

"Quit worrying. Her parents will love you."

She didn't know why she was worried. If they didn't like her, they didn't like her. That would have no bearing on her and

Cassidy's relationship. What she was really afraid of was that they wouldn't think she was a suitable partner for Cassidy. She was the yard girl, for God's sake. Cassidy was a professional. She had a real job. Laura? Well, she did have three yards now, but that hardly constituted a thriving business.

"Laura Sue, you're frowning. You've got to quit worrying about it. You are what you are."

"A yard girl," she said almost disgustedly.

Her mother laughed. "So tell them you're a writer."

Laura laughed too. "And what? I'm between books."

"Writer's block," her mother managed between laughs.

"Eight years of it!" she said as she broke into a fit of giggles. "God...what was I thinking?"

"You wrote a book. I've always been so proud of that."

"Thank you. But we should probably leave that in the past. And you're right. I am what I am. A damn good yard girl."

"What's all that giggling out here?"

Laura turned at the sound of Cassidy's voice and nearly fell off the float. "You're early!"

"I know."

"Like a day early! I don't have dinner planned."

"No problem. We'll do our fallback plan."

"Pizza? We're going to get so fat."

"No way." Cassidy gave her an exaggerated wink. "I think we get enough exercise...don't you?"

Laura felt a blush on her face which deepened as she heard her mother's chuckle beside her. Laura turned to glare at her, which did no good whatsoever.

"Maggie? Is it okay if we have pizza at your place?"

"Oh, that would be nice. I was about to leave anyway. Help me out, Laura Sue."

They paddled over to the shallow end, and Laura marveled at how comfortable her mother was in the water now. And at the progress she'd made over the summer. She walked unassisted up the steps—wearing her new flowery swimsuit—to take Cassidy's hand. Cassidy draped a towel around her shoulders.

"You're doing so good, Maggie."

"Thanks to you two." She looked fondly over at Laura. "She would have made a good drill instructor. She was relentless."

Laura smiled at her. "Maybe by next summer, you'll be able to ditch the cane too."

"I'm just happy I'm not tied to that dang walker. It made me feel old."

Laura watched her pick up the cane and make her way around the shrubs at the side. Laura stepped—dripping wet—next to Cassidy.

"So...you snuck away early again? Tanya let you off?"

"Yeah...she thinks she's the boss, all right." Cassidy was unmindful of her damp suit as she pulled her into her arms. "I missed you this week."

"I miss you every week."

"Oh, yeah?" Cassidy finally kissed her, long and slow, drawing out a moan from Laura.

"You have entirely too many clothes on," Laura said. She started unbuttoning her blouse. "You look kinda nice in your power suit, but let's take it off, huh?"

"We don't have time for this. Your mother—"

Laura put a finger against her mouth. "We have all the time in the world." But something caught her eye and she looked past Cassidy, seeing her mother standing beside the shrubs, watching them. "Mother!" she hissed and waved her away. Her mother was smiling as she left. Laura was smiling too as she looked at Cassidy. "She loves you, you know. She loves *us*."

"You're worried about meeting my parents this weekend?"

"I'm worried your mother won't like me. I'm worried she won't like...*us*."

"I told you...they're very normal, down-to-earth people. They're going to love you. If for no other reason, they're going to love you because I love you." She kissed her again. "Quit worrying."

Laura finished unbuttoning Cassidy's blouse and she ran her hands across her smooth skin. "Ooh...sexy bra," she murmured. "I love you in black." When she would have pushed the blouse off of Cassidy's shoulders, Cassidy stopped her.

"Move in with me."

Laura looked up, startled. "What?"

Cassidy smiled. "Move in with me."

"I'm practically living here now," she said, echoing her mother's words.

"Practically, yes. Let's make it official."

Laura swallowed. "Are you...are you sure?"

Cassidy frowned. "Are you not sure?"

Laura saw the doubt in her eyes and she moved closer, pulling Cassidy tight against her. "I love you so much. I'm sure of that." She pulled away. "But I don't want you to regret it later and then—"

"Laura, I want to marry you. I want us to be together... always."

"You want...you want to...to marry me?"

"Yes, I want to marry you."

Laura felt tears in her eyes and she tried to blink them away.

Cassidy smiled gently at her. "I want you to move in with me. I want to marry you. I want to love you for the rest of my life." She leaned closer and kissed her. "Please say yes."

Laura gave in to her tears as she nodded.

"Yes. Yes to all of it."

Bella Books, Inc.

Women. Books. Even Better Together.

P.O. Box 10543
Tallahassee, FL 32302

Phone: 800-729-4992
www.bellabooks.com